THE
MUSIC
AND THE
STRIFE

SUSAN ROOKE

The Music and the Strife
Copyright © 2025 by Susan Rooke

Holynok Press
Thorndale, Texas
srooke@susanrooke.net

ISBN: 978-0-9990872-4-4

Library of Congress Control Number: 2024926673

Printed in the United States

10 9 8 7 6 5 4 3 2

THE
MUSIC
AND THE
STRIFE

**A Record of Events Occurring
from May 1976 through April 1977,
Constructed from the Journal of Sophia McKean:**

I began keeping a journal in February of last year. I was in ninth grade, and it was a month after Dad died. I'd meant to start it sooner; I thought it might help me work through the hurt—maybe make it possible to bear what felt unbearable. But the shock was too huge, too sudden. Those first weeks, all Mom and I could do was cry. More than a year has passed now, and I understand better what people mean when they say that time heals all wounds. I can't call it healing, though. Time just makes the wound a little less raw.

When Mom and I moved away from the city, away from the place where the accident happened—a place we were forced to see nearly every day—summer vacation had recently started. It was about five months since we'd lost him, and by then I was in the habit of keeping my journal faithfully. I wrote about that summer as we settled into our new lives, about my fifteenth birthday in July, and the start of tenth grade in August. I wrote in it every day, as completely as possible, about what happened as fall became winter, and then spring. It's late April now, and I'm so glad I recorded what took place over the last fourteen months, especially since last August. Otherwise, I wouldn't believe it.

Now that it's behind me, I've tried to make something of these journal entries, leaving out the parts that aren't relevant and setting the rest in better order to make a connected story. I've remembered a few other things lately, and recorded them, too, while I still can. Because if I don't do it now, they'll be gone—faded into the past. The time is coming soon when I'll forget much of what's written here. Mom warned me about it. I know it's true, because I've seen how people around me forget. She told me it would be for the best, and she's probably right, but I'm doing this anyway. I have to at least make the effort to remember what happened to me. If I do, maybe it won't happen again.

I won't turn sixteen for three months, but already I feel years older. I learned some important lessons, though. For the first time, I realized just how much of what we see might be false—a front meant to deceive us while the truth makes its plans, conducts its secretive business out of sight. I learned not to trust too soon. And I learned about the darkness.

Also, none of what follows began at the bend in the River Buckle. It began much longer ago than that.

one

At the end of ninth grade, a couple of months before my fifteenth birthday, my mother and I left the city for a small town called Holm, three states away. When she first told me where she wanted us to move, I thought she said "home," and didn't realize my mistake until later when she showed it to me on a map. Even with the "l" it sounded welcoming, and I hoped it might make a good change for us. We'd be leaving the only place I'd ever lived, though, and that made me uncomfortable. I wasn't really sure I wanted to leave. But my father had died early that year, and Mom said she needed to get away. She wanted a quieter life outside of the city, fewer people, and fewer reminders of our old life before everything went to pieces. I understood her need. We had to pass the spot where Dad died nearly every day, and though we tried to look away, it ate us up inside. That orange spray paint the police use at accident scenes takes a long time to fade.

As the move got closer, she explained to me a little more about the reasons for her choice. Some of it was due to finances. She'd be selling our house, and she also had the insurance money from the accident, plus the money from selling Dad's half of the business to his partner. Even though it might seem like plenty, she told me, it wouldn't last forever. There would always be monthly payments to make, and it went way beyond just the mortgage and utilities. I could see she was simplifying, probably not telling me everything, but I didn't ask her for details. Financial discussions belonged to the adult world, and I was happier not knowing much about it. What it came down to was a need to live someplace where the money would stretch further. So in May, a few weeks before the end of the school year and after she'd put our house up for sale, she began making phone calls, searching for our new place in Holm.

She had two specific things in mind. It had to have a room with good light, large enough to serve as her art studio. She also wanted a backyard with space for a vegetable garden. When she described her ideas for the house to me, her eyes lit up. She was excited, and it was the first time I'd seen her that way since the accident. Even though I was still unsure about the move, especially about starting over in a completely unfamiliar place, I tried to seem enthusiastic. I wanted to be strong for her, to be who she needed me to be, and understanding of her feelings. I desperately wanted her to be happy again. So when she told me over breakfast one morning that she'd found the perfect place for us, I was able to give her a real smile.

———————

A few days before the start of summer vacation, she pulled into our driveway in a nearly new white Ford pickup truck she'd bought from Dad's business partner after signing her old no-frills sedan over to him and throwing in some cash. He needed a vehicle that was easier to get into after recently injuring his knee; she needed something with cargo space that could also haul a trailer. The fact that they both got what they wanted from the trade seemed to give her a boost.

We stood in the driveway, admiring her purchase. It *was* a nice truck.

"It's all going smoothly, Phee," she told me. "I found out today that the closing date on our old house is right before we leave for Holm. There won't be any loose threads to tie us here once we're gone." She turned to me, a shine that might've been tears in her sea-green eyes. "I keep thinking your father is looking down on us...helping any way he can."

I nodded, but didn't reply.

———————

We arrived in Holm in that pickup on a warm, late afternoon in June, a U-Haul trailer attached to the bumper hitch. It held the things Mom had saved back for us from the auction of our belongings. She'd bought our new house based on a handful of photographs sent by the realtor she'd found through the local chamber of commerce. I'd seen the photos, and the house looked pleasant, but all I really knew was that it was in a rural area outside of town, and the surrounding properties were mostly pasture and farmland.

After stopping in Holm to fill up the truck, she'd asked for directions from the gas station attendant. He seemed a little stiff and standoffish, but his directions were clear, which was helpful. The map we were using was missing a lot of details, and I don't know if we could've found our way through the webwork of country roads by nightfall.

When we pulled into the gravel drive, we just sat in the truck for a minute, looking at the front of the house. The windshield, clean when we left the gas station, was already dusty and smeared with bugs again just from the drive out of town, but I could see a roomy covered porch and some leafy shade trees. The front yard wasn't very big, which concerned me. I hoped the backyard would have enough space for Mom to have her garden. If it didn't, she'd be very disappointed. I stole a sideways glance at her. She looked pleased, even peaceful. She knew more about the property than I did, I reminded myself. So I kept quiet and tried to look expectant.

Mom gave herself a little shake and put the truck in gear again. "The realtor said there's an area to turn around in the back. We'll pull in there, and I'll get this thing facing the right direction. Then we can start unloading."

I groaned before I could stop myself.

She turned to smile at me and gave me a quick pat on the leg. "Don't worry. We're only going to take in our suitcases, a couple of boxes, and the bedrolls for now. We'll need a couple of kitchen chairs and tray tables, too. We'll leave the rest for tomorrow."

This was the very ordinary way our new life began.

———————

A few days later, we were already beginning to settle in. I'd stopped coming awake in the middle of the night, wondering where I was. We'd set up our beds by then, so sleeping was more comfortable. Doorways and light switches were where I expected to find them. Mom had taken command of the kitchen as if she'd cooked there all her life.

"This reminds me of being an Army wife," she told me as she put a box of Mason jars away in the pantry. "You get so used to transfers that you go right into an unfamiliar place and immediately make it your home."

"How could it remind you?" I asked. "You've never been an Army wife!"

"You're right." She set the box on a shelf and turned back to me, a small smile on her lips. For a second, I saw a faraway look in her eyes. "I just meant this is what I imagine an Army wife's life is like."

We finished emptying out the U-Haul that afternoon, and the next morning I went with Mom to turn it in. We had to drive ten miles to the next small town, since there was no place in Holm to do it. On the way back, we did a little cautious exploring, not wanting to wander too far off the routes we were gradually becoming more familiar with. I gazed out the truck windows and realized for the first time how beautiful the countryside was. Why hadn't I noticed this when we first arrived? Waving grass, a soft golden green, covered the low, rolling hills. The slopes were dotted with trees so big around, so heavy with twisted limbs, that the sight of them made me catch my breath. I'd never seen trees that looked so weary, so old. Others were much taller, their branches upthrust like arms raised to heaven. My shoulders began to relax as she drove, and I released a long, slow breath. I'd been so sad and anxious since Dad's death. Anxious about everything. I realized Mom and I had each been trying to be the strong one, to lift the other's spirits. That had been hard on both of us.

When we got back to Holm, we stopped at the same gas station. The same attendant was there, but he was friendlier this time. He obviously remembered us, which surprised me at first, until I realized there probably weren't many strangers passing through. Holm is miles off any major highway, Mom had told me that before we moved. It's not a place people travel through on their way to somewhere important. That's one reason it appealed to her.

This time, we put gas in the truck and bought another road map—a newer one with even the smallest roads marked. Then we went on our way.

When we got to the outskirts of town, I could sense Mom's tension easing as the houses fell away behind us, yielding to corn-fields with rows of stalks browning in the sun. It was feed corn, meant for livestock, she explained, and the farmers wouldn't harvest it until the kernels were completely dried on the cobs. As she drove, her right wrist rested on top of the steering wheel in the careless way I'd seen Dad do. He'd been a builder, and he used to drive me to the job sites to show me his latest projects. I'd ridden so many miles in his pickup. Mom owned a pickup herself in her younger days before she met him, and she liked to joke that she'd only married Dad for his truck. She and I both loved the feeling of sitting up higher, seeing farther down the road. When she bought the Ford, I was afraid it would bring back painful memories for us. It didn't seem to, though.

In fact, by then we were getting so comfortable with that truck that we'd given it a name: Steve, for Steve McQueen, my mother's favorite actor. I knew who he was from a few movies I'd watched with her. He was too old and not really my type, but I had to admit that he wasn't a bad choice for a movie-star crush. The sedan she'd recently sold to Dad's business partner had been Cary, for Cary Grant. He was even older and in my opinion, way less…well, way less everything. As I looked out the window, watching the countryside slide by, I wondered how she'd ended up with two such opposite choices.

I turned to her. "Mom, help me figure something out."

"Sure, honey, what is it?"

"I can understand the reason for Steve's name." I patted the truck's dash. "What I don't understand is why your old car was named after Cary Grant."

"Well, *that* question came out of nowhere!" Mom gave a little laugh and shook her head. "It happened because your father's business was doing well, and he wanted to present me with a dashing, elegant car. I told him thank you, but no. That was the last thing I needed. So I chose a plain, dependable car and gave it a dashing, elegant name."

I considered this. It made sense to me. "Okay. But why don't you ever give your cars female names, like most people do?"

"Because I don't want to drive a girl."

I smiled at that and she threw me a glance of impish innocence. Seeing her like this, more like her old self, tugged at my heart.

After a minute, she said, "Why don't you open up that new map and find Holm? It'll be lower central. Then look to the southwest, out by our house. There's a river not too far from there, and I'd like to see it."

I know plenty of kids my age—and a few adults—who can't read a map, and even some who don't know the points of the compass. Dad had made sure I knew such things from an early age, though. He told me both skills were essential in the city, where so many streets have names like North Main, or South Parkway, and will be east or west of someplace else. He thought having a sense of direction was important. He probably never imagined me using that knowledge in the country. When I thought of him, my smile evaporated. A tear ran down my cheek, and I quickly brushed it away.

I unfolded the map and tried to keep it from flapping in the breeze. We'd lowered our windows to the summer air, leaving the air conditioning off to save money on gas. It was too warm, but I was grateful that it dried my eyes quickly. Now that I'm older, I understand better why Mom was being so careful with expenses, but at the time it was still unclear. Even after she'd explained her reasoning, it seemed to me there was plenty of money. Since then I've realized that while I may have known my compass points, I had no experience with budgeting. I didn't understand yet how quickly money can seep away, disappearing like rain into parched earth.

"Oh," I said, "here it is. The River Buckle?"

"That's the one."

I peered more closely at the map. "It's not far from the turnoff for our house." I glanced over at her. "How have we not seen it?"

"Have you stood on the back porch and looked out behind our property?"

"Yes."

"Did you notice the thick line of taller trees in the distance beyond our fence line?"

"Sure, they're gorgeous. What does that have to do with—"

"That's where the river flows. I think they're pecan trees. At least that's what they look like from our house. Their roots drink from the river water. We can't see the river from our house because the ground slopes downward and the trees hide it, but that's where it is."

I dropped my hands, letting the map rest on my lap. "Oh, okay."

"Anyway," she went on, "I know where it is, but I don't know how to get to it. We haven't explored that direction yet." She pointed up the road. "Here comes a highway sign. Why don't you get us there?"

Before much longer, with only one wrong turn—my fault—we found ourselves on a dusty gravel road following a line of weathered wood posts strung with wire to our right.

Beyond that was a broad expanse of blowing grass, then farther, through gaps in the distant trees, we saw the glint of sunlight on water. My mother slowed Steve.

"That's a quarter, maybe a third of a mile away," she murmured. She pointed out my window, toward the river. "Our house is on the other side of that."

"Do you think we can walk to it from our house?"

My mother stopped the truck and leaned across me to get a better look at the land. "As a matter of distance, yes. It's not too far from us. But someone owns all this property. It may be divided into several plots, which means there are probably more fences between our house and the river. So…no."

Slowly, we started moving again. I eyed the wire strands, noting how some of them weren't stretched as taut as others. "We could probably get in from this direction. It looks pretty easy to climb through here," I said.

"Through the fence? Don't be silly. This land belongs—"

She stopped, and we both saw a sign hanging on the fence up ahead. As we drew nearer, I could read the bold red lettering on the white background.

PRIVATE PROPERTY
NO TRESPASSING
VIOLATORS WILL BE PROSECUTED

"Oh," I said.

Mom sighed. "I guess that's that."

two

The rest of the summer passed quickly as we unpacked boxes, hung pictures, and settled into our new home. I helped Mom get her garden laid out and the soil ready for planting, and the next day we filled the pickup truck bed with tomato plants from Holm's little hardware store and garden center. We were so busy that my fifteenth birthday arrived before we knew it.

That late July morning, we drove to the doughnut shop where Mom bought our favorite, two dozen plain glazed. We ate them only twice a year, on our birthdays, and it was a huge treat that we looked forward to. Much better than birthday cake, we agreed, even though we always overdid it by feasting the whole day on nothing but those two boxes of doughnuts.

Dad didn't have a sweet tooth, and he'd always enjoyed ribbing us about our craving. The last time had been in early January for Mom's birthday. When he got home from work that evening, we'd heard his voice call out from the kitchen.

"Where's the birthday girl?"

Mom hurried into the kitchen and I came after her.

"There you are, Livvy!" He beamed. "These are for you."

He held up a bouquet of roses in her favorite color, a pale shade of lavender. As she reached for them, he spotted the white cardboard box on the counter and went to it.

"Where's the second box? Gone already?" he teased. "I guess you two won't be wanting dinner." He flipped the lid back and gasped, pretending to be shocked. "What's this? No sprinkles?" Then he grinned at us, because he knew we both detested them.

Mom had looked him straight in the eye as she took the roses out of his hand. "Ian McKean! Don't you know what sprinkles are? That's what they give you in Hell and call the devil's candy!" She held the bouquet to her nose, inhaling deeply. "Mm… These are gorgeous, thank you."

Mom's comeback must have surprised him, because his mouth had dropped open, then he burst out laughing. "You girls," he chuckled, shaking his head.

Three days after that, he was gone.

So I guess it was inevitable that the shadow lingering over Mom's January birthday ended up clouding my fifteenth in July. The day started out well enough, but when we got back to the house and opened up one of the flat, white boxes, it changed course. I'd expected the sight and smell of all those doughnuts to nearly overpower me. It always had before. Seeing them then, though, their neat rows, the sugary glaze lavishly coating each one, made me miss Dad so badly my heart felt as if it would break. I looked up at my mother's face, and saw the grief there. We got two plates out anyway and went through the motions as best we could. We managed to eat a few during the course of the day, then left the rest. The next morning they were gone; I think she threw them away. We never talked about it, and when her birthday came the following January, we went for ice cream. I doubt either of us will ever want another doughnut.

The fall term was starting in August, only a couple of weeks after my birthday. Mom and I had seen the high school grounds when we went to enroll me, and my first impression hadn't thrilled me. I wouldn't call it a campus. That makes it sound too big, too carefully laid out. The main building looked grim and institutional, just a several-story brick block with windows in it. The gym was something Mom called a Quonset hut: a long, low metal building with a domed roof. Except for the athletic fields, the area was mostly asphalt, with patches of weeds here and there pushing through cracks. A week into the school year I looked out a window and saw the janitor dressed in khakis and a straw hat, using a weed whacker to shear the weeds down. He made them shorter, but they stayed ragged and unkempt. I found out later he was the school's entire groundskeeping crew. The athletic fields were maintained by parent volunteers.

The Music and the Strife

As the start of school drew closer, I began to get nervous. I still hadn't met anyone my age. If Mom had bought a house in town I might have, but out where we lived, there was hardly anybody. I'd never attended a school where I didn't know a single person. I'd read about small town clannishness, how people could be chilly and unwelcoming to newcomers, which added to my anxiety. I didn't mention anything about it to Mom, though. I didn't want her to have any reason to worry about me. Mr. Bligh, the man who owned the butcher shop in Holm, was very nice, and when I'd met him, he mentioned he had a son who'd be in my grade. I tried to hang onto the hope that his son was as nice as he was.

On the first day of classes, we were having breakfast when Mom suddenly jumped up from the kitchen table and ran out the front door. I looked out the window and saw her standing on the first step of the school bus, talking to the driver. Soon she waved goodbye, hopped down and came back into the house.

"What was that about?" I asked when she was in her chair again. I was picking at my food. An attack of nerves had wiped out my appetite.

"I just let the driver know that you wouldn't be riding the bus this morning. A friendly woman, you'll like her," Mom added. "I'm taking you today, though."

"Really? Why?" A feeling of relief washed over me as I forced down a bite of egg.

"I need to make sure the office has received all your records from the old school." Mom glanced at her watch. "That's why I let you sleep in a bit this morning. We do need to get going soon, though."

It was comforting to have her with me to start off that first day, but I wasn't looking forward to riding the school bus home that afternoon. On the drive to town, I tried to calm my anxiety with slow, deep breaths. My expectations weren't high, and I pictured myself as the awkward outsider, being ignored and treated as if I were invisible. Then I imagined that going on for the entire school year, and I started to quietly panic. I'd never been a fearful person before Dad's death. *You are now,* a voice in my head said. That was too much of an uncomfortable truth, and I sternly told myself to get a grip. I needed a more positive attitude. Then we pulled up to the high school, and a boy walked past and gave our truck an admiring glance. That made me smile a little. Mom had run Steve through the gas station carwash the day before, and secondhand pickup or not, he was looking good.

Mom went to the school office and I trudged to my home-room, giving myself a mental pep talk. I was the new girl in a small town; most of the others had probably grown up together I shouldn't expect much from anybody, not right away. As the morning wore on, I saw that they weren't unfriendly. Just kind of reserved, maybe cautious of strangers. The teachers were more outgoing, and some I liked immediately, a nice surprise. The world history teacher was a big, burly man with a matching over-the-top personality. He also turned out to be the head foot-ball coach. The Algebra II teacher was tall and lanky with a dry sense of humor, and he did double duty as the head baseball coach. This turned out to be a pattern: Everybody had more than one job. Even, as I saw a few days later, the janitor.

The Music and the Strife

The English teacher, Mrs. Gilpin, was my favorite, which made me happy since English is my favorite subject. At first, she seemed a little shy, peering at us with inquisitive eyes through her glasses, her penciled, reddish eyebrows lifted in a look of mild surprise. Then, by the time that first class was over, she had everybody eating out of her hand. She had a talent for voices and used part of the class period to read aloud from *Romeo and Juliet*. We'd be spending much of the first semester on Shakespeare's tragedies, she told us. She also led the Holm High book club. When she announced near the end of class that club members would be reading vampire literature that school year, I was thrilled.

"If you're interested, the sign-up sheet is on my desk." She arched an eyebrow playfully. "We'll have lots of fun this year. Among the books we'll be reading are Sheridan Le Fanu's *Carmilla* and Bram Stoker's *Dracula*. To finish out the year, we'll read something brand new. Can any of you guess what it is?" She scanned our faces with an expectant air.

I hesitated, then when no one else did, I put my hand up.

Mrs. Gilpin's bright eyes turned toward me and she nodded. "Welcome to Holm High, Miss Sophia McKean. What do you think that book might be?"

"Is it the one that takes place in Louisiana?"

Mrs. Gilpin gave me a delighted smile. "You're exactly right! Anne Rice's *Interview with the Vampire*."

"Wow!" I blurted, then blushed and put a hand over my mouth as a cute boy to my right turned to look at me. A few people laughed, but not in a mean way, and I felt the tips of my ears burning.

Susan Rooke

Embarrassed or not, I rushed to the front to sign up as soon as class was over. A handful of other girls and one guy were signing up, too, which gave me hope of making at least one friend from the people who enjoyed the same kind of reading I did.

As I walked back to my desk to get my books, I noticed the cute boy was still sitting at his desk, gathering his things together. He looked up as I reached him and smiled at me. When I smiled back, he held my gaze for a brief moment, and I had a quick impression of clear, steady eyes of a striking turquoise blue. Then he ducked his head, and dark blond hair fell to cover those eyes as he slid to his feet and left the classroom. When I followed him out the door a few seconds later, I was still smiling. Maybe high school in Holm wouldn't be half bad.

When the bell rang for lunch, I followed a group who seemed to know where they were going, and found the cafeteria. It was a sizeable, high-ceilinged room with dull, putty-colored walls and a linoleum tile floor that at first looked as if it had been mopped with mud. It turned out to be the grayish brown pattern on the tile, but I noticed it didn't match the floor tile in the hallway nor in any of the classrooms I'd seen. In fact, everything inside the school building looked like a collection of mismatched parts, as if it had been finished a little at a time over a period of years—maybe as the town's population grew.

I glanced to my left. A food line staffed by two women in hairnets extended along one wall. I wondered what their second jobs were. School nurse? Bus driver? As I looked around, I saw columns of stacked chairs lining another wall and a small stage

23

with steps leading up to it against a third. Even the cafeteria had a second job; it was also the assembly hall.

I walked to the far side of the room and took a seat at one end of a table for six. I had my back to the wall and a good view of the entrance, so I could watch everyone coming and leaving. Soon a boyfriend/girlfriend pair straggled in, went through the food line and took the other end of my table. They said hi to me—politely—when they sat down, which I hadn't expected. Then they drowned in each other's eyes for the rest of the lunch period. I doubt they tasted what they were eating, which didn't seem to be much of a loss. I looked over their trays, and nothing I saw made me regret packing my own lunch.

The remaining classes and free period were perfectly ordinary, so my first day was painless. Even gym was a pleasant surprise. It turned out I could fulfill that requirement by joining a walking group that spent each P.E. class briskly circling the track. Riding the bus home that afternoon, lulled by the deep growl of the engine and the rhythm of tires meeting the road, I was greatly relieved. For the past week, I'd been wondering if I'd have to beg Mom to homeschool me. Thankfully, it didn't seem that would be necessary. It would be nice to have someone to eat lunch with eventually, but I was a little more hopeful now that it would happen in time.

———

That time came about two weeks after the term had begun. The days so far had been passing much like the first one, and the cafeteria food continued to look unappetizing. I knew a couple of girls superficially from book club, well enough to say hi to.

A few people had come by my table at lunch or stopped me in between classes to ask about homework. Also, I knew the name of the cute guy who sat next to me in English; he turned out to be Jack Bligh, the butcher's son. We had two other classes together, world history and typing, but we weren't seated near each other. Which was a shame, because he always gave me a shy smile in English now as we got settled at our desks.

On this particular day, I was late to the cafeteria. I'd stopped off in the library to return a book and, as always happens when I go to a library, I got distracted by several other books I saw. By the time I made it to lunch, almost everyone else had finished and left.

As usual, I was alone at my table, enjoying some quiet time. I was eating a really good sandwich, made from the leftovers of a ham my mother had baked, and spread with her homemade whole grain mustard. While I ate, I let my eyes drift around the room as I daydreamed about Jack. That went nowhere, mostly because Jack wasn't there; he'd apparently left with the earlier lunch crowd. So I entertained myself by making up stories about the lives of the Holm High lunch ladies. I'd guessed correctly that one of them was a school bus driver. She drove my route, in fact, and Mom had been right. I did like her; she was quite nice.

The other woman dishing up food on the lunch line seemed nice enough, too, but she was still a mystery. I'd learned she ran the school kitchen with the help of a couple of volunteer parents, but judging from the cafeteria food, how long could that possibly take? She needed something else to fill the rest of her day, so I made up another job for her. She spent the hours of darkness,

I decided, as the school's night watchman. Her eyes were large and protruding, so I imagined her stalking the silent campus grounds, illuminating her way not with a flashlight, but with the light of her own glowing, bulbous eyes, which cast a pale, eerie light wherever they turned. I've since realized I must've been under the spell of *Carmilla*, which we were reading in book club that week.

I checked my watch and saw I still had about fifteen minutes before my next class. Very few people were still in the cafeteria. I noticed a girl standing in the food line on the far wall, waiting as the big-eyed lunch lady put a plate on her tray. The girl carried a mesh bag over one arm, and inside it was a brown paper bag holding something roughly the size and shape of a football. Even though she was facing away from me, I knew I'd never seen her before. Her hair was very dark, almost black, and curly, with long ringlets rippling halfway down her back. It was the hair I'd always wanted, imagined myself having in another life, and once I saw it in this one, I could never have forgotten it.

She turned to face the room, tray held before her in two slender, long-fingered hands, and I almost gasped. Her skin was a creamy milk white, and so smooth it seemed translucent. Against that skin her ink-dark hair looked as glossy as a black panther's coat. I knew it wasn't possible, but even from across the room I could swear I saw the color of her eyes in that white face. They were a rich, buttery caramel, large and wide-set. Until that moment, I hadn't known that in the fabled other life I imagined for myself, those were the exact eyes I wanted, too. She seemed unreal, a character straight from fiction. I could envision her as the ideal Anne Rice vampire. Her perfection was marred only by her lips. They were a deep pink, but a little on the thin side. It was the sole feature that made her seem approachable The mesh bag was the only other thing I saw. I have no memory of what she was wearing. A plastic garbage bag? I can't say.

Too late, I realized I was staring at her. Of course, she noticed, but instead of looking annoyed or superior, she smiled and headed toward me. Then asked if she could join me. One outsider recognizing another, I decided. Because from what I could see, though for completely different reasons, she didn't blend in there any more than I did.

"Sure," I said. Or something equally lame.

She set her tray down and put the mesh bag on the table beside it, then slid into the molded plastic seat across from me. It was putty-colored, like the walls. As she opened her drink carton—lemonade, I think—she smiled again, and her caramel-colored eyes shone. "You're new here, aren't you? I'm Holly. What's your name?"

I know I managed to get my own name right, because she repeated it back to me. It could have gone either way. Then I added, "But if you want to, just call me 'Phee' for short."

As we ate, I was able to get past my awe, and we started to talk. It was a bit stiff at first, but her genuine friendliness and interest in what I had to say made it easier. I told her my mother and I had moved into a house outside of town and we were new to the area. I didn't mention Dad's death. Not yet. If she'd asked me why it was just Mom and me, I would've told her, but she didn't, just gave a sympathetic nod. Warmth and understanding seemed to radiate from her, and she was polite, too, with a sort of old-fashioned courtesy. It made her seem a little formal, older than she was.

Before too long, though, we'd fallen into an easy, relaxed conversation. My mother's ham and homemade mustard broke the ice. We started talking about food, and it turned out Holly's mother was a whiz in the kitchen, too, unlike the mothers of most of my old friends, whose kitchen cabinets were filled with boxes of powdered mixes and cans of condensed soup. In fact, Holly had missed the first two weeks of school because she was helping her mother, who had a successful business running a small bakery out of their home.

"People all over town buy her bread," Holly said with pride in her voice. "You'd be surprised how hard she has to work to keep up with demand. She has out-of-town customers, too." Holly patted the mesh bag. "In fact I've got one of her loaves in here."

"Oh, could I see it?"

"I'm taking it to Mr. Parker after lunch, so I can't unwrap it, but I'll let you have a peek." Holly pulled out the paper bag and lifted a small section, revealing part of a golden loaf with a shiny crust. I caught a rich, yeasty smell.

I was impressed. "It's beautiful. I'll tell my mother about her." I picked up my sandwich and looked at it. "This is great, but on homemade bread, it'd be spectacular." I took another bite. "So who's Mr. Parker? One of your teachers?"

Holly smiled. "No, he's the school janitor. He scrapes by on his pay and doesn't have many luxuries, so Mama gives him two or three loaves a month."

This was a humbling revelation and made me realize how much I could stand to improve. Until that moment, I hadn't even known the janitor's name. "That's so kind of her," I said.

Holly gave a little embarrassed shrug as she carefully rewrapped the bread and set it aside. "She's had to slow down production lately. Before school started, she injured her wrist when she was filling a large order. So I did the steps she needed two hands for. Scraping dough out of the mixing bowl. Transferring trays of baking tins in and out of the oven. That kind of thing. Luckily she could do the kneading one-handed. I don't have enough experience with that."

As she spoke, Holly waved her fork in the air, and I looked at her hands. They appeared so delicate, the fingers so long, that I couldn't imagine them working with heavy bowls full of dough. "Do you see yourself joining her in the business one day?" I'd actually had that dream with Dad but I'd never told anyone about it.

"No. My thing is music."

I leaned forward as my attention sharpened. This sounded exciting, and I was imagining her fronting a band. "Really? What kind of music?"

"I play the violin."

I nodded, trying to appear interested, but my enthusiasm had deflated a bit.

She looked down at her plate, where the remnants of a limp cheeseburger lay. She seemed to sense my disappointment. "I've played for as long as I can remember. My parents tell me that from the time I could walk, a violin was put into my hands." She set her fork on the plate and pushed her tray away. "I compose, too."

My eyebrows shot up. This was getting interesting again. "That's so amazing, you can play your own music! I'd love—"

She put a hand up to stop me. "It's not anything special. Not like people are listening to these days. It's..."

"It's what?"

"The style is classical. Not completely, though. There's not a name for it."

Puzzled, I waited for her to explain. When she didn't, I prompted her. "Well, what do *you* call it?"

Her gaze drifted to the cinder block wall behind me, then higher, to where the fire alarm was mounted a few feet above my head. For a moment, she stared at it, as if mesmerized by its steel casing, painted a glossy red. Finally she said, "I guess I'd call it... music of the spirits." She lowered her warm caramel eyes to me again and shrugged. "That's as good a name as any."

I didn't know if she had meant to blunt my interest, make me believe that she was ordinary and her music dull, but her words had the opposite effect. They seemed to hang in the air and reverberate inside my head. A little tremor ran up my spine.

―――――――

That first lunch with Holly was soon cut short by the bell for next period. I did learn that she was a year ahead of me, and we didn't share any of the same classes. From that day on, we fell into the habit of eating lunch together whenever our schedules allowed, and soon it was as if we'd known each other for years. By then I'd told her about Dad's accident, and she responded just the way I'd hoped: with quiet, heartfelt sympathy. That eased my mind because until then, I always tried to hide how badly it had devastated me.

One day while I waited at the table and Holly stood in the line, I thought about how lucky I was. Things could've been so much worse. I'd been nervous about moving that far away, but I knew Mom desperately wanted new surroundings. Holm wouldn't have been my choice, but now I saw that it wasn't bad at all. It might even suit me. I'd already found a good friend. A friend whose family, as it turned out, lived in a house on the banks of the River Buckle.

I was floored when she told me. We'd come to that, "Where do you live? Really? That's so close to me!" conversation on the third lunch. Their house was only a few hundred yards beyond the back of our property. Though their property was considerably larger, their land, in fact, bordered ours. Immediately, we made plans to visit each other.

I remember Mom's face when I got off the school bus that day and practically ran into the kitchen. She was relieved when I told her.

"I'm so glad, Phee. I've been concerned that this house might be too isolated for you to find friends out here. I'm happy that's not the case." She put a hand up to her forehead, looking suddenly vulnerable, and my heart went out to her. She dropped her hand and sighed. "That's good news; I feel better about it now."

I went to her and put my arms around her. "It's going to be all right, Mom." I squeezed her hard. "Holly's invited me over this Saturday. Is that okay with you?"

Mom squeezed me in return, then released me and looked into my eyes. It was the first time I noticed that I was now a little taller than she was. "Holly? That's a lovely name. Not one you hear that often."

"Holly Miller," I added.

Mom nodded slowly. "Oh, yes, the Millers. I'm told they've lived in Holm for a long time."

———————

Late in the morning that Saturday, I struck out from our backyard, heading for the line of taller trees bordering the River Buckle. Our back fence marked the start of a gradual downhill slope, and it was an easy walk. It was nearly autumn by then, but the day was warm and humid, and flying insects buzzed around me under the trees as I walked. Birds startled as I passed by, and flew up to higher branches, squawking. Squirrels chittered in annoyance, and I would swear one dropped an acorn on me on purpose. I watched for Holly through the trees as I walked. She'd said she would meet me halfway and walk with me to her house. There was a fence to cross, she explained, and she needed to show me where the stile was.

The undergrowth wasn't as thick as I'd feared it would be, though I still couldn't see as much of my surroundings as I would've liked. Traveling through these woods at night would be a frightening prospect. My skin crawled as I imagined doing that. I was startled—and glad—when Holly's voice called out to me.

"There you are! Yay, you made it!"

She wore a big smile as she jogged toward me. Her dark curls were pulled up into a high ponytail that swung from side to side as she moved. I smiled back at her.

We fell into conversation as she led me forward, showing me a couple of obvious landmarks to watch for.

"I want it to be easy for you when you come on your own. I don't want you wandering around, getting lost in the woods," she said with a laugh.

That makes two of us, I thought.

Their fence was similar to the one Mom and I had seen from the road, but the posts were thicker and straighter, the rows of wire stretched tight between them.

The stile was a structure of four wide, smooth wooden boards, each maybe four feet long. Three of them passed crosswise through the fence, their length running perpendicular to the wire rows, so that about two feet of board extended on either side. They were stair-stepped, supported by sturdy wood posts. The fourth board topped the fence and ran lengthwise—a place to stand when turning to descend the steps to the other side. Next to the top board was a wood post that extended up above it as a handhold.

For several moments I stood admiring the stile. It delighted me. I'd never seen one in real life, although I'd read about them in books. I knew they'd been used for centuries and were meant to keep livestock fenced while allowing people to cross over without the need to build a gate. To me, it seemed ingenious, almost miraculous, like a magic door to some other world, a parallel dimension.

I was still gawking at it when Holly ran lightly up the steps to the top, then down the other side. She turned and waited for me, smiling.

With a little hesitation, I moved forward, put a foot on it, then with more confidence mounted the steps to the top. There I stopped and looked around. It was much steadier than I'd expected, and gave me the same feeling I got from riding in Steve. I had a different view, a farther view, and it was wonderful. With a cushion, a book, and something cold to drink, I could've spent hours up there. But Holly was waiting for me, so I descended the steps to join her.

Maybe the stile was a magic door after all. As soon as I'd crossed to the other side of the fence, the woods fell silent.

three

The unnatural silence continued as we walked. The woods thinned, giving way to yards of grassy ground open to the sky, and beyond, a thicket of tall trees. These were larger than the ones we'd been walking through, and looked like a single kind, their long leaves tinged with yellowish bronze, branches reaching to the clouds. I thought they were probably pecans, like my mother had shown me from the truck the day we'd gone in search of the river. They grew close together, making a kind of barrier before us. Some stood straight, others leaned against each other, looking ready to crumble. Holly led me toward them and pointed ahead. There were several ranks of them, but peering between their thick trunks, I saw another stretch of grass-covered ground on the far side. Beyond that, there was the sparkle of sunlight on water.

She gave me a secret, mysterious smile, then turned and slipped in among the trees.

I followed, and at once the warm breeze vanished. Trees towered around us. I halted, looking up, and saw splashes of blue and white sky between the topmost branches high above. There were no birds flying, no nests in the branches. I saw what I thought must be ripening pecans everywhere, roughly round shapes, almost golf ball-sized. Mom had told me the nuts grew encased in thick husks that would open when the nuts were ripe. These husks looked like they were splitting. The woods were deep and still. Holly had stopped to wait for me. Neither of us spoke. The quiet was profound, as if the shady aura of the pecan trees surrounding us allowed no sound to carry. I could've been in a sacred grove from antiquity. Even from myth.

After a few moments I became aware of Holly's eyes on me. "Sorry," I whispered. "This is just so beautiful." I knew how silly I must have looked, standing there gaping as if I'd never seen trees before. I was awed, and also a little uneasy. It seemed possible that a wolf standing on its hind legs like a man might step out from behind a deeply scored trunk and, with a sharp, white grin, block our way.

Holly lifted a graceful hand, waving my discomfort aside. Then she beckoned without speaking, and we moved forward through the pecan trees.

We emerged, and I felt the breeze on my face again. Before me was the River Buckle, and for the first time, I heard its purling, gurgling voice.

It was maybe forty yards across. The water was a deep blue-gray color and flecked with bright glints of sunlight. The shores on either side were covered in rolling green hummocks that sloped gently to the water's edge. They looked as if they'd be soft to lie upon, like pillows filled with down. Directly in front of us, the river took a sharp bend like an elbow. To the right of this bend was the oncoming current, heading straight for us. To the left of the bend, the current continued its flow away from us downstream. At the bend itself, just below the near bank, there was a torrent of boiling white froth where the water hit a tumble of boulders jutting above the surface. Before and after the bend, the river flowed swiftly, rippling, and for some reason I can't explain, it gave me the notion of great depth. It struck me as a beautiful, peaceful place, but with a cauldron of savage wildness at its center. As I stared at the water pounding against the boulders, my mind emptied of thought and filled with vague, formless darkness. When I came to myself, Holly was watching me with a knowing look.

"You felt it, didn't you?" she asked.

I swallowed, nodding.

"Not many people do." She swept her right arm out, gesturing past the Buckle flowing relentlessly toward us to point out a structure not far away. "Come on, let's get to the house."

On some level, I think I'd noticed it set back a distance from the bank, but the river had claimed my attention. I turned to look at it then.

I couldn't help myself. I studied it with the critical perception my father, the builder, had instilled in me over the years. During those times I'd accompanied him to job sites, he'd taught me about his trade. He kept a hard hat in his truck adjusted smaller, just for me. In the slower hours, under his close supervision, I'd used the tools, taken the measurements, even helped to mix mortar and lay a few bricks and tiles. I developed an eye for the most pleasing dimensions. As we walked toward the Miller house, I felt whatever expectations I might've had for it vanish in the reality of what I saw.

It was a three-story heap so broken down it could've been there since time began. Or just as easily, it could've been thrown up the day before by a crew of willing but inexperienced volunteers. It was made of a jumble of worn boards that looked like scrap lumber, and some kind of gray, pitted stone. The roof was jagged pieces of gray slate that looked as if a stiff wind would send them sliding down the steep pitch to shatter on the ground. There were windows across the broad front of the house, distributed in no particular pattern. They appeared to be old, even antique, the kind that would have bubbles in the glass. The impression the house gave was of great age, and that it had been added on to here and there over a period of centuries with no real goal in mind. It had an almost derelict look.

The front faced the river, and there was a yard planted with rows of vegetables and some herbs I recognized, and dotted with small fruit trees. Their branches drooped with green fruit, some round, some more pear-shaped, a few with pebble-skinned fruits that were turning yellow and orange. A driveway circled the garden, then turned to pass one side of the house and head off into the distance away from us, parallel to the course of the river. The driveway was surfaced with something dark in color, and I didn't think it was crushed asphalt or dirt. As we approached it, I crouched down to look at it more closely. It was powdery, a little coarse, and on impulse, I ran my palm across it and pressed. It was surprisingly soft and smooth. And thick.

I brushed my hand off on my jeans and stood up. "What is this stuff?"

Holly turned back to the pecan trees we'd come through, and lifted her arms to them. "Ground pecan shells."

My eyes tracked the length of the driveway. What I could see wasn't all of it, and I wondered how far it went. "How many hundreds of thousands of pecans would it take to pave this road in shells?"

"More like millions," she answered.

My head swam. "How long would it take to collect enough pecans to cover it to a depth of—" I took a step back and glanced down. "—five or six inches?"

Holly just laughed. "You wouldn't believe me if I told you."

I waited, expecting her to tell me anyway. Wasn't that what people usually did after making a statement like that? She didn't.

I tried a less direct approach. "Is it long-lasting?"

She shrugged. "Not especially. But we never run out of pecans, so…"

I stared out into the distance, down the dark ribbon that followed the river until I couldn't see it anymore. I couldn't imagine the amount of time the creation of this road represented.

When I tried to think of it, to hold it in my mind, it slipped away. Then my eye was caught by an unpainted, rusty mailbox that stood beside the driveway near the front of the house. It was the kind shaped like a tunnel, and it was mounted on a scarred wooden post. The flag was bent, hanging down only partway and jutting out at an angle. The flap was crooked, unable to close completely. Painted in faded black letters on the side of the box wasn't a name I'd expected: ARDEN. The box appeared to be as old as the house, as if it had been there since before mail service began.

Holly saw me looking at it. "Oh, we don't get mail here. We're too far from the main road."

"So who were the Ardens, then? Did they live here before your family?" I asked.

"No."

I stared at it, expecting her to elaborate, but she didn't. How long had the Millers lived there? And why did a mailbox with somebody else's name on it, a mailbox that never collected mail, stand by the front drive? My thoughts were beginning to feel like a snarl of saved string.

"Come on in!" Holly called.

I looked up and saw her standing on the front porch, holding open a screen door. Without meaning to, I'd been lagging behind. I hurried after her, walking quickly across the driveway, and felt it give a little beneath my feet, very unlike gravel or concrete. Joining her on the porch, I started after her into the dark interior of the house before remembering to catch the screen door so it wouldn't bang shut. I was only partly successful, and a small thud echoed back at me.

Susan Rooke

We were in a long, dim entry hall. Darkly painted walls and a dark wood floor gave it a somber look. A threadbare carpet runner with a pattern too dreary and worn to make out ran down the center to an opening at the far end. A tall, narrow window on each side of the front door did nothing to brighten the space. If it hadn't been for the amazing smell of baking bread in the air, the house might've given me an uneasy feeling, but the aroma was so comforting I set any doubts aside.

"Mama's probably in the kitchen," Holly remarked. "Smells like this batch must be almost done. Let's go see."

She went down the hall and I came behind, noticing several wooden doors on either side, the same color as the floor. They were all closed. At the end of the hall we emerged into what seemed like a different house—a space as welcoming as the hallway was steeped in shadows and gloom. There was Holly's mother, turning to greet us. She wore a sky-blue bib apron looped around her neck and tied at her generous waist. Her olive-skinned face was a little pink as she pushed curly hair back from her damp forehead with the back of one hand. Her hair wasn't as dark as Holly's. It was more like the caramel color of Holly's eyes, with streaks of gray through it. Her eyes were darker than Holly's, with strongly arched brows.

Mrs. Miller smiled kindly at me as Holly introduced us. She held up her right forearm, showing an elastic bandage wrapping her wrist. "I'm still healing, otherwise I'd shake your hand, Phee, dear. I'm very glad to meet you, though."

I ducked my head, feeling a little timid, for some reason. "You too, Mrs. Miller."

41

"Would you girls like a slice of buttered bread? I'm about to pull it out of the oven."

"I can do that, Mama," Holly offered.

"It's just one loaf, sweetheart, I can manage." Mrs. Miller chuckled. "I might make a mess of slicing it, but it will still taste good."

My mother made bread sometimes, but only rarely with yeast. Instead, she made batter breads, quickly stirred together, needing no rising—cornbread, gingerbread, and banana bread, mostly, and all delicious. When Mrs. Miller set her bread on the wooden cutting board, I could see at once that hers was in a different realm.

I watched as her left hand wielded the knife; her right forearm, resting on a folded cup towel to shield her from the blistering heat, steadied the loaf. When she set the knife to it, the bronzed, shining crust crackled and a shower of crisp flakes dropped to the board. She cut two thick, perfect slices, exposing a cotton-white interior that plumed with steam. Holly had fetched the butter dish and was now pouring us a couple of glasses from a clear bottle of milk. I tried to remember if I'd ever seen a glass milk bottle anywhere other than in movies. Even the refrigerator was exceptional, a monstrous stainless-steel thing with glass doors. It looked like something you'd see in a restaurant kitchen. Holly pulled a stool up to the kitchen counter and motioned for me to do the same. Impressed, a little dazzled by what was evidently a regular occurrence in the Miller kitchen, I did.

I'd never known anyone who made risen loaves of bread at home. At first, all I could do was hold my piece up and examine it. It looked like a photo from one of my mother's food magazines. Eating it was even better. It wasn't just good. It was probably the best bread I'd ever put in my mouth, and I said so. For a time, we sat there and devoured it, Mrs. Miller leaning back against the kitchen sink, looking pleased. When I finally slowed down, I glanced at the loaf and noticed a pattern cut into the top crust.

"Oh, how pretty!" I said. "I've seen pictures of loaves with the tops slashed, but this is way more decorative. It looks kind of like fancy embroidery stitches." I took another bite and chewed, studying the loaf. "How'd you do that, Mrs. Miller? Don't you have to use a really sharp knife to get those clean cuts?"

"Not a knife, exactly, but it's certainly sharp." She held up a finger. "Hang on, I'll be right back."

I watched her leave the kitchen, then looked at Holly. "Not a knife?"

Holly shook her head. "You'll see."

Mrs. Miller soon returned with a shiny metal implement in her hand. "It's a straight razor." She opened the steel casing and held it up so I could see it.

The blade flashed wickedly in the light from the overhead. I was taking a gulp of milk and nearly choked on it. When I stopped coughing and it was obvious I wasn't going to aspirate, Holly and her mother burst out laughing.

"I didn't know baking involved so much risk," I said, once I was able to talk again. "I mean burns happen, oven racks are hot, but…"

"You don't know the half of it," Holly said, and shot her mother a look.

Mrs. Miller was nodding. "That's right. It's how I hurt my wrist."

I gasped. "You cut it with the straight razor? A deep cut?"

"Deep enough," Holly said, her face grim. "She's lucky. It…she missed doing major damage. Not by much."

I noticed Holly's hesitation and wondered at the look that passed between them. Mrs. Miller had nearly done herself a serious injury, though, one that likely would've taken a long time to recover from. That probably explained it.

"Yes, I was fortunate, and I'll heal. I've had to make allowances, of course, simplify the patterns, but my wrist is already much better." Mrs. Miller folded the razor up and slipped it in her apron pocket. "I should be back to normal in another couple of weeks."

"I'm so glad," I told her. "After you're healed…" I paused, shyness getting in my way. "Well, would it be all right if I watch you make bread sometime? I'd like to know how you do it and see how you make those beautiful designs in the top. Your bread is incredible. It's a work of art."

She gave me a warm look. "Thank you. Of course, dear, I'd love to show you. Holly has her music, a true art form. Baking is more humble, but, I think, just as satisfying to do."

Holly rose from her stool and grabbed our empty milk glasses. "And you can't eat a violin. Thank you, Mama, that was wonderful." She put the glasses in the sink and motioned to me. "Come on, I'll find Papa and introduce you. Then I'll play you some music and you can pretend to like it. Deal?"

"What do you mean? Of course I'll like it!"

As Holly rolled her eyes, I thanked Mrs. Miller with enthusiasm and followed my friend from the room.

"Try the workshop first!" Mrs. Miller called to us as we left.

We found Mr. Miller in an outbuilding away from the house, closer to the river. Calling it a workshop doesn't really explain it. It was nothing like the shop my father and his partner ran their business out of. It didn't have pegboards on the walls with hammers, levels, different types of saws and wrenches of all sizes lined up, each one in its own penciled outline on the board. There were no stacks of lumber or sheetrock, no large wood- and metal-working machinery taking up the floor space—no lathes, drill presses, band saws, table saws, or the like. Mr. Miller didn't work in building construction and renovation. That much had been obvious from my first sight of their house. So what did Mr. Miller have in his workshop? I have no idea. There was no equipment visible on the main floor.

It was a building that looked much like the one they lived in, made of board wood and porous-looking gray stone. On the inside, the walls were unfinished, the wood unpainted, and the framing exposed. The floor was light-colored flagstone, swept clean. A push broom hung upside down from a double hook on one wall. In the middle of the floor was a large rectangular opening into which a set of sturdy metal stairs, shining with black paint, descended. They were nothing like lightweight fire escape stairs. The hand railing was at least two inches across, and the steps were broad and deep. They looked rock solid. From the workshop entrance, I could see the stairs turned at least once on the way down.

Holly led me to the opening, which had a substantial black safety railing most of the way around, with a gap to access the stairs. "I can hear him," she said. "He's down at the bottom working. I'll call to him and see if he can come up here. I'll have to yell. It doesn't sound that loud up here, but down there, it can get noisy." She put her hands to her mouth and leaned over the railing. "Papa!" she hollered. "Can you come up? I've got a friend for you to meet!"

There was a short pause, and a deep voice came booming up from beneath us. "I'll be there in just a moment!"

I looked down over the side. Mostly I saw the black stairs, which made several turns. At the bottom, I saw nothing but a little patch of flagstone floor. It looked well-lit, and the light had a golden cast to it. I could hear machinery at work. There was a cranking, ratcheting sound, made by some sort of metal. It wasn't a rough sound; it was well-oiled and smooth. I envisioned cogs and flywheels, like pictures I'd seen of the inner workings of old, handmade clocks—every piece with a job to do and fitted into place perfectly, turning, clicking, nesting for an instant before moving on. What on earth did he have down there? And what job did it perform?

The machinery slowed, coming to a gradual stop, and I heard the sound of heavy footsteps clanging on metal. Then the top of a dark head of shaggy hair appeared, rounding a turn in the stairs below. When he reached the final flight, a large, beefy man with huge shoulders looked up and gave us a big grin.

Movie-star white teeth showed beneath a thick, black mustache. "Holly, sweetheart, who've you got here?"

I smiled uncertainly back at him. Feeling strangely dizzy, I pushed myself back from the railing, away from the large opening in the flagstone floor. The workshop faded around me, and my thoughts drifted to another time, another place, to centuries ago, and a blacksmith, aproned in leather, working at his anvil in a sweltering hot forge, firelight flickering on mud brick walls. Then the forge grew smaller, receding, and my vision encompassed a larger view, an ancient city soaring nearby, agricultural fields, a blue ocean, its white-capped waves crashing against a rocky shoreline. Gradually, the vision dissipated, and I came back to myself to see Mr. Miller standing beside me. He and his daughter were watching me. They both looked gently amused.

After a moment, my head cleared and I stuck my hand out. "I'm glad to meet you, Mr. Miller."

"Welcome, my dear," he said solemnly, clasping my hand between both of his own in a firm, but not punishing, grip. He wasn't as tall as I'd thought he would be, but he was powerfully built. "This place has an odd effect on people sometimes. On those few who are fortunate enough to be receptive to its ... magic. I see you're one of them." He gave me a quick wink and another generous smile before releasing my hand. "Don't worry. You'll get used to it."

Holly was looking at me appraisingly. "That's the second time since she got here."

Her father raised his eyebrows. "My, my. That *is* unusual."

He smoothed his mustache with a fingertip as he gave me a thoughtful look. His eyes were a golden brown.

I watched the two of them, my gaze moving from one to the other. It was obvious where Holly's coloring had come from. "I'm so sorry," I said, "I don't mean to be rude, but I have no idea what you're both talking about. I must have missed something."

Mr. Miller barked a short laugh. "You haven't missed a thing. Quite the opposite, in fact." He turned back to the stairs. "Well, girls, I need to get to work. You two enjoy yourselves. And you, my dear—" He inclined his head toward me. "You will always be welcome here. I mean that."

For a moment I was speechless. There had been so much kindness, so much perception in his words and in his manner. As if he had looked at me and seen every sorrow from the past eight months laid bare. I suddenly missed my father terribly, and I was overcome. Tears sprang to my eyes. Finally I managed to say, "Thank you, sir. That means a lot to me."

He nodded, his lips pressed together, a sad smile in his own eyes. Then he grabbed the railing with one broad hand and clanked down the stairs.

I stood there unmoving for a moment, lost in reflections of grief and death. Holly's arm came around my shoulders, and she gave me a squeeze.

"Come on. We need to get some music in you."

––––––––––

A few minutes later, I was in Holly's room on the third floor. She'd left me there and run back downstairs to get us something to drink from the kitchen. "Feel free to take a look around, just don't wander out the door," she'd said cheerfully. "The upper floors are easy to get lost in!" Then she dashed out, shutting me in.

Everything about her room enchanted me. Her bed was a wooden four-poster set into a snug sleeping nook that paralleled the front wall of the house. The headboard was fairly tall, and the bed was strewn with gold-trimmed throw pillows in a rich shade of purple. A matching comforter covered it. The bedframe was carved in an intricate design that reminded me of the one in Mrs. Miller's bread. There was a window above the bed, and unlike the ones in the entry hall, this one allowed lots of light into the room. The nightstand held a brass lamp with a glass shade painted in amethyst and gold.

Two walls were lined from floor to ceiling with shelves. One set held a multitude of musical instruments and cases. Three were violin cases, which I assumed held their instruments. Among the other items, I noticed a triangle, a set of bongos made of ebony-colored wood with ivory-toned drumskins, a French horn resting on its bell, a zither, a stringed instrument with a slender neck and a belly shaped like a fat teardrop, a case lying open that held a gleaming silver flute, even an exotic-looking tambourine with delicate flowers painted around its wood frame. I guessed it was probably an antique. Beside it was something that looked even older. It was a metal stand on which was mounted a glowing, burnished gong made of the same metal—bronze, I think. It was maybe a foot in diameter, and two upcurved hooks below it held the mallet to strike it with. The handle was wood, and the rounded striking end was covered in a material with a soft, suede-like finish, possibly animal skin.

The shelves on the adjoining wall were stacked with books and papers. I wandered over to take a look. Holly's taste in reading material seemed quite different from mine. There was a large section on music, with several books on theory and stacks of scores and sheet music as well as books on composers. Some names I recognized, others I assumed were probably composers, too. I paged through a couple of scores. They looked like complicated hieroglyphics. Until then, I guess I hadn't realized just how advanced Holly's ability was. It became abundantly clear to me that I didn't know enough about music to know what I was looking at. Feeling more than a little lost, I moved on down the shelves.

Among the hardcover choices I saw Plato's *The Republic*, Bulfinch's *Mythology* (which is on our shelves, too), *The Golden Bough* by Sir James George Frazer, a history of ancient Greek art, a couple of versions of the Holy Bible (one of which looked old enough to crumble in my hands), a frightening sounding book called *Psychopathia Sexualis* by someone named Krafft-Ebing, *The Interpretation of Dreams* by Sigmund Freud, several books by Carl Jung and both volumes of Julia Child's *Mastering the Art of French Cooking*, which my mother also has. In the paperbacks I saw mostly fiction. There were a few Agatha Christie, more by a writer named Dorothy L. Sayers, and the entire Narnia series, which I knew from my own smaller collection of fiction. I smiled at this. The Narnia books have always been some of my favorites. Suddenly Holly's vast musical knowledge seemed a little less intimidating.

I heard footsteps outside the door and turned to see it swing open. Holly entered the room carrying two glasses dripping with condensation. She brought one to me, and I put it to my nose, inhaling. It was some kind of fragrant fruit juice concoction poured over ice. She sat on the side of the bed and grabbed a purple throw pillow, propping one elbow on it. I chose the armchair covered in forest green velvet near her nightstand.

I took a sip and thought my eyes would roll back in my head. The rich, sweet complexity was unlike anything else I'd ever tasted.

"What on earth is this?" I asked her. "Nectar of the gods? I've never had fruit juice this good."

Holly grinned. "Tastes like it, doesn't it? It's my mother's favorite. She blends it up out of the different fruits we grow, like melons, figs, strawberries, peaches… We grow lots of fruit, and whatever we don't use immediately, she preps and freezes or makes into preserves." Holly took a drink from her own glass and ran the tip of her tongue across her lips. "You wouldn't believe our basement. We have four big chest freezers and shelves covered with glass jars."

I took another sip and held it in my mouth before swallowing. "Do I taste bananas, too?"

"Yeah, she adds storebought bananas to give it body. She says it's got so many vitamins and minerals in it that you can't help feeling good when you drink it." Holly's face grew serious. "I hope you don't mind. I told her I thought you could use a lift."

I looked into my glass, then met her eyes. "No. I don't mind."

Relaxing, I sank back into the chair. It was such a relief to have a friend I didn't have to pretend with. It had been so different at our old home in the city. There, my friends tiptoed around my grief for a while, but not for long. Two months after my father's death, they expected me to be back to normal and were surprised that I wasn't. Not one of them had lost a person they were really close to. A few had lost a grandparent, an aunt or uncle, maybe, but they'd been too young at the time for it to make a big impact. Their memories had faded quickly.

I became the outsider in the group, and gradually these girls had started pulling away from me. I suppose I made them uncomfortable. When my mother decided we needed a fresh start, I knew I'd miss the people I'd thought were my friends, but not the people they turned out to be. No. My father was gone. If I couldn't have him, what I'd miss was my room, our comfortable old house, and the many places where we'd had fun together as the family we once were. Sometimes I need things to stay the same, but I learned the hard way that life can change in an instant.

I felt Holly's gaze on me and realized I'd been lost in thought. I smiled at her. "This is wonderful, thank you. I feel better already." Which was true...and surprising. I cleared my throat. "So how about that music you promised me?"

With a brisk, getting-down-to-business kind of nod, Holly put down her glass and went to the shelves housing the musical instruments. She studied the violin cases, then chose a dark burgundy one and brought it over, setting it on the bed. Unlatching the case, she opened the lid and exposed an interior of cranberry-colored fabric. I saw a gleaming, delicate instrument resting there, and caught my breath. It was so exquisite it made me think the music it produced would be the same. Holding it tenderly by the neck, she lifted it out, then brought out the bow. My anticipation increased. Yes, when we first met, I'd been a little let down after learning her music wasn't what I'd expected. Seeing her hold the violin, though, her confidence and experience made plain with every touch of her fingers, I knew this would be far more memorable. I set my glass on the nightstand, my senses trembling.

She crossed to the far wall, to the only other chair in her bedroom, moving with even more purpose and grace than I'd already seen from her. The chair was wooden, plain, straight-backed. It had no arms. She sat down, her posture erect but not stiff, her face serene and thoughtful. Her eyes were on the window, her gaze distant. I turned in my seat a little to see her better and watched while she fiddled with the tuning pegs, making adjustments I must've been incapable of hearing, since the stroke of the bow on her instrument already sounded beautiful to me. She lowered the violin then, and I knew from her face that she was considering what she would play. Her decision made, she lifted it again to her chin, raised the bow in her right hand, and began.

At once, the light in the room grew brighter. I thought I was imagining things, then I saw the shaft of sunlight stream through the window and fall across her bed, warm the lining in the burgundy case to a rosier tone, then streak across the floor until it stopped at the foot of Holly's chair. It quivered there in a golden pool as she played. I had the odd idea that she had called the light to her, and it had gladly done her bidding.

The notes she played were sweet and liquid, and I found them moving, so moving, yet in an uplifting way, not a sad one. As I listened, I thought this must be the first time since my father's death that I was free of sadness and anxiety. For months they had been always with me, either at the forefront of my mind or tucked away, hiding in the darkest corners. Now, for this moment, at least, they were gone. I felt at peace, my soul soothed. I shut my eyes to listen more closely.

When I opened them, the room was quiet and Holly was gone. The shaft of sunlight had withdrawn, and the violin case was back on its shelf, the instrument and bow presumably inside. I sat up straighter in my chair and gripped the arms tightly, unsettled. What was this place? Who were these people? How long had I been…unconscious? Asleep? What on earth had just happened?

A little unsteadily, I stood up and went to the door. When I opened it, Holly was approaching from down the hall.

"Good," she said with a bright smile, "you're back."

———

Soon afterward I started for home, first thanking Mrs. Miller, who kindly invited me to return any time. Holly walked with me to the stile to be sure I could find it on my own. She seemed concerned about me.

"Are you sure you can get back to your house okay?"

"Oh, yeah, it's not that far." I tried for a casual tone. I felt much better by then, almost normal, and it seemed important that I *sound* normal. I was a little disturbed by my behavior. I didn't want Holly thinking I was unstable. Or strange. What if she decided she'd made a mistake and wouldn't want to be friends anymore?

"I just meant you seem a little out of it. Some people are easily affected by the ..well, I call it atmosphere. We've always known there's some sort of charge in the air here. It affects some people more than others." She stopped in front of the fence and turned her head to look at me, her ponytail of black curls flipping over her shoulder. "You're especially sensitive to it, I think."

About to put my foot up on the stile, I froze. Was she getting ready to write me off? "You think so? I feel fine now, really."

"Oh, I know so. My parents could tell, too."

"Oh, God." I shook my head. "I'm sorry, I didn't mean to cause any worry. If you don't feel comfortable having me over, I guess I understand. I'd love to have you come to my house, though? If you'd still like to?"

To my surprise, she burst out laughing.

"Of course I still want to come see you! And don't you dare say you're sorry for your reaction. My parents told you you're welcome any time, and they meant it. So do I! Actually, the fact that you can feel so clearly the atmosphere of the place makes it much easier on us."

"It does? Why?"

"You've heard the expression, 'Never apologize, never explain?'"

"Sure."

"Well, now we don't need to do either one. You know our place has weird vibes. We know you feel it. That makes you more like us than anyone else around here. It's almost like you're long-lost family!"

I thought about this for a second and then felt my face nearly crack open in a big grin. "I love that!" Impulsively, I gave her a hug. "Thank you, Holly. And thank your parents, please. This is the best I've felt in months."

"You know why?" she asked me, suddenly serious. "Because you're where you belong. Maybe for the first time ever."

———

That evening, as I set the table for dinner, I described my visit to Holly's house to Mom. I told her about Holly's violin playing, praising her skill without trying to describe music I had no memory of hearing. I didn't tell her about passing out, of course, or whatever it was I did. That would worry her and possibly cause her to limit my visits there or even forbid them—a chance I didn't want to take. I also didn't tell her about the peaceful feeling that stole over me as Holly played. Though Mom didn't talk about it much, I knew she hadn't even begun to recover from Dad's death yet. I didn't want to risk hurting her by confessing how soothed the music had made me feel. In no way did I want to sound as if I was dismissing her grief.

As I carried two steaming bowls of black beans and rice to the dinner table I told her about the beautiful property, the river with the sharp bend in it, and Mr. Miller's workshop. Since I hadn't seen much more than a hole in a flagstone floor and a set of metal stairs, that part didn't take long. I wasn't about to bring up my peculiar vision of the village blacksmith.

Mom set down a sizzling plate of spicy cheese sausages from Mr. Bligh's butcher shop, then pulled out her chair. "How odd. I wonder what sort of equipment he could have down there. It's very close to the river, you said?"

I nodded, sitting down myself. "Surprisingly, it's not damp, not like our basement at ho—" I cleared my throat. "At our old house."

She looked thoughtful, and we both devoted ourselves to eating for a bit.

"Mom, you should see the bread Mrs. Miller makes," I said around a spoonful of beans and rice. "It was gorgeous, like something you'd see in a magazine. She even slashes designs into the crust."

Mom smiled at my enthusiasm. "Really?"

"Yes, she does it with a straight razor. It has a blade about like this." I held my fingers about six inches apart.

Mom paused with a spoon halfway to her mouth. "Oh, right. I've read that bakers often use razor blades."

"She accidentally injured herself with it before the start of school," I said. "She made a deep cut in her wrist."

Mom's eyes widened in surprise before narrowing. She frowned. "You've told me Holly's been helping her mother for a while. Is that why?"

"She's recovering now," I added, realizing too late that I should've left the reason for Mrs. Miller's injury unmentioned. "She'll be back to normal soon."

Mom said nothing, watching me as she chewed.

"She slashed the pattern in that loaf she made this morning,"

I said. "It was amazing—so sharp and clean. I asked if I could watch her make bread someday—you know, once she's got the full use of both hands again—and she said yes. I want to practice what she teaches me at home. Who knows what could happen after that? I might have a real talent for it!" I could hear myself babbling and forced myself to stop and cut a bite of sausage.

"Hm. My daughter, the professional baker," Mom finally said in a bemused tone. "I could see that." She picked up her wine glass and took a sip of rosé.

I speared the sausage and waggled my fork at her. "Just think of the fantastic breads I'd bring you!"

"I'd love that." She set her wineglass down and gave me a serious look. "But listen to me."

I tensed. "Sure. What is it?"

"You are not to use that straight razor. Understand?"

I relaxed again. "You don't need to worry, Mom. That thing scares me." I shook my head. "I won't touch it."

"Good. There are other ways to slash a loaf of bread. You can snip the top with scissors, for instance. It might not be as pretty—"

"That's fine with me," I said. "I'm more interested in learning to make the dough, anyway."

Mom nodded, satisfied. We'd both finished dinner by that time, but we weren't in a hurry to leave the table, so we talked about school for a while.

Finally, she said, "Well, I'm glad you had a good time with Holly. It's wonderful that you've met someone you can be friends with. You like her family, too, which is always a help.

Oh—" She snapped her fingers. "You didn't say. Does Holly have any brothers or sisters?"

My face grew hot. "I can't believe it. I've never asked. All the times we've met for lunch, too. How embarrassing. She must think I'm the most self-absorbed person ever."

My mother gave me a look of mild reproof and reached over to pat my hand. "Don't be so hard on yourself. Did she ask you about *your* family?"

"She didn't have to." I sighed, looking down at my empty bowl. "I told her about Dad not long after we met. And about our move to Holm. Since then, I think all I've done is talk, talk, talk. Mostly she likes to hear about what she calls 'life in the outside world.' You know, what it was like living in the city compared to here."

My mother stood up and began clearing dishes from the table. "It's fine, sweetheart. You can ask her about siblings the next time you see her."

I jumped up to help her, and that was the end of it for the evening.

four

"So I know your mom has her bread baking business," I said, "but you haven't told me about your dad. What does he do?"

"My father turns the river."

I stared at her. It was the following Saturday, and I was at Holly's house again. We were sitting out by the Buckle in a little picnic area—some wooden benches and a table in a small gazebo upriver from the bend. I'd brought us two cans of diet soda and some peanut butter cookies, and we were working our way through them. It was a pretty day, breezy with a few puffy white clouds to ease the warm sunshine. I thought I could feel fall in the air, though, which made me glad. It's always been my favorite time of year.

We hadn't seen each other much at school that week. We both had assigned papers to work on and spent our free time in the library. We'd rushed through lunch in the cafeteria together only twice. We'd been looking forward to the weekend, and I was determined to be a better friend than I had been. This time, I would not just talk about myself. I wanted to learn more about her and her family. So I'd asked her what her father did, assuming he must work in Holm somewhere. He was maybe in his late forties, fifty at the most. Too young to be retired. And that was her answer.

"He turns the river?" I repeated. "What does that even mean?"

Her mouth curved in an unreadable smile. It seemed to hold something like pity. "The course of the River Buckle sometimes needs changing. When sedimentary material builds up at the oxbow—"

"What's an oxbow?" I asked.

She pointed toward the river. "That bend you see there. Like an elbow."

My eyes followed the direction of her finger automatically, even though I knew what she was referring to. The bend was certainly distinctive. I'd never seen a river turn so sharply before.

"When silt and gravel and…other things carried downriver begin to build at that bend, a structure begins to form, almost a concretion."

As she talked, I watched her lips move. I wasn't just listening; I was also observing a change in her. She seemed suddenly older, an adult. I felt as if I were in class, listening to one of my teachers give a lecture.

"If too much time passes," she was saying, "that structure will build up to such a height that the river will overrun its banks in several places, upstream and down, and flood the land. Once this process begins, there's no way to be certain how much ground it would swallow. The countryside for miles around might eventually be underwater. So," she shrugged, "my father turns the river."

I could feel myself staring at her with my mouth open. I had so many questions. How long had this been going on? How often does the river get turned? Did somebody else turn it before her father? The biggest question, the one that weighed on me more than all the others, was, how do you turn a river, unless you're God? The whole concept sounded…biblical. Then an idea came to me. "Is that what the machinery in his workshop is for?"

Holly nodded. "What you see on the Buckle's surface is far from the whole story of the river. Long ago, a complex system of tunnels and channels was constructed, built deep down into the riverbank, and bored out under the riverbed. It's a bit like the locks used to adjust water levels so ships can pass from one body of water to another…but not." Her lips quirked, and, seeming more like herself again, she cocked an eyebrow at me. "Got it?"

She was having fun with me, I could see that, but I didn't mind. "Uh-huh. Sure." I grabbed another cookie and sipped my soda. I left the question of turning the river for another time. "What about the rest of your family? I've told you about me, but I don't even know if you have any brothers or sisters."

Holly took a bite of cookie and chewed slowly. After she swallowed, she said, "I have a brother."

"Oh, a brother! Is he—"

"These are great, by the way. Did your mother make these?"

"No, I did." When she looked surprised, I shrugged. "I'd like to get more into baking. I enjoy it."

"Well, they're delicious. We don't have many sweets. My mother doesn't bake them except around the holidays.. for customers." She licked cookie crumbs from her lips. "Unfortunately."

"Anyway, tell me about your brother. Is he older? Younger?" Her answer had surprised me. I thought if she had any siblings I surely would've seen something to indicate it. Wouldn't I have noticed toys or sports gear? Books or clothes? Heard a voice or a TV in another room? I'd seen none of those things, so I had decided she was an only child like me.

Then I recalled the previous Saturday, and how much time I'd spent unaware of my surroundings, and how little of her house I'd actually seen. Today I'd been in the house only long enough to say hello to Mrs. Miller. Mr. Miller wasn't around. He was in the depths of his workshop, no doubt. Probably "turning the river." Whatever that meant.

"He's older," Holly said.

Older. That could explain why I hadn't seen him. "So he's away at college?" Another thought occurred to me. "Or maybe married?"

"No."

The flat terseness of her answer caught me off guard. It seemed brusque, meant to put a stop to this part of the conversation. I felt I'd been slapped down when all I was trying to do was make up for my self-absorbed focus on my life, my problems. The expression on Holly's face, however, didn't match her reply. She looked pleasantly neutral, even placid. Still, I was taken aback, and I guess it showed, because she offered me a bit more.

"Ruminato travels quite often."

What an odd name. "Rumen what?" I said. Wasn't that a cow's stomach?

"Ruminato," she repeated, sounding out the syllables. "It's a family name."

She said this with a calm serenity, as if it explained everything. Maybe it did, only now I was more curious than ever. I turned it over in my mind. The name sounded exotic. Could it be Spanish? Italian? I almost repeated it just to feel my lips and teeth around it. It made me want to know more about her family, where they were from, how long ago they'd moved here. Ruminato. Was it a family surname? An ancestor's first name? I bit my tongue, though. I wasn't going to pry. If she wanted to share more with me, she would.

"Oh," I said. "Okay." I decided to switch gears. I'd been really enjoying Mrs. Gilpin's book club and I'd been urging Holly to sign up, too. "Hey, have you thought any more about—"

"So that's our family," Holly said, as if unaware I was speaking. "That's all there is to know."

Something about the way she said this made me certain that was far from all. She was staring at the river, and her mind could've been a thousand miles away. In the breeze, her long black curls twirled around her shoulders like serpents.

"But..." I hesitated, fearful of saying the wrong thing.

"You haven't really told me much." If anything, I knew less than before.

She turned to look me in the eyes. "Yes, I have." She held up a long, white hand and extended her index finger upward. "My father turns the river."

This again? I thought, but I said nothing. There was a robotic quality to her voice that disturbed me.

She held up her middle finger beside the first one. "My mother bakes the bread."

I nodded and smiled a little, even as I noticed her phrasing. "The bread." Not simply "bread."

She extended her ring finger to join the other two. Her thumb held her little finger down. "And I must bring the music." She dropped her hand into her lap.

The smile froze on my face as I stared at her. "'Must?' You mean...you *have* to bring the music?"

"Oh, yes." She nodded, her face serious. "There is no one else to do it, and the music is essential."

My mouth dropped open, and I forgot my determination not to pry. "No one else? Well, what about your brother? Ruminato? What does he do?"

Holly dazzled me with a warm, compassionate smile. It transformed her face, making her look like herself again. "That is why the music is essential," she explained slowly, as if to a small child. "My brother—" She raised her hand again, this time extending four fingers, her thumb crossed over the palm. "My brother brings the strife." Then she closed her hand into a fist.

The Music and the Strife

I debated asking Mom's opinion on the latest conversation with Holly, then decided to keep it to myself. If it sounded strange to my ears, I could only imagine how it would sound to hers. By then, I was on fire with curiosity. If before I'd been too preoccupied with telling Holly my life story, now I'd become too preoccupied with hers. Not that I meant to be nosy. I really wanted to spend more time at her house, though. The way she had talked about—or avoided talking about—her brother was odd, to say the least.

Fortunately, the Millers didn't seem to mind my visits. They always welcomed me gladly, and Mrs. Miller stuffed me with her luxurious bread. I had the impression they were as pleased Holly had found a friend as my mother was pleased for me. And Holly and I were pleased to have found each other. We were like two peas in a pod. Two oddball peas.

I went to her house almost every time. She wasn't unwilling to come to mine, but she pointed out that her instruments and music were in her own house, and daily practice was an important part of her schedule. She didn't need to convince me. She was capable of magic, as I'd glimpsed that very first time, even if I didn't remember most of it or understand it. Holly had brought to the room something that should've been impossible, and I'd been fortunate enough to be in its presence. She brought the music. Maybe she was right. Maybe she really did have to bring it…because Ruminato brought the strife.

One school night, I lay in bed trying to sleep but kept thinking back to what Holly had said in the gazebo that day and the way she looked when she said it, like something supernatural, with the gold flecks in her serious caramel-colored eyes, her skin so luminous, her hair so alive and dark. I knew the music she brought had power. The first time I heard it, it had commanded the sunlight, and it had put me to sleep, as if casting a spell. An unsettling thought occurred to me.

Could she be right about her father's power to turn the river? If so, did that mean her mother might be more than just a baker who made astonishingly good bread? Was it possible that the powers her parents and her brother brought to the table equaled her own? I had the feeling that Holly meant exactly what she said. Her mother's purpose was to bake "the bread," to create works of art with which to nourish people. Bread had been known for centuries as the staff of life. Her father's purpose was to preside over an apparently ancient complex of machinery that could change the direction the River Buckle ran. Her older brother brought "the strife," not some nameless, everyday strife. "*The* strife." Was it of a kind so dreadful that no one wished to speak of it?

And Holly brought the music, something that none of the other three could do. The longer I thought about it that night, the more obvious it seemed. Her music tamed the strife, directed it, just as it had tamed and directed the sunlight that first day.

Who were these people?

———————

In another couple of weeks, the weather had finally turned a little cooler, and Mrs. Miller's wrist injury was healed. She asked me if I still wanted to watch her make bread, and of course, I jumped at the chance. She'd been forced to cut back on her production while she recovered, but now she resumed making all the breads she offered in the quantities her customers had come to expect. Each loaf, I felt certain, was a work of art.

The first thing she did when Holly and I entered the kitchen that Saturday morning was to shoo one of us back out again.

"Holly, let us have some space for Phee to have her lesson, please. Go find something to do."

Holly gave her a blank look. "Why?"

"Because you know more about bread baking than Phee does, dear. I don't want your familiarity with the process to make her shy. I want her to feel free to speak up and ask any question she likes."

My eyes moved from one of them to the other. I felt like a child among the grownups, but I appreciated Mrs. Miller's suggestion.

Holly gave an exaggerated groan, but left the room without further protest.

"Now, then, Phee dear," Mrs. Miller said briskly once Holly had vanished through the doorway, "go ahead and take off your jacket. Give yourself some freedom to work. You'll warm up quite soon, I promise."

Surprised, I unzipped my windbreaker and hung it over the back of a chair. "I get to help you make it? I thought I was just going to watch."

She smiled at me. "Of course you're going to help me. Hands-on lessons are the best kind in baking. Today's lesson is Irish soda bread."

With that, we got to work. Mrs. Miller was true to her word. She made certain I had my hands in everything, a part in each task. The time flew by, and in less than two hours, I was pulling a handsome, rustic round loaf with an X slashed into the top out of the oven.

"Very nice," she murmured in approval as she set the loaf on the breadboard. "Now that you've got your feet wet, we'll aim for something a little more complicated next time. And we'll use yeast for leavening instead of baking soda. Here you go. You do the honors." She handed me a long, serrated knife and watched me position it on the loaf. "A little thicker... There, perfect."

Hesitantly at first, I cut into it, and a warm and mighty fragrance arose, making my mouth water. The texture was a bit coarse, which created plenty of surface area to absorb the lightly salted butter I was soon swiping across my slice. Holly entered the kitchen just then, drawn by the smell of baked bread, and together we sat down to enjoy it. I forced myself to eat mine slowly and savor it.

One thing made me curious, though. The only marking on this loaf was the X on the top. I asked Mrs. Miller about it as Holly and I ate.

She untied her apron and hung it on a hook on the pantry door before answering. I had the idea she was using the time to think about her response. She walked back to the counter where Holly and I sat.

"I know you particularly want to see that part of the process, Phee, and you will. I'll show you in future lessons. This loaf here, though…" She patted the thick, dark brown crust. "This is strictly a practice loaf. Meant as demonstration."

"Don't forget eating!" Holly put in with her mouth full.

"Of course." Mrs. Miller smiled. "However, the patterns on the loaves I make to sell, and for us to eat here at home, serve a purpose that wasn't necessary for this loaf."

"So they aren't just for decoration?" I asked. "Are they to tell one kind of bread from another?"

She hesitated, then nodded. "They do both of those things. But you're right, their true purpose is more than ornamental. Those patterns are for protection—for healing, for defense against harm. I don't take them lightly. I make them with intention, specific to each need, exactly the way I mean for people to eat my bread."

I was so surprised that I stopped in the act of taking a bite. "Mrs. Miller!" I exclaimed, more loudly than I'd intended. I heard Holly snort with laughter. "You mean like a *spell?*"

Mrs. Miller's face flushed, and she chuckled. "You could call it that, I suppose."

"Do your customers know?"

"Not really, no. I've never mentioned it to anyone outside our family. Until just now, to you." She gave me a mock-severe look. "So there's no need to spread it around. I'd rather no one knew. My customers are good people who've been buying from me for years, but they probably wouldn't understand and might even misinterpret. I could lose business. So don't tell anyone, Phee. The only thing that's important is that my customers know how the bread makes them feel."

In the brief silence that followed this statement, I wondered why, then, she had decided to tell me about it, a fifteen-year-old she'd known for a matter of weeks. Something else bothered me, too. "What about my mother? Is it all right if I tell her?"

Mrs. Miller caught me in a piercing gaze that seemed to go on too long. She looked at Holly and raised her eyebrows.

"I'm sure it's fine, Mama," Holly said. "Mrs. McKean doesn't seem like someone who'd be offended by what you're trying to do for people."

Mrs. Miller pursed her lips, finally nodding. "Then, yes. You can tell your mother. No one else, though, dear. I need to keep doing the most good that I can."

She looked so serious and determined she seemed almost fierce, like a she-wolf protecting her pups. I had a momentary glimpse of her strength, and felt as if an aura of safekeeping surrounded the three of us, filling the kitchen. It was another of those moments I was getting used to having in the presence of the Millers. Instead of panicking or trying to fight it, I lost myself in it. When I was able to think clearly again, I found myself staring at the slice of bread in my hand. In my head, I heard Holly's words: "My mother bakes the bread." I took a bite, trying to hang onto the feeling of safety.

I wished Dad had been lucky enough to have such an aura around him, but it was far too late for that.

five

I persuaded Mrs. Miller to let me take the rest of the Irish soda bread home. She was reluctant at first, pointing out that the loaf had already been cut into and it didn't bear one of her special patterns.

"I want your mother to see a perfect specimen, Phee. Why don't you wait until next time? I'll give you a lovely loaf of yeast bread to take home."

I thanked her, but said that Mom would especially enjoy eating the first loaf of bread that I'd helped to make. Mrs. Miller understood and wrapped it up for me. At the time it didn't strike me, but looking back, I think there was more to the conversation. She didn't want me to have the loaf because it offered no magic. If she'd known I was going to take it home, she would have endowed it with its true purpose.

Mom loved it, of course, and was pleased to know I enjoyed the lesson. By that point, I think she really was envisioning a daughter who owned her own bakery, and I wanted to believe that, too. In any case, we both ate too much of it with dinner and finally stopped because we wanted some of it toasted the next morning. So maybe it was the sheer quantity I ate and not the loaf's lack of protective symbols. I don't know. Whatever the cause, I slept restlessly that night and had a strange dream.

I found myself in a space that I recognized at once as the entry hall of the Miller house. It was night in my dream, and so dark and still that the atmosphere had a heavy, velvety texture to it, as if I were being smothered with a cloak. The hall looked different, though. In the often-illogical way of dreams, it stretched on and on, easily twice as long as I knew it to be in real life, and the wood floor was bare. At the far end, the black opening of the kitchen doorway squatted, like the mouth of a cave. Silence muffled everything. As hard as I listened, I heard nothing, not even the hum of the refrigerator, until I heard the soft click of a knob turning down the hall. Someone was opening a door.

I froze, holding my breath. I heard something coming toward me, but the hallway was so dim I saw nothing definite, only a dark shape. Footsteps bumped softly on the wood floor. At first, I thought whatever was coming wore slippers, but the sound was too big for slippers. That makes no sense, I know. The best way I can describe it is to call it a swishing, bundled thump, as if whatever came up the hall had its feet wrapped in something thick that disguised noise. I thought of the gong in Holly's room and the mallet with animal hide wrapped around the striking end. Whatever was coming had its feet—however many feet it had—bundled just like that stick. For some reason, that terrified me.

As it drew nearer, I heard it breathing. It was labored, with a faint, high whistle to it, as if its nasal passages were obstructed and it couldn't get enough air. It reminded me of a boy I'd known in elementary school who had a deviated septum. His nose whistled when he breathed. Except this breathing came from something taller—the height of a man. Now I thought I could make out a form in the middle of the hallway—just a vague outline of a thing, like an upright figure wearing a baggy robe.

I felt a swirl of air and a sudden slight warmth. It was closer, and God help me, though I still couldn't see it clearly, now I could smell it. A rank odor that made me think of sweat…and of barnyard animals. I tried to open my mouth, wanting to scream, unable to do it. Then the hallway lit up. There was no sound, no click of a switch, no lamp or light fixture that I could see. Remembering the dream later, I realized there were no shadows, either. It was as if the light came from everywhere at once.

When I saw what was in front of me—too close, closer than I expected—I felt as if I'd been punched in the chest. It wasn't some monstrous thing, not exactly, but it was awful, and impossible. I saw a tall young man wearing what looked like a long, grimy blanket, wrapped so that only his head and neck were exposed. It took me a moment to realize it was the hall carpet runner. His eyes were as dark as strong coffee, so dark brown that I couldn't tell iris from pupil. His skin was very pale, and his hair was nearly black, cut short and ragged. His brows were black slashes above his eyes, and they slanted up at the outer corners, giving him a devilish look. From his eyes up, he had a human face. Below that, I couldn't tell what he was. Was he wearing a mask? That seemed the only explanation. Something creamy white, stiff like starched fabric, molded into the shape of a flower, covered the rest of his face from nearly the bridge of his nose down, hiding his cheeks and jaws and chin. I saw petals, rounded and flared upward a bit at the outer edges, like an open blossom. In the center, over the area where I guessed his nostrils and mouth would be, was a protruding, dense circle of yellowish filaments, just like the heart of a flower. It jutted toward me, quivering, as if it were tasting the air around me—tasting me. There was something lewd and foul about that grotesque thing. It disgusted me in ways I can't describe.

The young man had halted when the light came on, and I thought at first it had surprised him, too. Now, as he resumed his muffled tread, his whistling, labored breathing, closing in on me, he seemed to be smiling—a mean smile. It was impossible to tell for sure, since I had only his eyes to go by, but I thought I saw a gleam of malice in them. Then I knew the purpose of the light. He wanted me to see him clearly, to see the cold, white bloom that passed for his face, and be afraid.

In the way that some dreams have, I tried to move, and couldn't. It was as if my feet were nailed to the planks of the wood floor. When I tried to turn my head away, my neck muscles didn't respond. I couldn't even close my eyes and was forced to watch his slow, deliberate advance. In my mind, I screamed for help, praying that something, or someone, would come to save me. There was no one in that hall but the two of us.

As I stared at him, I could also see past his shoulders, to the end of the hallway and the dark cave of the kitchen. I wasn't focused on it, though; my fear was of him and what he would do when he reached me. Then without warning, a cloud of something exploded from the kitchen doorway and surged up the hall toward us. It was as black as calligraphy ink, and it filled the space, swirling, obscuring everything behind it, gobbling up the light.

Inside, I was panicking, fighting to escape, but outside I was a stone. The blackness was coming nearer, and I could only watch, helpless. The young man seemed unaware of what was advancing up the hall, and his eyes were still locked on me. The thing behind him seemed to move with purpose, as though it were a consciousness possessing intent. It blotted out the walls, the doors, the floor as it flowed up that impossibly long hall. It had slowed, and now its behavior gave me a flash of hope. I didn't believe it was coming for me.

It wasn't. It stopped just short of engulfing the young man, then began fitting itself against him from behind, oozing up around him, conforming to his wrapped shape, leaving only the front of him exposed. He looked like he was pressed into a large mold filled with gelled midnight. His brown-black eyes had gone wide with shock. Then he was drawn slowly backward down the hall, an inch at a time.

I could have wept with relief as I watched the young man retreat in the relentless grip of that thing that was the very opposite of light. I never saw how the dream ended, though. In the next instant I woke up, my eyes flying open. I was in the comforting, familiar darkness of my own room at night, in my own bed, my pulse racing. Before another thought could drive out the one I was trying to hang onto, I rolled over and jerked the chain on the bedside lamp. I opened the nightstand drawer and pulled out a notepad and pen, trying not to dwell on the animal reek that seemed to linger in the air. I jotted a note to myself and turned off the light. It would be there in the morning for me to think about.

Ruminato? it read.

The next day was Sunday and a busy day at home. What seemed like a massive quantity of Mom's tomatoes had ripened, and she wanted to put them up so that none would go to waste. I'd been helping her do the canning and preserving since I was tall enough to stand at the kitchen counter, so I knew what she needed me to do without her telling me. When we lived in the city, she'd shopped for seasonal vegetables and fruits at the farmers' markets, and now she was excited to have grown her own. She was in a happy mood as we worked, talking about what she hoped to achieve in her garden over the next year. I smiled at her. It was good to see her enjoying herself. At one point, she stopped stirring the large pot of tomatoes bubbling on the stove and set the spoon down.

"You know what's funny?" she asked.

"I don't know," I said. "Could it be the fact that you grew enough tomatoes to feed us for the next three years?"

She laughed. "They're not all for us. I plan to give some away...to the Millers, for instance."

"Oh, good. I mean, I love tomatoes, but..." I stopped in the act of washing another batch of jars and lids in the sink and gestured with one soapy hand at the countertop. It glinted with bright, tomato-filled glass containers. "This was just getting ridiculous!"

She cast a critical eye over it all. "It kind of is, isn't it? No, what I started to say was about you and baking with yeast. I know it makes you a little nervous, but there's no need to be. I'm not nearly the expert Holly's mother is with yeast, but I know enough not to be afraid of it. One thing that helped me get past that when I was your age was what you and I are doing right now."

"What do you mean?" I asked.

"Take a look around. See the different steps, the precision we take with the timing and temperatures, the sterilization of the jars, the care we use to seal them properly?"

I nodded. "Sure."

"These tasks scare a lot of people silly. Not because of the work it takes, although it takes plenty. It's because if they do it wrong, they'll end up with something inedible, or worse, something dangerous."

"But it's so easy to do it right!"

"It seems that way to us because we're used to it," Mom pointed out. "You've been doing it half your life already." She turned back to the stove. "I'm just saying, don't be afraid of yeast. Many, many people who are comfortable with yeast would never dream of attempting this."

Dream. That reminded me of mine. I murmured something in agreement as a terrible flower face appeared in my mind's eye.

six

Holly and I met in the cafeteria for lunch the next day. As we caught up with each other, I passed on the tomato message from my mother to hers. She jumped on the suggestion.

"Homegrown tomatoes? We'd love some, thank you! You've seen our garden; you know Mama grows lots of fruits and vegetables, but we never have enough tomatoes." She closed her eyes, a blissful expression on her face. "Tomato soup on the first really cold day. Lovely!"

Her enthusiasm made me laugh. "Great, I'll tell her. She grew enough tomatoes to feed everybody in Holm. She's missed having a garden for so long that she went way overboard."

"Not a problem," Holly said. "We're happy to take any surplus you want to give us." She looked down at her food tray, and her blissful look vanished. She picked up her uninspiring cafeteria lunch with her fingers, studied it a moment, then took a bite. It looked like some kind of pizza turnover, and when she set it back on the plate, gummy red sauce leaked out. A few pale orange carrot sticks garnished the plate.

I eyed her tray with distaste. "I promise you the tomatoes will be better than that."

Holly nodded and rolled her eyes. She was chewing with obvious determination.

"I have to ask," I said. "Why on earth do you eat the cafeteria food when I know you could bring two slices of any kind of your mother's fabulous bread and be so much happier? It's not because you like this stuff, is it?"

She shook her head and finally swallowed. "It's complicated."

"How? We've got time, so why don't you explain it to me?"

She gave me a look of mild irritation and then sighed. "Fine. Phee, you know a bit about us by now. Not the whole story, of course. But you've been around us long enough to have a feeling for some things. You can tell that we aren't your normal, small-town heartland family, and that there's more to us than meets the eye." She took a sip of her lemonade. "You aren't like most people that way, and that makes you—" Holly laughed. "That makes you kind of abnormal, too."

I nodded, conceding the point. I've never thought of myself as normal.

"So when I tell you this, I think you'll understand." She

stopped and gave me a searching look.

"Yes?" I prompted.

"I *have* to eat their food."

I noticed the way she stressed the word "have," as if eating the cafeteria food was an unpleasant duty to fulfill. Today, it certainly appeared to be. The next thing that struck me gave me a very odd feeling. "'*Their* food?'" I leaned toward her and lowered my voice. "Holly. You make these people sound like aliens."

"I know. I don't mean it in a disparaging way. To my family, though..." She shrugged. "They kind of are."

I stared at her in disbelief. "Okay. I've known almost from the beginning that you and your parents are different from everyone else I've met here. But why do you have to eat their food?"

"It's how I..." She wiped her mouth with a flimsy paper napkin, then balled it up and tossed it on her tray. "It's how *we* monitor the situation. It's kind of like when you go to the doctor and the first thing they do is check your vital signs."

I cast my eyes around the cafeteria, looking for a hint as to what she meant. The sight of Jack at a table near the lunch line distracted me momentarily. He was talking to his friends, though, not looking my way. I suppressed the disappointment I felt and returned my focus to Holly. "Everything looks like it always does," I said. "Exactly what 'situation' are you monitoring?"

"Ohh, boy," she muttered. She stared down at the table for a moment, then looked up again and met my eyes. "The state of humanity."

Her answer was so unexpected it rocked me back.

"Think about it, Phee," she said earnestly. "So much of this world is expressed in its food—whether good, bad, or indifferent. The way people eat, the things they choose to try to nourish themselves with, it's all indicative of their mental and emotional state. Of whether they care about themselves, or care about others. It's about so much more than throwing a pizza turnover in the oven just because it's convenient."

"What about the people who can't afford to feed themselves properly? That certainly doesn't mean they don't care."

Holly's expression darkened. "That's a huge part of it, too. We keep tabs on all of it."

"'We,'" I repeated. "You and your family."

She nodded.

"What did you learn from monitoring me, then?"

For a moment she looked blank, then she understood. "The peanut butter cookies."

"That's right."

"I learned about your grief, your anxieties. Your fear for those you love." She sighed. "Nothing I didn't know already."

I considered this. It wasn't as if she'd learned anything surprising about me. I'd already confided most of it. It still made me a little uncomfortable, though. After a pause, I nodded toward her lunch. "So what *is* the state of humanity?"

Holly pushed her tray toward me. I looked down at the doughy, oozing remnants of her lunch and the dry, curling carrot sticks accompanying the flabby turnover—as if anyone would ever eat them.

"What do you think?" she asked.

That day after school was Mrs. Gilpin's book club, held in the small meeting room in the school library. On my way there, I thought about how my efforts to convince Holly to join had failed. I'd tried again at lunch, before we got on the subject of food. When she told me the genre didn't interest her much, I was bewildered.

"Why? Vampire literature has a long history—it's such an important part of gothic fiction!" I said. "Don't you at least want to join so you can read *Interview with the Vampire*? People across the country are talking about it! Even my mom's dying to read it after I finish with it!"

She'd only shrugged, so I gave up.

To be honest, I was a little annoyed with her. I didn't know why her family would need to "monitor" the human race, but her attitude seemed patronizing and intrusive. The more I thought about it, the less I liked it. "We keep tabs on all of it," she'd said. Oh, did they, now? She made it sound as if she and her family were some sort of otherworldly beings with superpowers. Yes, they were different, but so different they weren't even human? What kind of gullible idiot did she take me for? I decided she could wait a long time before I baked her any more cookies.

In book club, we were wrapping up *Carmilla* and moving on to *Dracula*. Mrs. Gilpin had turned the meeting over to the students who wanted to share their opinions of the first book. Most of them were girls who seemed to have a vampire crush and had joined strictly for the Anne Rice book. A couple of them expressed impatience that they had to wade through the other books to get to it. Others were surprised and impressed with the one we'd just finished. I was listening, enjoying myself and feeling a little more sophisticated and well-read than they were—I'd read *Dracula* once before and was looking forward to reading it again—but also still feeling awkward as the new girl in school, so I kept quiet.

Deb currently had the floor. I knew she was a couple of grades ahead of me, and she was articulate and smart. As she spoke, it became clear that her vampire absorption was more than just a teenage crush. She'd done some study of the subject and at the moment was comparing the vampires in gothic fiction from the late 1800s to the vampires of old movies. Specifically, the monstrous vampire portrayed in a silent film that Deb told us came out in 1922.

When she said the movie was called *Nosferatu*, I sat up straighter. It made me think of Holly's brother. The name Ruminato sounded similar to Nosferatu, sharing some of the same vowel sounds and accented syllables. I thought of the young man in my dream—his dark hair and brows, his dreadfully pale face—as so many vampires are described. For that matter, Holly fit that description, too. In the days since I dreamed of him, I'd grown certain—reasonably or not—that he must be her brother, the one she would clearly rather not talk about. I didn't believe he looked like that in real life, of course. I thought the awful creature I saw must represent the sort of person he was, and that my subconscious conveyed this by using the coded symbols of dreams. Maybe he appeared to me as horribly inhuman because that was his true nature.

Thinking about this, I lost track of what Deb was saying. I'd suddenly realized that the strange qualities of Holly's mysterious family would make more sense if they were viewed through the prism of a vampire novel. The Millers were certainly different. Maybe Holly's brother was the most different of them all. What if claiming he traveled a lot was just a cover? What if, in reality, they were keeping him hidden away because, unlike the rest of his family, he was too odd to pass for normal? *And what could be odder than if he believes he's a vampire?* I thought. The idea gave me chills, and I shivered. Luckily, no one noticed, because Deb had just caused a small stir in the meeting room. She'd held up a black-and-white photo of the actor who played the vampire in *Nosferatu*—in full, hideous makeup.

Even as I had these thoughts, I was cringing with embarrassment. My imagination was obviously running away with me. Maybe Holly was right in her sense of superiority. Here I'd been congratulating myself for being more grown up, so much less foolish than some of these book club girls wasting their time drooling over vampires.

Then I grew cold as I remembered his vile flower face and the obscenity of that small, quivering, dense mound of filaments in the center. None of them would ever drool over Ruminato. At least, not the creature I'd seen in my dream.

Stop it, I told myself. I forced him out of my head, focusing instead on listening to Deb. *Nosferatu* did sound like an interesting film....

Midterms were coming up in a couple of weeks, and with the extra work and study required, I wasn't spending much time with Holly. We waved at each other passing in the halls, and that was about it. We did make plans to get together at her house that weekend, and by the time Saturday came, I was looking forward to seeing her again. I was completely over my annoyance with her and couldn't really remember what it was that had bothered me. She wasn't being superior. She was just being Holly—a little advanced for her age, a little offbeat in her view of the world.

She met me at the stile that day to help with the tomatoes. I was carrying two canvas tote bags, each half-full of jars carefully wrapped in sheets of newspaper. I handed them across the fence to her, one bag at a time, then climbed the stile and joined her. Each of us holding a bag, we started walking through the woods, talking nonstop, catching up on the conversations we hadn't had that week. We hadn't yet reached the clearing before the pecan grove.

As I was blabbing away, not being the least bit careful of what I said, I mentioned *Nosferatu*. I told her I'd been so intrigued by Deb's description that I'd looked it up in the library later in a book I found there on old movies. In it there were more stills from the film, which I pored over for several minutes, fascinated. The vampire character was monstrously ghastly, frightful. He was light years away from the vampire in *Carmilla*, who was quite lovely. I was describing to Holly the way he looked, the arching crest at the top of his bald head; the low-set, pointed ears; the sharp teeth that seemed to fill his mouth; the bright, vivid, tiny-pupiled eyes that lay like boiled eggs in the inky pools of their sockets. The more I talked about him, the more carried away I got. I didn't stop until I suddenly realized Holly wasn't beside me anymore.

I laughed and turned to walk back to her. "Okay, okay, I'll stop talking about it. You don't have to hide from me! I just never knew anything about silent movies, and I thought it was—" The words turned to dust in my mouth when I saw the thing facing me.

It wasn't Holly. It was Ruminato. His awful flower blossom face looked exactly as I had dreamed it. Too stunned to move, I stood and stared at it, and as a shaft of sunlight stabbed down between the trees, illuminating his features, I noticed something I hadn't seen in my dream. The pupils of his dark eyes were rectangular, horizontal. They looked like two coin slots set into his head. Horrified, I tore my gaze from them, and only then realized he was naked from the waist up. From the waist down he wore a ragged, stained pair of blue jeans. Gripped in one hand was a piece of fabric. It was brown and loosely woven, like burlap. *A sack, he's holding a sack,* I thought, and it was hanging slack and empty. My eyes were drawn downward to his feet, and at first I was relieved to see that they weren't bundled in cloth the way they'd been in my dream. It took me longer to see what they really were. What I'd thought were shoes on human feet were hooves.

––––––––

The next thing I knew, I was in the gazebo with Holly on the bench beside me. I felt nothing: no fear, no shock, no sense of lost time. My mind was so empty I couldn't form words. I could only sit watching her. Finally my head cleared a little. "What happened?"

"I don't know." Her eyes were wide and distressed. "One second you were with me, and everything was fine, the next second you were gone, like a big hand had come down from the sky and grabbed you up."

I tried to think carefully about this. It was difficult to sort my thoughts into some sort of order. "How did you find me?"

She swallowed hard and glanced away. "By following the screams."

When she said that, I remembered hearing the screaming. It had been mine. A sudden memory of blackness filled my mind then, a memory of an icy gulf streaked with distant falling stars. Cold certainty overwhelmed me. Wherever that was, however far away it was in time and space, however briefly, *I had been there*. Something had taken me there. This should have terrified me, but for some reason I could think of it with detachment, as if it had happened to someone else.

"You were in the woods," Holly was saying, "not far from where you vanished. You were in bad shape when I found you. Crying and babbling about dying alone in the dark, and for some reason about that movie vampire you'd been describing to me, making no sense. I was finally able to calm you down and get you back here by playing music for you. To soothe you."

When she said this, I realized how odd it was that I felt much calmer than I should after experiencing something so horrifying, almost as if I'd been anesthetized. I was beginning to feel more like myself, however, and a cold knot was forming in my stomach. What had just happened to me? Thank God for Holly and her music.

Her hands were empty, so I glanced around, but saw only the two canvas totes of jarred tomatoes. *At least we still have those,* I thought. "You played music? On what?"

She reached into a pocket in her sweater and drew out a set of small wooden tubes. They were hollow, of different lengths, and strapped together. "On this."

I stared at it. A word popped into my head, and I said it aloud. "Panpipes?"

"That's one name for it. I call it a syrinx. This one is a simple version, with fewer pipes. It's so compact I can carry it with me."

She put it to her lips and blew a few soft notes on it. The tone was sweet and ethereal, and as I listened, the knot of unease in my stomach faded into nothing. I thought about all the instruments on the shelves in her room.

"Is there anything you *don't* play?"

She gave me a faint smile, and the expression in her eyes seemed a little sad. "I tend to stick to the portable ones."

"So, no pianos?" When I heard that question come out of my mouth, I was surprised. I sounded normal to myself, which didn't seem possible.

"No organs, no kettle drums, no calliopes…" This time, she laughed. "I could keep going." Her face grew serious. "I need to ask you, though. These woods can be strange, I know. But the way you just disappeared? That was a first for me. Can you remember anything about it?"

I looked down at my lap and saw that my hands had clenched. In my mind, I was again in the woods, and that unnatural hooved creature was confronting me. I raised my eyes to hers. "I remember what happened just before it."

"Okay, good, that's a start. What was it?"

"I met Ruminato."

Holly gave me a disbelieving stare at first, then shook her head in protest. "That's not possible. And how could you even know it was him? You don't know what he looks like."

"Does he wear a white mask shaped like a flower?"

Her face drained of what little color it possessed. Even her lips blanched as she sank back against the picnic table. "Oh, God," she breathed. "I'm.. I'm so sorry. I didn't know he was...here."

I watched her for a minute, not sure if I should say anything more. There was so much I still needed to know, to understand. What did she mean by "here?" Outside? Back home from someplace else? Where did he spend most of his time? Finally I had to ask. "Holly, the reason I was babbling about Nosferatu when you found me..." I stopped, aware that I was about to make myself sound crazy. "Look, something's been weighing on my mind, and I have to just come out with it. I've been wondering if, just maybe—" She already knew what I was going to say.

"The movie vampire? Seriously, Phee? I thought you were more evolved than that. No. We are not a family of vampires, okay?" She clicked her tongue with impatience.

The "evolved" remark stung, but I relaxed a little. "Good. You can kind of understand why I ask, though. Your dark hair and eyes, your good looks...your pallor. Your freaky strangeness, honestly."

Holly snorted. "You can see my reflection in shiny surfaces, and you've watched me eat my weight in my mother's bread and butter. Vampires don't do that. You've been in my house, my room, you've seen all the windows—"

Yes, and most of them are caked in dirt, I thought.

"Not to mention we're sitting out here in broad daylight," she went on. "Vampires don't do that, either."

"We're under cover." I pointed up at the gazebo's octagonal ceiling.

She gave a scornful toss of her head. "Oh, stop. You're letting your imagination run wild." Then she turned her eyes on me and leaned so close I saw a red pinpoint in each black pupil. "I should suck your blood just to teach you a lesson."

I backed away and stared at her open-mouthed.

"Gotcha!" She burst into delighted laughter. Soon she grew sober again, and her jaw tensed. "But really, I need to apologize. My brother had no business being out in the woods, and he certainly shouldn't have intercepted you and scared you half to death. I'll have my parents speak to him. He's an odd one."

Holly had said this with an air of finality, and now I had the feeling she was washing her hands of the subject of Ruminato. Her parents would take care of him, and that was that. Or, at least I think that's what she wanted me to believe. I wasn't prepared to let it go so easily, though. Too much was being left unsaid.

"This wasn't the first time I've seen him."

Her eyes widened. "What? *Where?*"

I sighed. "It was in a dream."

Her dark brows drew together in a frown, which deepened as I told her about the Ruminato I'd seen in my sleep. When I finished, she said nothing, dropping her gaze to the panpipes she held in her lap. I'd described the way he came relentlessly toward me, the light that showed him so clearly. Then I told her about the blackness that took hold of him and pulled him backward down the hall. I emphasized seeing his face, the white blossom he wore on it. It was so clear in my dream, but I needed her to confirm my guess. When she didn't, I asked her outright.

"It's a mask, isn't it, Holly? Please tell me that's what's covering his face!"

She didn't look at me.

"How else could a human being look like that?" I'd considered asking her about his inhuman eyes and the hooved feet that I'd seen in the light of day only a few minutes before. Her silence made me decide against it. For now, at least, I would keep that to myself. I didn't think to ask about the sack he carried. That seemed the least of his strangeness.

"Okay, then, tell me this, Holly. How did he make me disappear? Where did I go? What would have happened if you hadn't found me?"

She shook her head, lips pressed together, as if she wasn't willing to consider that possibility.

"I was alone in the dark, you know. I remember that. Somewhere out in the blackness between worlds, light years away from my home."

She made a sound of disgust. "Come on, Phee, don't you think that's a bit—"

The Music and the Strife

"Let me finish," I said. I stopped and took a breath, forcing myself to ask a question that might have a horrible answer. "If you hadn't found me…would I be dead now?"

seven

Holly never did answer my questions that day. Instead, she just gave me an excuse, saying she thought I should be fully re-covered from my awful experience before we talked more about it. The real reason, I think, is that she wanted to leave the explaining to her parents.

So we sat together in the gazebo for a while, both of us staring out at the blue-gray waters of the Buckle, not talking much. Every so often, she played a sweet tune on the pipes. Then she emptied the totes, lining up the jars of tomatoes on the picnic table, and walked me back through the woods. When we got to the fence, she crossed the stile after me. I was surprised and said so.

"I want to see you get back to your house with my own eyes," she said, handing me the bags. Then she came with me almost to the edge of my backyard before saying goodbye.

"Please tell your mother again how grateful we are for the tomatoes."

I told her I would.

"We'll save the jars, and Mama will fill them with something from our garden for you when we give them back."

She smiled at me then, and I couldn't help smiling back. Returning a full container was something my mother had taught me—the polite thing to do when someone gives you food, a like gift to show how much you've appreciated the food they worked over and shared from their heart.

———————

The following week, Holly and I were able to have lunch together just once. We talked about unimportant things. Nothing was said about my vanishing—my *abduction*—by her brother. We hadn't talked about it since that day, and then I hadn't told her everything I'd seen. I'd asked only about his masked face. Which seemed less awful to me now than his even more shocking features. How did he come to have those eyes? Those hooves? And what sort of beast did they make him?

I sat across the lunch table from her, stewing with resentment and hiding it. Our conversation felt stilted. It was hard for me to leave so much unspoken. Now that a little time had passed, the trauma was affecting me much more deeply than it did that day in the woods. I needed someone to listen to me, to really hear what I had to tell. It would be a bit longer before that happened.

By then, the fall days were getting noticeably shorter. On weekday afternoons, once the bus had dropped me off, my routine was first to finish whatever schoolwork I hadn't completed on the long ride home. The midterms were now less than a week away, so I was mostly going over my notes. I felt reasonably prepared, especially for English and Spanish, but I wouldn't relax until all the tests were behind me. Daylight was usually beginning to fail by the time I finished studying. If it was close to dinner, I helped Mom with the prep and cooking. If there was still time to spare, I went into her studio.

It's a wonderful, creative workspace, and from the moment she set it up, I've enjoyed hanging out there, soaking it in. It's perfect for her needs, big and light-filled, and her art is everywhere I look. The bold paintings always catch my eye first, but there's so much else to see, like her watercolors, pastel sketches and pencil drawings. There are several easels in the room, some holding works in progress. Art supplies are in cabinets and on shelves, and there are drop cloths on the floor as well as draped coverings protecting some pieces. From what, I'm not sure. Too much air? Light? Or maybe from view, if she feels they aren't ready to be seen. Paper constructions hang from the exposed beams at the ceiling. At first glance, the room might seem chaotic, filled with a riot of unrelated, random objects, but it's a place where making art is an important occupation, deserving its own office, so to speak, and the artist's focused attention. Mom's art is not a hobby, or a whim to be indulged when the mood hits.

The Music and the Strife

On this particular afternoon, less than a week had passed since I'd seen Ruminato in the woods. As twilight approached, I'd walked into the art studio, intending simply to sit among these symbols of Mom's creative life in the hope they'd bring a little calmness to my spirit. She wasn't home; she'd left coffee off the grocery list and gone back into Holm to get some. I figured she'd be back soon.

I looked around, taking pleasure in how the character of the room shifted according to what she's working on and what's most prominent. Just a couple of days before, she'd told me something thrilling: She had an exhibition coming up early in the new year. Holm has a tiny, artsy section downtown on Main Street, and a gallery there had expressed interest in her work after she'd brought a few pieces by to show them.

I was so proud and so excited for her. Her talent awed me; I hadn't known how far-reaching it was until after Dad died. Though she's never said so, I think she put her own creative gifts on hold to raise me and to make the best home she could for the three of us, and I felt a little guilty about it. Since our move, though, I saw that she was coming to know herself better, something I'd never realized she needed to do. I mean no reflection on my father when I say that; they adored each other, and each wanted nothing more than to see the other happy. But I don't think she'd felt really free to be her true self until we moved. How I prayed for her to thrive.

As I scanned the room, wondering which pieces she'd choose for the show, my eyes were drawn to a couple of wax models she'd started working on soon after we'd settled in to the new house. One was a wary fox, about one-quarter life-size, turning to look over its shoulder, and the other was a larger ram's head with curling horns, so detailed you could even see the rectangular pupils in its eyes. Those eyes had fascinated me before. After seeing Ruminato's, they made my skin crawl. I knew she wasn't planning to have these pieces cast. It was an expensive process, and the finished works took up more space than canvases and were more difficult to transport. It was a shame, but I could see the reason for her decision.

I glanced to my left at the large windows and saw the darkness gathering out in the backyard. I thought she'd be home already. I wondered what was keeping her. I crossed the floor to look outside, hoping to see the glow of headlights approaching. Instead I saw the bird feeder and a lone male cardinal perched there, his bright scarlet fading in the gloom. Seeing him triggered a thought that jolted me. I couldn't remember ever seeing birds—or any animal life—after crossing the stile at the Millers' fence. I'd noticed the abrupt silence in the woods the first time, but then I forgot about it. I thought back, but came up with nothing. That couldn't be right. I had to be mistaken. Next time, I vowed, I'd pay closer attention.

I moved to a sturdy wooden armchair on casters and sat down, spinning it to face the room. In our old house, it had been Dad's desk chair in his home office. Now it was lightly freckled with paint spatter. I rested my hands on the arms where the finish had been worn through by his big hands. I'd seen him in that chair many times. The knowledge of his absence hurt so badly at that moment I thought I'd start to cry. I squeezed my eyelids shut, willing the tears away. I didn't want Mom to get home and find me like that. When I opened them again, feeling more in control, my eyes met the coin slot pupils of the ram's head. They were as clear as if sunlight streamed through the windows. The sculpture was looking at me.

It was so unexpected I jumped. My pulse beat faster, and as shadows crept across the floor, I saw in them the lithe shapes of fearsome beasts, slinking nearer. I knew I was being ridiculous, and before panic could really take hold, I spun the chair around again, scrambled out of it, and dashed to the wall switch. Light flooded the room, and at once, I felt better but also upset with myself. That ram was a piece of my mother's sculpture. She'd held the wax in the warmth of her hands, forming it into something beautiful. Nothing she made could ever hurt me. I was certain of that.

I went to the head and studied it. To someone who's grown up on a farm, or spent time around farm animals, maybe the eyes wouldn't seem so strange. To me, they looked unnatural, and horribly so in a human face—if anyone could call Ruminato's face human. Who knew what the white flower mask might be hiding? What strife those alien eyes had seen?

Strife. That word screeched across my mind like a violin bow sawn across catgut strings. Sharp. Discordant. I didn't want to, and would've done anything to avoid it, but I understood strife too well. Better than Holly thought I did.

I glanced down at my watch. Mom definitely should've been home already. She was at least fifteen minutes past the time I'd expected her back. A voice whispered, *I hope nothing's hap-*

pened to her. It was so clear it startled me, and I whipped around to be sure I was alone in the studio. No one was there. The voice had been in my head. But it didn't sound like me. Or at least, not like the old me…the me before Dad died. The new me jumped at shadows.

Just then, I saw Steve's headlights flash across the windows as Mom pulled into the driveway. I left the studio, flipping off the light switch behind me, and hurried to meet her at the back door.

———————

That Saturday, one week after Ruminato had snatched me away, I had another bread-making lesson with Mrs. Miller. I'd had several by now and was feeling more comfortable with the process, even the yeast, which I'd killed only once. Holly was waiting for me at the stile and waved at me cheerfully, as if nothing unusual had happened the last time. I still needed answers and wanted desperately to talk about what happened, but like a coward, I wanted to avoid creating awkwardness between us. After a week of barely seeing her, I was starting to miss her. I had no idea what to expect from her today, but she put me at ease.

"Hi, Phee! Mama's getting everything ready in the kitchen. I think she's looking forward to this as much as you are."

Holly was present when her mother had promised to show me in the next lesson how she slashed the loaves. "It's one of the easier patterns," Mrs. Miller had said, "but very beneficial, meant to promote good health." After her demonstration, I'd be trying my hand at it for the first time, but with a sharp knife instead of the straight razor.

The Music and the Strife

I smiled at Holly, glad that things were okay between us. We started walking toward the river. "I'm excited to see how she slashes the loaves," I said. "A little nervous about doing it myself, though."

"You'll be fine," Holly said. "Just have fun with it!"

As we walked, she casually reached in the pocket of her sweater and pulled out the panpipes. Putting the instrument to her lips, she blew a few low, quavering notes and let them hang in the air. Then she blew again, a more sustained breath, her fingers dancing across the tops of the hollow tubes. The notes gathered strength and became higher, lilting. They seemed to float up and rest among the treetops.

I looked up at the branches that laced together over our heads. Many were nearly bare of leaves now, while others showed their fall colors of rust and bright gold. The ground was covered in leaves that swished and swirled under our feet as we walked. It was a beautiful setting on a perfect autumn day. Even as I admired it, I remembered my vow to pay more attention. So far, it was just the two of us. I saw nothing else with legs, nothing with wings. Not even anything creeping underfoot.

I wondered where Ruminato was, and imagined the sharp sound his hooves would make on that dry, leafy carpet. Holly had caught me between classes in the hallway the day before, though, and told me she'd make sure I reached her house without another incident. "I'll be waiting for you at the stile, and when you're ready to go home, I'll walk you back to it. So you can relax. No need to worry." Then she'd rushed off to her next class. I was grateful to have her with me, enclosing the two of us in the world of her music. I felt protected.

———

While the dough was on its first rising, Mrs. Miller and Holly and I went to sit outside in the backyard. It was a little cool, but sunny. Mrs. Miller had a lined notepad and pencil, and Holly carried a violin and bow, as well as a small, cloth-wrapped cake of rosin, which I'd seen her use before. Strange to say, though we'd spent plenty of time in the gazebo by the river, I'd never been in their backyard. I was intrigued to see a sundial standing in the middle of a broad, grassy clearing, and I crossed the yard to examine it more closely.

The base was a pillar about three feet tall and carved from pink-gray stone, probably granite. Its shape was graceful: wider at the bottom, narrowing up to a slim neck, then curving outward again at the top. It reminded me of the pawns in a chess set of Dad's, but oversized. The flat disc on top was some kind of metal, maybe bronze; it had a green patina of verdigris from long exposure to the weather. The Roman numerals on it were worn, which made me think it must've been very old. The pointer, which I learned later is properly called the gnomon, was casting a shadow. What it meant was a mystery. I'd never seen a working sundial before, but I thought telling time would be easy, sort of like reading a clock face. It wasn't like that, however, and the lack of minutes was only part of the problem. I watched its weathered face for a moment, long enough to see the shadow shift ever so slightly. I felt as if it was trying to tell me something about the days and years it had seen, how it had come to be there at that moment in history.

On the dial, below the gnomon, was an inscription, worn like the numbers, but still legible. It read: "Your back to the shadow. Your face to me." I puzzled over it, at first sure it was meant to read: "You're back to the shadow. You're face to me," but that didn't make much sense. I read it twice more before the meaning became clear.

Turn your back to the shadow. Turn your face to me.

It was a warning. A command. After studying it a bit longer, I moved away, feeling the chill in the air, uncomfortably aware of the sundial standing behind me.

Holly and her mother were seated under a shade tree and I went to join them, sitting down in a low-slung, wooden Adirondack chair with broad arms. Mrs. Miller was drawing a design on the notepad. Holly had finished rosining her bow and making small tuning adjustments to her violin. Now she seemed to be just noodling around on it, plucking random strings, but somehow it sounded like a complex composition. I wondered how much music she held in her head and if she would ever play this piece again.

Mrs. Miller held out the pad to show me. In a low, serious voice, she said, "Phee, dear, act as if you're listening to me describe how to cut this pattern into the bread. Nod your head every so often."

I played along. "That's lovely, Mrs. Miller. Do you really think I can do this on my first try?"

She raised her voice and smiled. "We'll just have to see how it goes." With her pencil, she indicated different places on the paper, lowering her voice again. "This is not the design I want you to make. It's just meaningless squiggles, lacking protective powers. I'll show you the real design once we're back inside."

I nodded, focused on the paper like an earnest student. "I see."

"We're out here because it's less likely we'll be overheard."

I tensed, waiting for her to go on.

"Holly told her father and me that Ruminato is threatening you," Mrs. Miller said. "She told us about the dream in which he first appeared to you." She tapped a different spot on the paper and raised her voice briefly. "This part is a little more complicated, as I'm sure you can see."

"I do." My eyes were fixed on the pencil marks as I wondered uneasily if Ruminato was in the house. If that was the reason we were outdoors playing this game of pretend.

"She also told us about that terrifying incident in the woods last weekend," Mrs. Miller went on, "and we are so very sorry you had to endure that. It's absolutely unthinkable."

I glanced down at my hands and saw them trembling. I pressed them between my knees to still them. Holly continued playing her violin, and I tried to concentrate on its soothing tones.

"She said you vanished from sight without warning and that you don't remember anything until you were safely back with her."

That's glossing over a lot of what happened, I thought. "Did Holly mention the darkness I saw?" I was still smiling and nodding, trying to look normal.

"She did. And Phee, while I'm sure that feels like a memory to you, it's not. Not really." Mrs. Miller gave my knee a quick, reassuring squeeze. "It's something your mind created to fit what the experience felt like to you as it transpired. What really happened, although frightening enough, is something far less drastic, thankfully. I want to put you at ease about that."

"Um…okay."

"He brought you here. To the house."

"Here?" This shocked me so much that I'd raised my voice without thinking. I had the sense to put my finger at a random spot on the paper.

Mrs. Miller nodded and pointed her pencil at the same place. "Here," she repeated. "He kept you here for a short time before returning you to the forest. That's where Holly found you. Upset, but safe."

Her eyes rested on me with calm concern while I thought this over. It would've been a relief to think I hadn't been kidnapped to some other plane of existence, but I couldn't quite believe it. The blackness? The brilliant silk threads of shooting stars? I'd seen them. He had taken me there. I was sure he could easily take me anywhere he pleased. Ruminato seemed capable of anything. Thank God he'd returned me. This time, at least.

The longer I thought about it, though, my eyes still on her notepad, on the pattern she'd drawn, the more I felt the nudge of uncertainty. Could she be right? Was my "memory" just another of those weird episodes I had around the Millers? Finally I looked at her. "What makes you think he brought me to the house?"

"Because, Phee," she murmured, "that's what Ruminato does. He brings the strife. That means he captures the shadow beings that travel between worlds and brings them home."

I had to force myself to keep my eyes on her and not look at the house. Maybe this was my chance to better understand what Holly had told me about her family. "Can you explain that a little more?"

She gave me a tired smile. "Well, you see, dear, there are…things that our family must guard against. It is our duty. Sometimes these things have no solid form, being only emotions or thoughts. Mere energy, in other words. There are other things which do have a true form, being just as much flesh—or substance, if you like—as you or I. Then there is still another class which only appears to have form but is nothing but deceit, and often is able to change its appearance at will."

She paused and seemed to expect a response. After a hesitation, I nodded again.

"We imprison these things that Ruminato brings us. It's the only way we can protect people from them. And there are so very many." She sighed, shaking her head.

I was beginning to grasp what she was telling me. I saw her glance at the house, so I allowed myself to look at it, too. It was a hulking, old thing. Three stories or not, I couldn't imagine there was enough room to store these things she spoke of, nor, in its ramshackle condition, any way the house could possibly imprison them. I mean, really. Not even the mailbox would close. She seemed to read my thought.

"I know you're wondering where on earth we put them. I can only tell you that the house is far larger than it appears from the outside."

"I see. How do you keep them here?"

"Holly's music. It's the balm that soothes them; it's the lock that binds them."

I caught my breath, remembering sunlight running like golden syrup across the floor of Holly's bedroom as she played her violin.

"So we believe that Ruminato brought you here, but before caging you, so to speak—" Mrs. Miller gave me an apologetic look. "—he must have decided to release you. Then return you, for whatever reason. Perhaps he feared being caught. Holly did say you were…putting up quite a fuss when she found you."

I watched her in silence. Her eyes went back to the notepad, so I followed her lead.

"If you'd simply escaped," she continued, "if Holly's music had momentarily failed, there would've been others."

"But why me?" I said, keeping my voice low. "Why did he invade my sleep? Then why did he *take* me?"

"We don't know." Mrs. Miller pursed her lips. "He must have thought you were a being of shadow…of strife." She tore the design out and handed it to me, then closed the sketchpad. "We also don't know how he was able to steal you in our woods. There are many places he can go freely, but we've had to limit his movements here."

I pretended to look closely at the drawing. "Why is that?" I asked.

The violin sounded a long, low, trembling note as the bow was drawn slowly across a string. The music ceased.

"Because he doesn't just bring the strife," Holly said. "He *is* the strife."

I looked at the two of them, mother and daughter. There were resemblances, but Holly was more like her father. Still, it was clear to me that the three of them fit together, that they were a family, even if they weren't a normal one. But Ruminato? Not even close.

"Is that why he looks the way he does?" I pointed at the drawing, trying to keep my voice level and calm. "His face?" I slid my finger lower, stopping near the bottom of the paper. "His *hooves*?"

Holly's eyes widened in surprise, and she shot her mother a tense look.

Mrs. Miller appeared less shocked, but her mouth tightened to a thin line. "What exactly did you see, Phee dear? Leave nothing out, please. I need to know it all."

I did as she asked. When I finished, there was a heavy silence. Then Mrs. Miller tilted her head toward Holly, who unsteadily tucked the violin beneath her chin and began to play once more.

eight

The rest of the bread lesson passed in the more usual way, although Holly stayed in the kitchen with us, softly playing her violin until the finished loaf emerged from the oven. Mrs. Miller was distracted for a time. She was as competent and kind as always, but her mind was clearly somewhere else. At one point, she made a sound of exasperation as a sudden thought occurred to her. "Oh, Phee, I keep forgetting to call your mother. Could you thank her for those beautiful tomatoes? And please tell her I apologize for not doing it sooner. We haven't had the chance to eat any yet, but I know they'll taste as good as they look."

"Sure, Mrs. Miller, I'd be happy to." I barely registered

what she'd said; I was preoccupied, too. Why were they so surprised by what I told them? They had to know what Ruminato looked like. They lived with him, after all. Or were they shocked that he'd revealed his hooves to me?

By the end of the first rising, however, Mrs. Miller was back to her normal self. First she had me shape the loaf as she watched I was getting faster at it. Once I had it smoothed, plumped and patted, I turned it over and pinched the seam together on the bottom. Then I turned it right-side up, slipped it into the buttered loaf pan and stood back to admire it.

"Very nice," Mrs. Miller said with a smile. "You've become quite good at shaping. Are you ready to practice slashing the top?"

I looked at the pristine loaf I'd just made. I'd been eager to learn her technique, but I was nervous. "I hope I don't ruin it."

She laughed. "You'll gain confidence with time."

She'd kept aside a wide strip of raw dough, and as we waited for the loaf to rise, she used it to show me the depth and angle of the cuts. I noticed she held the razor lightly and sliced the dough with a fluid motion. I did my best to imitate her technique with the knife, covering the dough with cuts, balling it up and re-smoothing it, practicing again and again. Then as she talked me through it, I slashed the design into the loaf. When I finished, mine wasn't as precise as hers, of course. The knife blade was duller and thicker than the straight razor, so my design looked like a picture drawn with a crayon versus a picture drawn with one of Mom's graphite sketch pencils. My design was clearly the same as Mrs. Miller's, though, and I was satisfied.

The Music and the Strife

When the loaf came steaming out of the oven, filling the kitchen with its homey fragrance, Holly set down her violin and the three of us gathered around to see the result of my effort. The pattern had enlarged, the cuts opening somewhat in the heat, but for my first try, the loaf looked good, and Mrs. Miller and Holly both congratulated me. I was proud of it and thrilled to take it home and show Mom what I'd made. As Mrs. Miller bagged it up for me, I remembered what she'd told me at the last lesson.

"So this design is for good health, right, Mrs. Miller?"

She shook her head. "I changed my mind, Phee. This one is to keep you safe."

———

Sunday was just an ordinary day. For breakfast, Mom and I had pork sausage links from the butcher shop, and French toast fried up from the loaf I'd made the day before. Before Mom sliced the bread, we admired the pattern I'd cut into the top. I didn't tell her its purpose; that would've required me to explain about Ruminato. I couldn't face that yet, and I didn't want to worry her with something she had no control over.

After breakfast, we cleaned up the kitchen and went to do our own activities. Mom spent the rest of the morning in the backyard and the garden, harvesting the last tomatoes and planning the layouts for the spring beds. Later, I heard her come in and go to her studio, where I knew she was working on a new painting for her upcoming January show.

While she was still in the garden, I went up to the attic to look through the boxes of Dad's things. I didn't tell Mom beforehand. Again, I didn't want to explain or worry her. I'd tell her later, when the time felt right. Maybe.

It didn't take long to find the box I needed. In black marker, Mom had labeled it, "Clothes, Ian's Dresser." That would mean the folded items, like T-shirts, socks and shorts. Kneeling on the attic floor before it, I slit the top open carefully with a knife from the kitchen, and began removing stacks of clothing. Smaller items were on top, but closer to the bottom were Dad's T-shirts. These were the ones with holes and frayed necklines that he wore on weekends with shorts or jeans for simply hanging around the house, or tinkering with something in the basement. I found the T-shirt I was looking for and held it to my face, inhaling a scent of laundry detergent and dryer sheets. I might've been hoping it would still smell like him. It didn't. But it was soft and smooth from many, many washings, and against my skin it reminded me of all the times he'd pulled me into his arms for a hug.

I sat back on my heels, and for a time just held the shirt in my lap, lost in grief. When I finally felt ready, I unfolded it and held it out before me. It was black, a little faded, with white lettering on the front:

"There are dark shadows on the earth, but its lights are stronger in the contrast."
—*Charles Dickens*

I read it aloud, and my voice broke. *If only that were true,* something inside me whispered. I tried to push that thought away and read the quotation again. My voice was steady the second time, and as I spoke the words, I held their meaning in my mind. I put the other items back in the box and resealed it with a roll of duct tape I'd brought with me. Then I went back downstairs to my room and approached the bed.

I moved the two pillows aside. Beneath them on the comforter were my favorite nightclothes: a purple T-shirt with bright yellow butterflies and a pair of gray cotton jersey shorts, both of them butter-soft. I folded Dad's Dickens shirt and put it in the purple one's place on top of the shorts, then gave it a little pat and set the pillows back on top. "I love you, Dad," I whispered. "I always will."

I'd been thinking about it since getting home from the Millers' the day before. I didn't know how much confidence I had in Mrs. Miller's protective design. She meant well, and was trying to help me, but the family was deluding themselves, I thought, believing they had more control over Ruminato than they actually did. That told me I needed extra help. I needed Dad.

I dabbed at my eyes with the butterfly T-shirt, then went to drop it into the washing machine.

Later that afternoon, I joined Mom in the studio to hang out with her. Watching her at her easel always quiets my mind and helps me realize that there are more important things in life than schoolwork. I understand nothing about technique, about the layering of colors, the effects she produces as if by magic. Painting is like alchemy to me. Even though midterms would start the following day, all I wanted to do just then was watch the mesmerizing process of my mother making something come alive on a canvas with brushes and paint. It had been a quiet, peaceful Sunday, and the unsettling conversation I'd had with Mrs. Miller and Holly on Saturday faded into the background.

Monday came in on a wave of cold air, the first really sharp temperature plunge of the fall. It took us by surprise, and we woke up without the heat on in the house. The crisp air in my bedroom had me hurrying to dress when I jumped out of bed. Shivering, I dug through my dresser and pulled out a dark blue turtleneck sweater that I hadn't worn since before Dad died. That with my black jeans, black tennis shoes, and a black wool vest made me feel ready for the chill. I made my bed, then folded up my shorts and Dad's Dickens T-shirt and put them under my pillows. I'd slept well, feeling comforted, as if I'd been wrapped in his hug all night. In the kitchen, Mom had a bowl of hot oatmeal ready for me and was pouring scalding milk over the top as I walked in.

"The butter and sugar's already in it," she told me, setting the bowl on the table.

She sat with me, reading the newspaper and drinking coffee. As I ate, I paged through one of my notebooks, doing some last-minute studying. Algebra II was my first exam that day.

I was scraping the bottom of the bowl with my spoon when I glanced up and caught her smiling at me over the top of the newspaper. "What?" I asked.

"Nothing." She shook her head. "It just makes me happy to see you enjoying your breakfast."

Grinning back at her, I jumped up and set my bowl on the counter with a clatter, then gave her a hug and dashed out of the room to brush my teeth before the school bus came. When it pulled up, I was already running outside to meet it, feeling much warmer—inside and out.

––––––––––

Midterms were held in the classrooms, and regular classes were canceled to accommodate the exam schedule. When we weren't actively taking an exam, we were free to go to the gym, study in the library, or hang out in one of the open classrooms under the watchful eye of a teacher. During my first free period that day, I'd visited the science classroom where Mr. Cruz taught chemistry to most of the tenth graders, including me. Even by Holm High standards, Mr. Cruz was a busy man. He was also my Spanish teacher, plus he taught engineering mechanics to an older class as well as welding to an after-school group. At the moment, he was conducting an impromptu discussion about the feasibility (or not) of building a perpetual motion machine. Listening to the engineering nerds get worked up over that while Mr. Cruz played the devil's advocate was entertaining for a while, but when it started to get too loud for me, I headed to the library.

In the reference section I soon found the book I was looking for: an Italian-English dictionary. I knew the library would have one because for a small-town school, Holm High had a surprising variety of language courses available. Most were taught by Mr. Ferguson, an old man who drove to the school a few days a week from a town twenty miles away. He taught languages at a community college there and was fluent in half a dozen, at least. At the high school, he taught Latin, Italian, French and German. I knew

Susan Rooke

Jack was taking German from him, which sometimes gave me a twinge of regret for choosing Spanish.

I sat down with the dictionary at a long, empty table and looked up the word "ruminato." I didn't see it, but I did find "ruminare," which in English means to ruminate. So I grabbed an Italian grammar book off the shelf, and after poring over verb endings for a while, it appeared to me that the Italian word "ruminato" translated to "ruminated" in English.

He "ruminated.' Is that how Ruminato came by his name? Through pondering? Brooding? By careful consideration of the shadows to bring back to the Miller house?

Now that I understood better what his name meant, it seemed to give him more weight, a sort of heavy inevitability. Like Fate. I leaned back in my chair, imagining Ruminato traveling between the worlds in the shadowed borderlands, gathering up the strife to take home. *That's what the sack is for,* I thought. *And it must be like the Miller house. Much, much larger than it looks.*

That rang a bell. I was certain I'd heard of such a legend before. I replaced the Italian language volumes on the shelf and searched once more through the reference books. I found one called *The Encyclopedia of World Folktales.* There it was, near the beginning of the "S" section. The Sack Man—a tale found in many variations throughout the globe. This time, in its malignant form, contrasting with the benign version associated with Christmas—essentially, the Bizarro World version of St. Nick.

Carrying his bottomless sack filled with strife. To store until the end of time in his bottomless house. Ruminato. The Sack Man.

Suddenly cold, I crossed my arms over my chest, wishing I'd worn a jacket instead of a vest.

————————

When I got home from school that afternoon, Mom was in the kitchen, making hot chocolate. I set my schoolbooks down on a kitchen chair and went to hug her. She asked me how the first day of exams had gone, and we talked about it for a bit. I noticed she seemed preoccupied. Something else was on her mind, and twice she opened her mouth as if to speak, but then shut it again. Finally she made a start.

"Phee, honey…"

"What is it, Mom?"

She didn't answer at first. She had turned back to the stove and was stirring the chocolate in a deep saucepan, a wooden spoon in her hand. An irresistible smell filled the room.

"Do you want me to stir for a while?"

"How about you put the marshmallows in the mugs for us?"

"Sure." I opened a cabinet and got out two white ceramic mugs, then grabbed the marshmallows from the pantry. "What were you going to say?"

"It's just…I've been thinking." She paused while she turned off the burner and pulled a ladle from a drawer beside the stove. Then she turned to face me, leaning against the counter, the ladle still in her hand. "How would you feel about having another dog?"

It had been about two years since we'd lost our beloved Chow Chow to cancer. Pickle's death had broken our hearts, and trying to replace him had been unthinkable. We'd had him since I was barely able to walk. Like fools, the three of us had believed his death would be the hardest thing we'd have to get past for a long while. Then came Dad's accident, and Mom and I learned how devastatingly wrong we'd been.

I thought it over as I put a handful of miniature marshmallows in the bottom of each mug, then set them beside her. To have and love an animal was to mourn it, sooner or later. *Could I even handle that pain again?* I wondered. Aloud, I said, "Do you miss having a dog, Mom?"

"Well…" She shrugged one shoulder, then said nothing more until she'd filled the mugs and brought them to the table.

I got us a couple of teaspoons and joined her. "Well, do you?"

She stirred her chocolate, her face pensive. "I have to say I do. The house seems pretty empty some days. It was fine during the summer because we were both here. Now that you've been in school for a while, though…" She broke off to spoon up a miniature marshmallow and blow on it before popping it in her mouth. She nodded, looking more sure of herself. "Yes. I really think it would be nice to have a dog for company again. How do you feel about it?"

I hesitated only briefly. Reading her expression, I knew she was ready to take this step, and I needed to follow her example. It could brighten our lives again, even bring us joy. "I think it's a great idea," I said. No dog could take Pickle's place, but it would be good for both of us to have an animal to spoil and love. The house would be livelier, and so would we.

My mother picked up her mug and smiled at me. "Wonderful."

"Wait a minute." I gave her a suspicious look. There was a light in her eyes that I'd known well in our old lives but hadn't seen for a while. I could describe it as a twinkle. "Why do I think you've got a dog in mind already?"

She looked a little flustered, then laughed. "Okay, you got me. Mr. Bligh has some puppies he's trying to find homes for. He asked me when I bought the sausage links if we'd be interested in taking one. I told him I'd get back to him after talking to you."

"I knew it!" I grinned at her. "How old?"

"About three-and-a-half months. Part chow, too. They've got blue tongues."

"That's great!" I exclaimed. "We've never had a dog with a pink tongue. After all those years with Pickle, it would look strange."

My mother nodded, looking pleased. "I thought so, too. Okay, I'm glad that's settled. I'll come get you from school tomorrow afternoon and we'll go pick out our new puppy together!"

———

When I put my school things in the pickup the next afternoon, I saw a bag of puppy kibble and some canned dog food already in the back seat. There were a couple of metal dog bowls, too, and peeking out from underneath them I could see the bright colors of a toy of some sort. Coiled up on the bench seat in the front was a leash and collar.

I climbed in and fastened my seatbelt. "You've been busy!" I said.

Mom put Steve in gear and headed out of the parking lot. "It was fun picking out things for a new puppy. I've got a vet appointment scheduled for tomorrow morning, too. I'm really glad we're doing this, Phee. I think it'll be good for both of us."

Mr. Bligh was a kind, easygoing middle-aged man with close-cut dark blond hair going gray at the temples and a bushy blond mustache. Each time I went in the butcher shop with Mom I hoped I'd see Jack there, but no luck so far. When we entered, setting the bell over the door jingling, Mr. Bligh greeted us with a jovial hello and a wave.

"I bet I know why you two are here," he said. "Come on back, I'll show you where they are."

He had the puppies in a storeroom at the back of the shop. The door was open and the entrance was blocked off with a baby gate. "This way, I can hear if they need me," he explained with a shake of his head. "Believe me, they're a handful! Three girls and a boy." He pointed to a corner of the room where a section of the floor was thickly covered in butcher paper. "I've been paper training them. Hopefully, you won't have much of an adjustment when you get one home."

He left us to play with them and went back up to the front. I looked around. Stacked and shelved around the storeroom was an assortment of supplies. At a quick glance, I saw rolls and rolls of butcher paper, gallon bottles of soap, butcher twine, sanitation equipment and sturdy boxes of spices and seasonings. My mother and I sat down on a couple of these and started getting acquainted with the puppies.

The Music and the Strife

They were adorable, excitable balls of thick fur, their faces wrinkly from the Chow Chow part of them but starting to show signs of the adult dogs they'd become in their somewhat longer bodies and legs. We'd gone in without having a strong preference for one sex over the other, but it didn't take long for us to decide on one. We chose the dog that chose us. He was the one who abandoned his sisters as soon as we came into the room, who stood up on his short hind legs, and put his front paws on our knees, begging to come up into our laps. He was our dog from the moment we walked in.

Toulouse, we named him, after a French artist from the 1800s whose work Mom greatly admires. Toulouse the puppy had a medium-length, very thick coat of rusty black fur, pointed ears, and a relatively short muzzle. His eyes were brown, radiating intelligence, and he gazed at us with a ferocious love. His tongue was bluish-black, which suited him perfectly. We adored him immediately.

Within days of bringing him home, Toulouse was the most spoiled dog on the planet. Mom and I had taken another step on the long, difficult journey of healing.

nine

Things got busy with the new puppy, and I didn't go to Holly's house for a couple of Saturdays. At school I saw her less often, too. Everything was fine between us, though. The sincere way her mother apologized for what happened that awful day when Ruminato kidnapped me in the woods—and how seriously she took my concern—gave me some comfort. My wellbeing seemed to mean something to the Millers, and that helped me feel easier about the situation.

Then one day when Holly and I met for lunch a couple of weeks before Thanksgiving, she told me—casually, as if it was the sort of thing that happened all the time—that her father was going to turn the river that afternoon.

"Would you like to come over?" she asked. "I like watching it, and I thought you might, too."

"I'd love to," I told her.

"Great! Dress warmly. We'll be sitting outside for a while."

"Okay." I hesitated. "Um…will you be at the fence to meet me?" I was a little less concerned than before, but I didn't want to take chances.

"There's no need. My brother is…" She pinched her lips together. "He's away. You don't have to worry."

So at a little after five o'clock that day, I was climbing over the stile and jogging through the woods to Holly's house.

I was crossing the grassy clearing and had almost reached the pecan tree grove, when, like a creature in a fairytale, Holly stepped from behind a tree trunk. She was dressed in a form-fitting, full-length black coat made of cloth, buttoned all the way down. Her hair was loose, and fell rippling over the coat's high collar, which was covered in what appeared to be tightly curled black fur. Her hair and the coat collar looked so alike it was hard to see where one ended and the other began. With her dark hair and attire and her white face, Holly could've been an illustration from an old story-book come to life. Her sudden appearance startled me, and I skidded to a halt, half-expecting her to offer me some magic beans or a small purse filled with gold coins. She wore a look of anticipation and silently beckoned to me. When I reached her, I scanned the almost leafless branches before me and glimpsed the roofline of the Miller house in the distance.

We quickly made our way between the trees toward the oxbow in the River Buckle. Neither of us had spoken yet. I felt as if I were about to witness a solemn ritual, and speaking out loud would be like talking in church. When we emerged from the pecan trees, there was the river, and it looked to me like it usually did. The water boiled up against the jumble of boulders at the bend, and the rest flowed swiftly but calmly, with only small waves. It made a soft chuckling sound. Three Adirondack chairs that might have been the ones from the Millers' backyard stood side by side on the riverbank. The green fronds of grass lining both sides of the river had browned since the last time I'd been there. Winter was on its way.

"Where's your dad?" I asked, keeping my voice low.

She pointed to the outbuilding nearby. "In the basement of the workshop," she said softly. "He plans to start the turn about five-twenty. Sunset is about twenty minutes after that, so we should have a good view of it."

Curiosity about the turning process was gnawing at me, but I was shy about trying to satisfy it. My impression that this was a ceremonial occasion grew stronger, and I didn't want to be the outsider who asked naïve or ignorantly offensive questions. Hoping I'd get her to volunteer information, I said, "So you've seen him do this before, right?"

Holly threw me a swift, sidelong glance before looking back at the river. I thought I'd caught something strange in that glance. Her pale face above the dark, high collar looked momentarily imperious, regal. It was as if I'd seen a second person superimposed on her familiar features—a second person who looked like her, but older. Much older.

"I have." The corners of her mouth lifted in a small smile. "Many times."

Maybe I imagined her emphasis on the "many."

"Why don't we sit down?" she suggested. "Mama will be out here to join us soon. She likes to see the turn, too."

So we sat facing the river and waited in respectful silence, and before long, I heard the sound of someone striding through the grass toward us. Holly and I rose to our feet and turned to see Mrs. Miller approaching from the house. She was wrapped in a long cloth coat that was covered in embroidery. Stunning images of creatures, stitched in crimson and white, lilac and golden yellow threads rippled against a peacock blue background. As she moved toward us, I had a quick, unnerving impression of horns and wings and hooves and reptilian things flitting and slithering across the fabric. They made me think of mythical beasts, and reminded me of some of Mom's paintings.

When Mrs. Miller reached us, she greeted me quietly and gave me a hug. Her coat seemed so alive I was almost surprised not to feel it moving between us. The first time she hugged me was the day of the Irish soda bread, my first lesson. It had felt like being wrapped in the comfort of a warm, heavy blanket. There was something powerful about her hugs, and I don't mean from the strength of her arms. It was true that she was quite strong, no doubt because of all the kneading she had done over the years, the thousands of batches of bread dough she'd pummeled and formed into loaves. This was a different kind of strength. More like that of a building that has stood for thousands of years, enduring the endless punishments of time. When Mrs. Miller hugged me, she felt eternal.

We sat down, I on one end and Holly on the other, with her mother between us. We gazed at the river expectantly.

"Phee, dear, I'm so glad you'll get to see this with us," Mrs. Miller murmured. "There's no telling when it might need doing again. It could be next week or ten years from now."

"Me too," I replied. "I've been so curious ever since Holly told me about it. I can't really wrap my head around it. It sounds almost like magic."

Mrs. Miller smiled. "Only if you think our largely forgotten abilities from antiquity were magic."

"Or that the pyramids were built by aliens," Holly added.

I stopped looking at the river and turned to them. "What do you mean? Are you saying that Mr. Miller's got some kind of...I don't know, ancient equipment in his workshop?"

We'd been speaking softly, as if we were in a concert hall waiting for a performance to start. Now I'd raised my voice without meaning to, and Mrs. Miller put a cautionary finger to her lips to shush me. She was smiling, though. "No, no, the equipment is more modern than that. Relatively speaking." She cleared her throat.

"It's the engineering that's ancient," Holly said.

I gaped at them.

"Oh, it's going to start soon!" Mrs. Miller spoke with low urgency. Her eyes were on the river as she reached a hand toward me and clasped my arm.

I looked back at the water, but I saw no difference. "How can you tell?"

"The sunlight on the waves."

I stared hard at the Buckle. Behind us, the sun had begun a swift descent toward the horizon. As the angle of the light changed, the tips of the waves began to glow like flaming match-heads, turning a brilliant reddish yellow. Before I knew it, I was looking at a river of fire. I inhaled sharply.

Holly leaned forward to look at me. "That's the sign that it's time for the turning."

I nodded at her, my mouth open, and quickly looked back to the river. I didn't want to miss anything.

"Watch, now…" Mrs. Miller whispered.

I sat up straighter and gripped the arms of my chair, intent. At first, I saw no other change. Then the beginnings of a swirl appeared on the surface. It was a few yards out from the nearer riverbank and looked like a whirlpool was forming. I had the sudden imagining of a huge catfish on the riverbed, twisting, twirling, hollowing out with her tail a shallow impression in which to lay her eggs. Then, all at once, the whirlpool grew from a few feet to several yards across, and into this whirlpool the water was spiraling downward, as if circling a gigantic drain, rushing down to the bottom of the river.

As I was still trying to grasp what I was seeing, I became aware of another movement thirty or forty yards upstream from us. I focused my gaze on it, and was astonished to see that the water had begun to churn ferociously there, boiling upward, shooting high into the air, as if a monstrous beast straight from myth were rising to the surface. It was the reverse of what was happening downstream near the three of us.

I gasped. I was barely aware of Mrs. Miller patting my arm.

I don't know how long it lasted; I was caught in the moment. I stared, mesmerized, as the water upriver continued to foam and thrash and bubble. At some point, the geyser rocketing upward in that section of the river dropped lower, even as the whirlpool close to us began to slow its swift circling, growing calmer. Now I could see the bottom of the whirlpool rising until, at last, there was only the slightest eddy at the surface. And then that, too, subsided. Upriver, the explosive turmoil was almost done. Finally, the water there resumed its swift downstream course.

I relaxed my grip on the chair arms and sat back, thinking everything had returned to normal, to the way it had been before the "turning." There was something different about it, though. I looked at the bank on our side of the river, where boulders lay in the bend of the oxbow. The torrent of fast water that typically crashed against them had given way to a mere ripple of white bubbles, and it was farther toward the middle. The water that flowed into the oxbow had become a thin stream that puddled around the boulders, forming calm pools.

I stared at it. The current of the river had changed the sharp angle in its direction, becoming a gentle curve instead. On the far bank opposite the bend, I saw water creeping upward, erasing the shoreline that had been easily visible when I first sat down. The river was wider. The river was slower. The river was climbing up the dry land across from us, and if it didn't stop, it would soon reach the tree line.

I looked at Holly and her mother. They were watching the water's progress with serious faces, not as if they were witnessing something miraculous, which was how I viewed it. It was as if they were satisfied that something desperately needing attention had been set right. That fate—not just the river—had taken its proper course. Mrs. Miller gave a little nod.

"That about does it, then," she said. "For a while, I hope."

I looked again at the land on the far side. An increasing amount of it was now underwater. "How much farther will it go?" I asked. "Are there any houses beyond it that might flood?"

Despite the astonishing thing I'd seen, what I was most focused on, I remember, was the thought that Mr. Miller had put into action an event that might have terrible consequences, and change the course of innocent people's lives. Maybe it was my family's tragedy that pulled my thoughts in that direction. I'm not the kind of person who puts the needs of others above their own, except when it comes to my family. I love them so much that it can be painful, and it's often all the emotion I can spare. The river's new course worried me, though. As a result, despite my liking for the Millers—for these three, anyway—I felt at that moment a slight coldness toward them. Then another thought struck me. Was that how this family viewed the human race, with a distant coldness? I thought it might be. Because at some point over the past few months, I'd come to the conclusion that they were nothing like me or my mother, and nothing like anybody else on this Earth.

I don't recall if either of them answered my question, or if they spoke at all. A minute or two, maybe more, is missing from my memory. The next thing I can remember is the three of us sitting together in the gazebo. The sun had disappeared below the horizon, but shafts of deep red light still speared the western sky. The floodwaters on the far side of the river mirrored the sky as they continued encroaching inland, and the red seemed to wash everything in its path, even the roots of the trees, as they had fewer leaves to shade their feet from the bloody sky. On the near side, the water was still and calm, well below the top of the bank. I couldn't imagine how this had been accomplished.

The light was now failing rapidly. Through the dusk, Mr. Miller trudged slowly across the grass from the direction of his workshop to sit with us. He wore a dark peacoat with a double row of buttons down the front and carried a kerosene lantern with a glass shade. He set it on the picnic table when he sat down. He put his broad hands on his knees and lowered his head between slumped shoulders. He looked exhausted.

Holly and Mrs. Miller watched him with concerned faces. "Are you all right, Nick?" Mrs. Miller asked.

"Yes, I'll be fine. Thank you. It was harder than usual, that's all." Mr. Miller raised his head and stared out across the river. "I may have waited a little too long to turn it this time."

Someone drew a sharp breath at this; I don't know if it was Holly or her mother. I had no idea what Mr. Miller meant by "too long," but I sensed tension in the air, and it made me uneasy. Things were being left unsaid because they weren't meant for my ears. That was awkward, and the certainty that I didn't belong there grew in me until I decided it was time to go. But it was now fully dark, and I realized something I should have thought of long before then: I had no way to light my walk home. Although Holly had assured me that her brother was "away," he'd already appeared in other places they hadn't expected him to. The thought of going back to my house alone through those woods, trembling under the growing certainty that Ruminato was stalking me and drawing nearer, made me break into a cold sweat. I didn't want to ask for help getting back, though. Something inside of me warned against appearing weak.

In the heavy silence, I stood up. "Thank you all for allowing me to see this with you." I tried to keep the nervousness out of my voice. "I don't understand any of it, but it was beautiful. Just amazing."

At first no one replied. Their faces were blank as they looked up at me, as if I were so insignificant that I didn't need to be remembered, much less bothered with. My stomach dropped when I saw this, and I felt as if any protection their presence might've offered me against Ruminato had been stripped away. Then, to my huge relief, Holly jumped to her feet.

"You can't go home by yourself. I'll come with you!"

I was weak in the knees when I thanked her.

"You'll need a light. Take the lamp, girls," Mr. Miller said.

"Yes, by all means," Mrs. Miller agreed. "Your father and I will be in the house when you get back, Holly."

She and Mr. Miller both rose to their feet, and she gave me a hug, which was just what I needed at that moment. When she released me, she stepped back and pulled her extraordinary coat more tightly around herself.

"Good night, Phee, dear. We're so glad you had the chance to see this. Don't worry. The floodwaters won't rise far enough to impact anyone on the far side of the river. We wouldn't allow such a thing to happen."

Mr. Miller smiled down at me. "Over the next few days I'll ease the turn, and the river will revert to its normal course. Remember, the purpose is to avert harm, Phee." He put a firm hand on my shoulder and gave it a pat. "Never to cause it. So set your mind at ease on that score."

I stared up at him for a moment, not sure how to respond. "Yes, sir, thank you," I finally said. My head whirled with questions clamoring for answers.

When I turned to Holly, she had the pipes out of her pocket. She smiled as she held them up for me to see. "I've got my syrinx. Ready?" The kerosene lantern was already in her other hand.

Her easy manner made me feel better, and I nodded. "I am."

As we set off, she blew a complicated series of tootling notes on the pipes. It was unlike anything else I recalled her playing, and reminded me of a black and white movie I'd seen when I was very young. There'd been a huge stone pile of a castle— probably nothing more than a Hollywood stage set of sticks and cardboard and painted backdrops, I realized later—and a king, a queen, and some knights. To announce the arrival of some new visitor to the throne room, a page with a trumpet had played a fanfare a lot like what Holly had just played.

But we're departing, not arriving, I thought uneasily. Were fanfares played for departures, too? Or was Holly announcing our imminent arrival in the woods to her brother, the strife collector? Ruminato, the Sack Man?

I didn't need to worry; Holly walked me all the way to my back door. Every so often, she played a few notes on her panpipes, and seemed unconcerned. Perhaps this time the Millers really knew for sure that Ruminato posed no threat. I imagined him a wormhole away, collecting a shadow thing from a crossroads between four worlds, his white flower mask casting a sickly, phosphorescent glow out into the darkness. A wave of nausea hit me, and I forced the thought out of my head.

Mom opened the door when we arrived. "Hi, Holly, what a nice surprise. How are you and your folks doing? Do you have time to come in for a bit?" She didn't get to see Holly often, since I usually went to the Miller house. She opened the door wider, a welcoming gesture that allowed Toulouse the chance to streak out onto the porch and start running circles around us.

"We're fine, Mrs. McKean, thank you. Maybe just for a minute," Holly said. She laughed at the sight of Toulouse jumping up, trying to leap into my arms.

"You're still a little too short for that, big boy. Would you let me give you a belly rub instead?" She set the lantern down on the porch railing and extinguished the flame, but Toulouse was too excited to hold still. When she bent down to reach for him, he squirmed away and raced back into the house, his toenails clattering on the floor.

As we watched him go, a mouthwatering aroma wafted toward us through the open door.

"Here's a thought," Mom said to Holly. "Why don't you stay for dinner? I was just about to take it out of the oven. Roast chicken and potatoes tonight."

Holly's eyes widened, and she rocked back on her heels. "Wow, may I? Yes, please. That smells amazing! If I could just use your phone first, I'll call my parents to let them know."

Mom smiled. "Of course."

It was a first. Holly had been invited to meals the few times she'd come to my house. She'd never stayed for one, and I wondered why she was making an exception. Then it occurred to me that maybe she'd always refused for fear of what she might learn about us from eating our food.

I watched her during dinner, though, and it was obvious any fears she might've had for our mental and emotional well-being were put to rest. On her first bite, I saw an odd look cross her face before she closed her eyes and leaned back with a rapturous expression. She cleaned her first plate and accepted another without even pretending to hesitate.

"Mrs. McKean," she said, "thank you so much. You have no idea what a nice change this is."

"From what?" Mom asked as she dished up Holly's second plate.

"From peanut butter and jelly sandwiches. Mama's been too busy with customer orders to cook. I couldn't face another one tonight."

"On your mother's bread?" Mom laughed. She set Holly's plate before her. "That's not so bad, is it?"

"I guess not," Holly agreed. She popped a bite of potato into her mouth. "We could be living on canned sardines."

We all laughed, and I was especially glad to see Holly

enjoying her dinner so much. It made me feel that Mom had made a good choice by moving us here. We were working through our grief, getting by the best we could, caring for each other and experiencing the new life we were making together. We'd settled into our own small, quiet pocket of the universe, and it showed in her food.

Toulouse had curled up under the table, not begging for morsels, just content to be there with us. After the disquieting awe the turning of the river had inspired in me, the rest of the evening turned out to be fun, filled with good companionship and laughter. I didn't know it then, but I wouldn't have another one like it for a while.

ten

The next morning, before my alarm went off, I had a long, tangled dream. That's usually the time when my dreams are the most vivid, often filled with images that seem symbolic. I'll try to decipher them once I'm up, usually without success. That morning's dream took place in a forest, but not a living one. This was a grim forest of dead trees, many of them so decayed they leaned on their neighbors to stand. Some were only husks: hollow shells of deeply grooved bark surrounding a damp, musty emptiness that once held wood. None had fallen, no matter how fragile the trees' remains were.

For what seemed like hours, I wandered this place full of tree ghosts, looking for something I'd lost. The search was frustrating, and I felt sad and helpless because I couldn't pinpoint what I was missing. The object I was seeking changed every few minutes. First it was my wallet, the brand-new leather one I'd saved my allowance for, so much more adult than the yellow plastic smiley face coin purse I'd been using. Then abruptly, the lost object became the plush stuffed bunny that Mom and Dad had given me on my first birthday. I loved that bunny with its soft gray and white ears and its puffy white tail. I'd carried it everywhere, then left it behind in a motel room when I was four years old. For days I cried, inconsolable. I knew all this in the dream, knew the bunny was long gone, but I hunted for it anyway. No matter what changeable thing I looked for, it was vital that I find it.

On and on this went, until, at last, the dream settled on the object I knew I'd been meant to find all along: a necklace with my birthstone, sardonyx, set into a pendant. It had been a gift from Dad on my fourteenth birthday, the one before he died. Locating it was my true purpose. So I persisted, wandering among these lifeless trees, feeling more defeated and less hopeful of ever finding the pendant as the dream wore on.

Crumbled bark and dry twigs covered the forest floor, and the crunching of my footsteps was so loud it made me fearful of what I might not be hearing. Dark things could be hiding among the trees. I listened closely but heard only my breathing and my trudging feet until, gradually, I became aware of a different noise. It was a low, rhythmic *thunk* coming from somewhere ahead of me. It sounded like something blunt striking a hollow log. The noise was so peculiar and out of place that it raised goose flesh on my skin. It paused between each beat, and at every pause, I prayed that it was over. It wasn't. Although I didn't want to walk toward it, I had to. Some force compelled me, and I couldn't stop.

My progress got abruptly slower as my feet sank into boggy ground. Whatever the source of the rhythmic noise was, the forest was making me work to reach it. Slick, decaying matter squelched beneath my tennis shoes. I lost one of them to the sucking ground and looked down to see it resting in a hollow filled with brown water. When I bent to retrieve it, the hollow opened wider like a wet, toothless mouth and then closed, swallowing my shoe. I snatched back my hand, shuddering. Still, I had to keep struggling forward.

Finally, a few yards ahead, I saw a tree unlike the others, and I knew it was the source of the noise. This tree was alive, with a sparse canopy of broad, dark, leathery leaves that swayed silently in the still, moist air like gently waving hands. Facing me in the trunk of the tree was a tall, jagged hollow, a couple of inches across at the top and gradually growing to about a foot-and-a-half wide where it met the ground. Inside a brass pendulum hung, much too bright in the heavy gloom. The pendulum was so long it reached almost to the bottom of the hollow, where I saw a knot of thick roots like muscular snakes.

I'd stopped on first catching sight of the tree, but now I was compelled by the unknown force to move forward again. I tried not to look at the bottom of the hollow where the tree roots lay. I thought I'd glimpsed them slithering over and under each other. Instead I looked up as I approached and saw a clock face above the top of the hollow. It was oval, roughly hacked into the bark, and had no hands. Where the numerals should've been, there were teeth. Real teeth, it seemed to me, yellow-ivory in color. As I drew closer, I saw that in each place where a single digit should've been—one through nine—there was a long, curving canine tooth. For each of the others—ten, eleven, and twelve—there was a large, heavy molar.

The tree's leaves waved to the motion of the pendulum. The pendulum swung slowly, ponderously, left to right, then back again—a grandfather clock keeping time in this place where time meant nothing. First a tick, then a tock, echoing out into the forest from trunk to trunk, making that thunking noise I'd heard. What was it marking, if not the hours?

Then the force that had been pushing me forward released me, and I jerked to my senses, frantic. I had no idea how I'd come to be surrounded by dead trees, nor how to find my way out. Gradually, I realized it was the sound of my alarm clock ringing that had wrenched me free, and I reached out blindly with one hand to shut it off. As I struggled to the surface of wakefulness, still feeling the presence of the dead forest all around me, I spied a bright flash. It was a broad, cream-white face bearing shapely petals like a flower blossom, and it peeked out from behind the clock-tree.

Now fully awake, I sat bolt upright in bed, shivering, and hugged myself. I was glad to feel the worn softness of Dad's old T-shirt hugging me, too. The dream was a warning, I was sure, and unlike most of my dreams, the symbolism was plain as day. Ruminato was coming for me, and it wouldn't be much longer. I threw back the covers and went to get what my dream had been urging me to find.

———————

I'm one of the first students on the school bus in the mornings and one of the last dropped off in the afternoons. A couple of others, both eighth grade boys, live even farther out like Holly, and they were already on the bus when I boarded that morning. Holly didn't ride the bus, though. I'd asked her why, thinking how much more quickly the long drives would pass if she were there to talk to. Her reply was vague, something about her mother delivering bread for customers in Holm, or her father having business in town to take care of. She'd told me early in our friendship that her mother's customers usually came to their house (though I'd never seen any there), and when I'd asked her what her father did, all she'd said was that he turned the river. What sort of business did he have in town, I wondered? Her answers just didn't make much sense to me.

The morning after the river's turning, the morning of my grandfather clock dream, I was thinking about Holly's explanation again as the school bus bounced along the pot-holed road. Most days, I didn't see her until school had started, but a couple of times I'd seen her walking from the parking lot to the school building. She'd wave when she saw me and break into a jog to catch up to me. I never saw where she'd come from. No car had dropped her off. One moment she wasn't there, and the next… she was. I knew she didn't drive herself to school. In fact, she didn't drive at all, and I doubted she even had her license. I was looking forward to getting mine, and when I told her Mom had promised to teach me on Steve, Holly had given me a blank stare, followed by a nod and a smile. It was the sort of look you give someone after not understanding a word they just said, but you're too embarrassed to admit it. Holly was just odd sometimes. I sighed, leaning my head against the window, and tried to put it out of my mind. It was too bad Jack didn't ride the bus, but he didn't need to. He lived so close to school, he usually walked there.

As always, I was at the very back of the bus, sitting where I could see what went on in front of me and not be watched without knowing it. It was a habit I'd fallen into after Dad died, when I would catch my friends looking at me, first in sympathy, then later in irritation. They seemed to think I was allowed a short time of mourning, but after that, I should put his death in the past where it belonged. Whether caring or annoyed, they would always be shaking their heads and whispering together, so by the end of the school year I was sitting as far as I could from them. Now I didn't have to put up with it anymore. Hardly anyone knew my past, but even if they did, I couldn't imagine the kids at Holm High doing that. They were more polite—nicer, really—than the ones at my old school. Just the same, I preferred that no one had the chance to watch me without my knowledge.

I looked out at the scenery. We were in farmland, the road winding between fields lush with winter wheat, waving like velvety green fur as the bus rumbled by. It was a huge improvement over the feed corn growing there when we first moved. In those early days, I was ignorant about things like crops and livestock, and Mom had to tell me what everything was. In our "before" lives, the three of us had gone camping a few times as a family. Then when I was about five, Dad had begun taking me fishing at an old rock quarry outside the city limits. I loved fishing, and looked forward to those trips, but I'd still been mostly a city kid then.

Now, I'd lived in the country long enough to observe some of the patterns in rural life. Long enough to know what to expect next August when the feed corn was again ready for harvesting. I wasn't looking forward to it. It would be bleak. The stalks would be brown and papery, and windblown. For weeks and weeks, that's all there would be, field after field, sweeping up and over the surrounding hills, each one covered in withered, dead cornstalks. At least, that's how it had seemed to me. Dry as wept-out grief.

As I rocked along, my head resting against the bus window, my mind wandering, the dead forest dream popped into my head, and I went cold all over. Quickly I fumbled with the collar of my jacket and thrust my fingers inside. For a second, I was afraid that finding my sardonyx pendant had been only part of the dream. I relaxed when I felt it against my skin. The first thing I had done that morning after awakening was to retrieve it from my jewelry box. I'd lifted the chain out and held it up to the dim, pre-dawn light leaking through the gap between the curtains. Sardonyx is a beautiful stone. Mine is oval, polished smooth, and banded in a pattern of reddish brown and dusty, pinkish off-white. Some of the darker bands are the deep brown-red color of dried rose petals.

On the day he gave it to me, Dad had handed me the small box wrapped in glossy white paper. "Happy Birthday, Phee," he said, then watched me with a big smile on his face as I opened it, ripping the tape away. He fastened it around my neck for me, then kissed the top of my head and turned me around to face him. "You know why I bought it?"

"Because it's my birthstone?" I suggested.

"Yes, but the real reason is because it reminds me of the color of your hair."

After his death, I'd put my present away. Wearing it made me cry. I needed it now, though. That morning's dream had sent me a clear message. Once I found the necklace, I'd watched the stone twirl at the end of its fine gold chain for a moment, then with clumsy fingers, fastened the clasp around my neck.

The bus driver slowed, and I came out of my thoughts to see we'd reached the stop where a narrow gravel road intersected the bus route. A few kids bundled in jackets, a couple with satchels, and the rest clutching textbooks to their chests stood waiting for us. They'd walked from houses down the road, and watching them board, their breath hanging like fog in the cold air, I was thankful that all I had to do was run out of my house to the end of the driveway.

The bus picked up a little speed again. Time seemed to be dragging this morning, the ride taking much longer than usual. We were coming to my least-favorite part of the journey, so to distract myself, I grabbed *Julius Caesar* out of my pile of books. I opened it to Marc Antony's stunning, beautiful speech that he made after Caesar's death. I loved that speech so much I'd memorized it, and I was looking forward to the class discussion in English that day. *O judgment! thou art fled to brutish beasts*, I read, *and men have lost their reason.* I savored the words in my mind. Some things are always true, I guess.

I tried to keep my eyes on the page. We were nearing the rift in the land where a one-lane steel bridge waited. Mom had told me that its design made it a truss bridge, and that it was the oldest steel bridge in the area. It was painted black but had faded to charcoal gray. Its heavy steel struts formed a cage over the road where the bridge crossed a swirling, muddy green creek. Both ends of the road where it met the bridge were blind, and a vehicle approaching from either direction would need to slow to a crawl and cross with caution. "One Lane Bridge" the diamond-shaped road signs read at either end, the black lettering sharp against a yellow background even in head-lights at night. Warned or not, people could still be careless. Racing up to rush across the creek, they could end up meeting their maker in the middle. I knew it had happened at least once. Every so often, a new, neon-bright bouquet of red plastic carnations would replace an older, sun-bleached version placed high on the creekbank at the Holm end of the bridge. Beside it was a cross hammered into the ground, along with a picture of Jesus with his sacred heart exposed. The heart wore a crown of thorns. I felt the pain of those people who'd lost their loved one. The orange spray paint at Dad's accident scene was still too fresh in my mind.

The school bus was almost to the bridge now, and I set Shakespeare aside. After the first time Mom and I crossed it from the Holm end and glimpsed the red flowers, I always braced myself, no matter which end I was approaching. Enormous trees grew along both sides of the creek and down close to the water, and both banks were littered with the thick trunks of the fallen ones. It made me think of an elephant graveyard. All those trees meant the road at both ends of the bridge was even more blind than it needed to be, but the county, whose job it was to take care of such things, according to Mom, rarely did the necessary trimming. As the school year wore on, I'd begun to think it was only a matter of time before the bus would take a hit. Mom didn't like the bridge any more than I did, and we'd begun taking a different, longer route when we went into Holm. The bus driver had no choice. There were students to pick up along this road.

I reached down and gripped the bench seat under me. No one was paying attention, so I bowed my head and closed my eyes. If danger was coming, I didn't want to know until it was over. I held tight and waited for the telltale bump when the bus came to the change in the pavement. That would tell me we were on the bridge. Then I'd wait for the bump at the other end before opening my eyes. Thankfully, it was a narrow creek and a short span.

The bus slowed. I didn't feel the first bump and thought I'd missed it. I still kept my eyes closed, sure I'd feel the one at the other end, and mentally counted off ten overlong seconds, at least twice the time it would take to cross the bridge. No bump. We should've been on the far side of the creek by then. I knew I couldn't have missed both of them. I also knew we hadn't stopped; I could still feel us moving. Yet I heard no engine noise, no gears grinding when we gained speed again, no low chatter from the students. I was riding to somewhere, though. Through…what? Time? Space? In complete silence, as if I were in a soundproof room. This alarmed me, but before I could get too frightened, my awareness faded away.

When I came to, my eyes were still shut tight, and my head was spinning. I was so dizzy I thought I might throw up. I had a sense of lost time, and though silence still surrounded me, I had the odd feeling that while I was unconscious, chaos had ruled. We didn't seem to be moving anymore. Cold dread gripped me by the throat. What had just happened? What would I see when I opened my eyes?

"You look like you're praying," a sly voice whispered in my ear. "It won't help, I'm afraid."

My head jerked up, and my eyes flew open. I whipped around, looking everywhere for the source of the voice. I knew it was Ruminato. It had to be, even though I had never, to my knowledge, heard him speak. I could swear I'd caught a whiff of a rank, barnyard smell—sweating animals packed too close together, manure. My eyes swept frantically over the scene before me, and at first it was difficult to grasp what I was seeing.

I was alone on the bus. Ruminato was nowhere in sight, and neither were the handful of other students and the driver. I wasn't sure I could believe what my eyes were showing me. Then—and this was worse, somehow, than those vanished people—although I could see everything in the bus easily, like on any other ordinary morning, outside the windows there was only blackness. It was as if, while I was unconscious, the bus had plunged into the deepest trench in the ocean. Why was I alone? And where in God's name was I?

I panicked. Suddenly, I couldn't breathe, and I was terrified that all the oxygen in the bus had been used up. I started gasping for air, and my heart felt as if it would burst from my chest. A new wave of dizziness engulfed me as I struggled to my feet. I grasped the top of the seat in front of me and held on for dear life. As my head cleared, I concentrated on trying to slow my breathing. Maybe I'd have enough air if I could just calm down.

Gradually, I gained some self-control, and my fingers released their death grip on the seat. I looked around. Did I dare search the bus? Did I really want to know if something was hiding behind a row of seats?

I put a shaky hand to my throat. Anything could've happened while I was unconscious. The pendant was still there, and I held it tightly to feel its comforting smoothness against my palm. A soft warmth began at my fingertips and crept upward, past my wrist. Swiftly, it gathered speed and heat and surged up my arm and soon had flooded my entire body. *Dad is with me,* I told myself. I could feel his presence. He was watching over me. Whatever was happening, I was sure Ruminato was behind it. He would keep trying to frighten me. But with Dad to help me, I would get through it.

I left the last row and moved slowly to the front of the bus, sweeping my gaze from side to side, alert for a glimpse of faded denim, listening for movement. I saw no one. Maybe Ruminato's voice was a trick of my overheated imagination. What about the animal odor, though? Had that been my imagination, too? I whirled around to look behind me, half-expecting to catch an alien flower face watching me over a back seat, but I was alone. Then I caught a flash of something outside a window to my left. A pale thing that briefly rose into sight out of the blackness before vanishing.

My first impulse was to cover my eyes and pray it went away. I knew simple avoidance wasn't going to help me, though. So instead, I watched the window, willing my nerves to stay steady, and waited for it to reappear. When it did, it was two windows closer to the front, closer to me, shirtless, visible from the shoulders up. Only a few feet and a pane of glass separated us.

The monstrous creature wanted to take me by surprise, of course, wanted me to scream and jump back. That wasn't going to happen. I'd gained tight control of myself by then, and no matter where it popped into sight, I would've been ready.

I held my gaze on the perverted flower petal face of the sick creep holding me hostage, focusing on that obscene, quivering nest of fibers at the center, and waited for him to speak first. Something told me that tactic would drive him crazy. As I stared him down, I could feel my fury building. Who in the hell did this freak think he was?

At first, he said nothing. Maybe he was trying to outwait me, or maybe my lack of fear took him by surprise. His eyes only narrowed a little, and I think he was giving me a malicious smile. Since the mask hid his mouth, it was hard to tell.

"I told you praying wouldn't help, didn't I?" His voice held a sneer.

I could hear him as clearly as if he stood beside me, just as I'd heard his mocking whisper about prayer. The pane of glass made no difference. I realized something I'd been too frightened to notice earlier. Ruminato had a speech impediment. He had difficulty with the letters formed by putting the lips together. As I turned this over in my mind, he grew impatient.

"Didn't I?" he repeated.

There was a note of petulance in his voice now, and that gave me the confidence to give him a smartass answer.

"You sure did," I agreed with a bland smile and a nod. "When you're right, you're right."

I can't express the triumph I felt when I saw him back away from me. His petal face got a little smaller for a moment before it came close to the glass again. The pursed cone at the blossom's center was twitching violently.

"Are you *mocking* me?" he shrieked, his voice quavering.

I shrugged. "Not yet, but I can if you want me to. Just say the word."

I must've touched a nerve. He did say a word. Not one I was expecting, though.

"BITCH!" he screamed, and slapped his palms flat against the window.

It was surreal, the white flower face looming, the splayed hands on either side of it, the brown sack dangling limp, draped over one thin, bare arm pressed against the glass. The darkness beyond so stark and dead. I could hear him struggling to breathe and wondered again what horrific face the mask must be hiding.

As I stared at him, that brief moment stretching into infinity, I thought I saw something swirl in the void behind Ruminato. It was an inky pool against the darkness, growing as I watched, until all at once it was immense, rearing up behind his back, ancient and formless, blacker than a night sky wiped clean of stars, clothed in the absence of all light. In that instant, Ruminato disappeared from the window. He didn't get smaller and recede out of sight like a car speeding past on a highway. One moment he was there, and the next, he was gone, sucked into a vacuum, as if he'd been snatched at the speed of thought to the far side of the universe. Shocked, I stared at the window, wondering what I'd just witnessed, and then my conscious mind blinked out.

eleven

The next thing I knew, the bus had arrived at the high school. I scanned the rows of seats. Many more students filled the bus now: the few who'd been on board at the bridge, and all the others who'd been picked up along the rest of the route. Where had I been? I'd missed every bit of it. The bus driver sat attentively in her seat as she always did, turning the big horizontal steering wheel as she pulled into the parking lot to drop us off. No one paid me any notice. I was still sitting at the back, and strangely, I still gripped the seat beneath me with both hands, bracing myself for the crash on the old truss bridge that I was sure one day would come. Where had I been for the last few minutes? Had I really seen Ruminato, or just some awful vision manufactured by my brain? Clearly, my ride had nothing in common with everyone else's that morning. Then a horrible thought struck me. Was something physically wrong with me?

I sat there shaking, feeling very alone as the bus came to a wheezing stop. I reminded myself of what Ruminato had already done to me. There was no disputing that, and it gave me the courage to believe in myself. I'd seen something, I was sure of it. Some monstrous being had taken Ruminato. What was it, and where did it come from? If Ruminato was the strife who traveled between the worlds capturing the shadow things, the thing capable of capturing *him* must have power beyond imagining. What would happen to us all if Ruminato was gone forever? Who would collect the strife?

I gathered my things together, trying to think about this rationally. A few months ago, I hadn't even met the Millers, I reminded myself, and now I was swallowing everything they told me. How did I know they weren't feeding me a bunch of lies? I'd experienced strange, frightening things, but maybe there was another explanation. Maybe I'd been hypnotized, even drugged. On the other hand...what if everything I'd seen was real?

The rest of the school day passed in the usual way, I guess. I didn't really pay attention; my mind was too preoccupied with what I'd seen that morning. I did notice that Holly was absent, which surprised me. She'd seemed fine at dinner. Was her absence connected to Ruminato's disappearance?

On the bus ride home that afternoon, I was waiting for it, watching for the bend in the road and the steel truss cage that yawned there, ready to swallow us up. I half-expected another incident and was nerving myself up for it. Somewhere in my mind a voice was chanting, *Look out, look out.* Nothing happened, and a few minutes later, I walked through my own front door with a feeling of relief. I first checked in with Mom and Toulouse, who were both in the art studio. Then I called the Miller house. I would ask about Holly first. I wasn't sure about mentioning Ruminato.

As I waited, listening to the ringing phone, I began to imagine that something terrible had happened. Expecting catastrophes, always jumping to the worst conclusions, was an upsetting habit I'd fallen into after Dad's death. It wasn't who I used to be, and it was wearing me down. "I just want to feel like *me* again," I muttered into the receiver. By this point I'd convinced myself that no one would pick up, so I was a little surprised to hear Mrs. Miller's voice. She sounded mostly normal, just kind of tired and distracted.

"Hi, Mrs. Miller, it's Phee. I'm just checking to be sure Holly's okay since she wasn't at school today."

"Holly's fine, Phee. Thank you for asking about her. We've just had…"

There was a sudden, crackling silence on the other end, and at first I thought the phone connection had failed. In the country, telephone lines are often strung farther from the main roads to the houses, and longer lines, I'd learned, could lead to problems. The Miller house had to be at least half a mile from the road. As I was about to hang up and dial again, I heard a muffled noise that sounded like cows bellowing. I wondered if

Mr. Miller was watching a Western on TV. The Millers certainly didn't have a cow, or any other kind of livestock. No pets, either. From what I'd seen, not much lived at the Millers' house but the Millers.

The bellowing was followed by a *clunk*, as if Mrs. Miller had dropped the receiver, then I heard her voice again.

"Hang on, Phee, please. I'll just be a minute."

There was another *clunk*, and I pictured her dropping the phone on the kitchen counter and rushing to pull a loaf of bread from the oven. Then came silence that dragged on and on. As I waited, I realized it wasn't completely silent, though. There was a low, distant whooshing in the background, like the sound a seashell makes when you put it to your ear. It made me think of wind rushing down long, empty passages or of someone breathing. I had a sudden mental image of the Miller house as a living thing. That this was the noise it made as it breathed.

"Phee, are you there?" Mrs. Miller was back, sounding breathless.

"I'm here. Is everything okay?"

"It could be better. We're having a little excitement today."

A hunch came to me. I stretched the telephone cord down the hall to be sure Mom was still in her studio. She was.

"Does your 'excitement' have anything to do with what Ruminato collects?" I asked. "The things Holly's music keeps locked up?"

"Not those specifically, no. They're still…safe."

"Okay, good. I asked because this morning—"

Mrs. Miller cut in. "Don't worry, it's nothing to—"

She broke off, and I heard what sounded like something enormous crashing into a wooden fence. Or a wall. Then she was back.

"Phee, I've got to go. We've got this under control. Or we will very soon. It will be fine."

She hung up.

I held the receiver for a moment, thinking, and reached a decision. It was possible that whatever was happening at the Miller house—pandemonium seemed like a good word for it—was connected to what had happened at the bridge that morning. I had to tell them what I'd seen; it was the right thing to do. It looked like the only way to do it was to go over there.

I went into the studio, and Toulouse bounced up to me. He dropped to the floor and rolled over, front paws resting on his chest, asking for a belly rub. I bent down to oblige him, but my mind was on the phone conversation. "Mom, I'm going to Holly's for a few minutes. She was absent today, and I just want to see how she's feeling."

Mom turned from her easel to give me a motherly look. "Okay, honey, just don't get too close if she's ill. It's flu season, you know."

"I'll be careful, don't worry. It won't take long."

I left the studio, feeling a little guilty. Why was I still keeping all this from my mother? I hadn't told her anything about the Millers, and their…oddities, or about what I'd experienced. At first, it was because I didn't want to worry her, but it was past that now. I had to tell her soon. If I didn't, she would think I'd been deliberately deceitful, and I didn't want her trust in me destroyed. There wasn't time to tell her now, though.

I grabbed a jacket and headed out the back door.

I halfway hoped I'd see Holly waiting at the fence with her panpipes, which was silly, since no one knew I was coming. I hesitated just a moment, then put a foot on the stile and climbed over. On the way there, I'd made a promise to myself that I was never going to let Ruminato frighten me again. Especially after seeing his insecurities on full display that morning when I'd made fun of him. His meltdown made it obvious that he was nothing but a bully who got his thrills from scaring others, and it wasn't going to work on me anymore. I didn't think he was anywhere near the Miller house anyway. It was more likely that he was still in the clutches of that dark... thing that yanked him into some other reality.

As I passed through the grove of pecan trees, I glanced down at my feet and noticed something missing. Shouldn't the ground be littered with ripe pecans? The husks had split, and I'd been seeing an increasing number of fallen nuts. That afternoon there were none, when there should've been hundreds or even thousands. Had the Millers gathered them already? That seemed like an impossible task until I reminded myself that impossible tasks were evidently what they did best. I shrugged it off. Compared to everything else I'd witnessed, this was nothing.

I spied the roofline of the house ahead. Nothing looked out of the ordinary, but that wasn't especially reassuring. My sense of urgency increased. I hurried on, wondering what I might see when I emerged from the trees.

The River Buckle caught my attention first. It looked different, but I couldn't pinpoint the reason. Then I saw it. It was a gray, gloomy afternoon, but even without sunlight, there were fiery tips on the waves, just like the evening Mr. Miller turned the river. Did it need turning again so soon? If it did, I wondered if it had anything to do with Ruminato's disappearance. Then I realized I didn't know why Mr. Miller ever had to turn the river. Vague hints had been dropped, but no one had truly explained the process or the reason for it. That wasn't why I was there, though, so for the moment I tried to put it out of my mind.

The house stood before me, looking the way it always did—like a rambling heap of stones and boards. I knew better, though. It held a horde of secrets no one would ever dream of. At this thought, a chill ran up my spine, and I wondered if I should go back home. *You don't need to be here. You don't need to do this,* my mind insisted. "I have to," I said aloud. "It's the right thing to do."

I ran up the front steps to the porch, and before I could change my mind, I opened the door and went into the Miller house.

The entry hall was dark and empty, the doors on either side closed. I'd never seen them open. "Is anybody home?" I called out. "It's me, Phee!"

At once I wished I hadn't been so loud. What if I'd announced my presence to something that shouldn't know I was there? I walked down the hall to the kitchen, hoping I might find Mrs. Miller, but the lights were off, and the room was cold. It was obvious she hadn't lit the ovens that day.

I continued through to the back door and stepped out onto the porch, taking a quick look around. The sundial was nearly in shadow; the afternoon was growing shorter by the minute. If I didn't find someone soon, I'd need to give up and head back home.

I came back into the kitchen and shut the back door, listening. The silence was so complete it unnerved me. Where could everyone be? What was the commotion I'd heard over the phone? There was no sign of a disturbance. I stood in the entrance to the kitchen, hesitant, indecisive, my eyes tracing the shabby hall runner to the front of the house. Now what? Should I just start knocking on doors? The thought of doing that made me uncomfortable. They could be anywhere, even in the basement. Holly had mentioned it, but I had no idea how to find it.

For a moment, the hallway seemed to loom before me, distorted, impossibly long. I blinked and looked again, trying to focus, and it returned to its simple layout: a ruler-straight line between the front and the back of the house to the kitchen, and through to the back door. The other first-floor rooms were on either side of the hall. I wasn't imagining things, though. The hallway really was oddly long—longer than I remembered—with so many doors. I'd never noticed how many there were. The door closest to the kitchen hid the stairs to the upper floors. I eyed it now, wondering if that's where everyone was, but I wasn't about to find out. Never in a million years would I have gone up there by myself. The upper floors were designed nothing like the first. Instead of a central hallway, they each had a jumbled hodgepodge of rooms that led into and out of each other, maybe opening on a short hall here or there, perhaps a bathroom or two. Holly had allowed me a few brief views but only with her by my side, guiding me. She'd warned me not to try going upstairs on my own.

"You'd never find your way out," she said. "People have been lost for days."

At first, I'd thought she was kidding, although she didn't look like she was. "Lost for real?" I'd asked her. "But you don't mean since your family's been living here, do you?"

She looked at me a moment, eyebrows raised, a puzzled look in her caramel-colored eyes. "Not since my family's lived here? I don't follow you. This has always been the Miller house."

Remembering that gave me goosebumps. She seemed to be implying so much that was beyond the scope of anything in my experience.

I heard a noise behind me in the kitchen and whipped around, my heart racing. The back door that I'd closed just moments ago was standing open. I must not have shut it properly. I went to close it again, this time making sure it was firmly latched. Then I crossed the kitchen and started back up the hall, fighting the urge to look over my shoulder at the back door. I would try a couple of rooms, I told myself, and if I didn't find anyone, I'd go home. I was regretting my impulsive decision to come.

The room nearest the front entrance was closed off by a pair of sliding doors that met so tightly in the middle not even a sliver of light came through. Holly had mentioned this was the living room. I knocked three times, then put my mouth close to the seam between the doors. "It's Phee," I called quietly. In that silent tomb, I couldn't bear to raise my voice. I listened for a response, but heard only my own words in my head. A light, breathy draft stirred the ends of my hair. Where could it have come from? I stepped back and looked in both directions down the hall. The back door I'd shut a second time was still closed, and so was the front door.

I needed to get a grip on myself. Putting my fingers to the recessed handles in the living room doors, I slowly slid them apart and stepped inside. I saw no one, but embers glowed in a fireplace on the left wall. Someone had been in there, although probably not recently.

I started to turn and leave, then something caught my eye, stopping me. Why didn't I notice this right away? The dimensions were wrong. The room was at least forty feet wide, yet the door to the next room down the hall was just five or six feet from the entrance to this one. From where I stood, it was obvious that the living room had one doorway: the one I'd used. What did the next door down the hall lead to, then?

I heard a faint hissing and tensed. It sounded like a pot of water coming to a boil somewhere to my left. I decided it must be coming from the fireplace and looked toward it, half-expecting it to burst into flames again. It didn't, but the embers seemed a little brighter. That could explain the hissing. Relieved, I left the living room and slid the doors shut, then went to confront the next door down the hall. Holly had never told me what was behind it.

I knocked, then called out softly as I had before. "It's Phee. Anybody in there?" I was glad to finally hear a voice answer me in this immeasurable, empty pile of stone and wood.

"Phee," it said. At least I think it did. The voice was so faint I couldn't be sure.

I pressed down on the latch, half-expecting the door to be sealed shut, a false door. Impossibly, it opened on another room, and I stepped inside.

A single lamp was lit on the opposite wall. It was so far away that it did little to illuminate the gloom, but I saw enough to know that no one was there. The room had no windows, and like the living room, it was much wider than it should've been. I remembered what Mrs. Miller had told me in the backyard: The house was far larger inside than it appeared on the outside. I now understood what she was talking about. This gave me such an unpleasant feeling that I left the door to the hallway open in case I wanted to leave in a hurry.

At first, I simply stood, my eyes wandering around the room. When I'd left my house, I'd thought it would be easy to find Mrs. Miller or Holly, but I was wrong. Since I had no intention of trying to find Mr. Miller in his mysterious workshop, it was now time to leave. Having seen so little of the house in my visits, though, I couldn't help being a little curious. Mostly, this room just seemed to feature a lot of bric-a-brac: little figurines, vases, lidded silver pots, and porcelain bowls on every table and shelf.

Then I heard the whisper. A single word from somewhere to my left: *alone.*

I spun around to search the left wall, but saw only more knickknacks like those I'd already noticed. Then another whisper came from the direction of the wall opposite the door, where the lamp cast its weak glow. The word was so clear, so sharp, as if the thing that whispered it stood beside me.

Useless.

I froze, listening, and was horrified to hear words burst into being from all different parts of the room, flinging themselves at me. *Dread empty powerless failure no one always fear gone helpless never nothing.* Then one that made me cold inside: *harm. Harm harm harm harm.* It came from everywhere at once, hammering at me, until in desperation, I stuck my fingers in my ears, blocking it out.

My pulse had started to race, but silencing the whispers calmed it and my breathing, too. After a few moments, I cautiously unplugged my ears and listened. The room looked the same as before, but the voices had ceased.

I was done. No more lingering to satisfy my curiosity. I'd overstayed my welcome. Now it really was time to go. Then, already moving to the door, I spotted something from the corner of my eye and turned. In the center of the room was a small, round, marble-topped table.

Its three legs were metal, maybe iron, and they curved gracefully, their three feet touching the floor on only the smallest of tips. For the first time in ages, I thought about the handful of ballet classes I'd taken when I was around six years old. All I wanted was to learn how to dance *en pointe*, and I was disappointed to discover that those lessons were years away. I lost interest in ballet classes soon after that. Now, alone in this poorly lit room, staring at those elegant legs, I felt a deep pang of regret for an opportunity lost, and wondered why I had given up so easily.

I moved a couple of steps toward the table. On its marble surface was a glass object in the shape of an egg, set upright on its larger end. It was about the size of an ostrich egg and looked quite fragile. It also rested on three feet, each only a small glass ball. The glass shell was thin and clear and had an iridescent sheen, like a soap bubble. I could see through it to the marble tabletop. It was enchanting, so lovely, that it made my heart break to see it, and all at once I was overcome with sadness. Why had I never been able to follow a dream to its end?

I stared at the shimmering egg, remembering. I thought of the elaborately appliquéd jeans I'd meant to create for myself at the start of the previous school year, but had tossed aside after decorating them with a few gold and copper sequins. And the sewing classes I'd quit taking when I was eleven. I hadn't completed even one skirt, because I didn't have the patience to pick apart and restitch my mistakes. Or the guitar lessons I'd abandoned at twelve, when I couldn't be bothered to keep my fingernails short. No. Ballet was only one of the things I'd given up on because it was too hard, or took too long to master, or was unlikely to ever be mastered by someone like me. Why couldn't I just do something for the joy of learning, without weighing it down with an all-or-nothing importance?

So many chances I'd had, always with my parents' encouragement, and each time I had let them—and myself—down. I hated myself for that. How could I have treated them so badly?

Now it was much too late to make up for it. My father was gone forever.

Looking at that egg, I felt bleak, blasted inside like a powerful funnel cloud had roared through me and laid all my plans and desires to waste. Before I knew it, I'd begun to cry, sobbing as if my heart would break. Agony filled me. I knew in my soul that I was destined to fail, that my whole life would be this way, and I would die unfulfilled, never having realized a single precious dream. Worst of all, I'd wasted any chance I could've taken to tell Dad how sorry I was for disappointing him. How could I have been so selfish?

I cried until I was wrung out. When I had no tears left, I used the sleeve of my jacket to wipe my eyes. I dropped my hands to my sides, exhausted. I was standing just beside the table, which somehow didn't surprise me, though I would've sworn I'd stopped several feet away. I took a step back and stared down at the egg. A thimbleful of darkness lurked in the center, like mold.

twelve

"Regret casts a long shadow," said a voice from behind me.

Badly startled, I turned so quickly I lost my balance, and a strong hand reached out to steady me.

"Mrs. Miller," I gasped, "I didn't hear you come in."

"Phee, dear, what on earth are you doing here?" She looked surprised, and not especially glad to see me. "This probably isn't the best time for a visit. I told you on the phone we had things under control."

"I know, but something happened this morning that I thought you should know about."

She frowned. "What was it?"

"There was another…" I took a deep breath and blew it out, willing myself to calm down, "…another incident with Ruminato this morning."

"What happened?" Her mouth tightened and she gazed at me intently.

I told her everything I remembered, about the truss bridge, the vanishing of everyone but me, the terrible darkness outside the windows. Then I told her the last thing I saw, when something black and vastly larger than Ruminato came from behind him and appeared to engulf him. That was when I saw the color drain from Mrs. Miller's normally flushed olive skin, leaving her cheeks sallow, her lips white.

We were still standing near the table where the glass egg was. She pushed her hair back from her forehead with the back of one hand and looked behind her to the nearest chair. I took her by the elbow and helped her to it.

When she was safely sitting down, I said, "Let me get you a glass of water, Mrs. Miller. I didn't mean to upset you like that; I'm sorry."

She hesitated, then nodded, her skin yellowish and sickly. She looked dazed when I dashed off to the kitchen.

Standing at the white porcelain sink, filling a glass with ice-cold water from the tap, I wondered again where Holly and Mr. Miller were, and just how big the house really was. There were so many mysteries at work. By the time I got back to Mrs. Miller, she looked a little better, and I was glad to see it. Her hand was steady as she took the glass from me and drank.

"Thank you, Phee."

"You're welcome." I waited a moment, then asked, "Do you have any idea what happened to Ruminato?"

She nodded slowly, staring into her glass. "I'm afraid I do."

I waited for her to speak, but she didn't. Finally I asked, "Did it have anything to do with Holly's absence from school? I was worried for her."

"No. You don't need to be concerned about that. Holly was helping out here at home."

Again she was silent, and I remembered her words when she first entered the room. "What did you mean when you said, 'Regret casts a long shadow?'"

She lifted one hand toward the marble-topped table. "I saw you with the egg." She shifted her eyes to me and waited. She seemed to expect me to understand, but I had no idea what she was telling me.

"What does that have to do—"

"Regret is one of our most potent griefs. You were overcome with it when you looked into the egg, were you not?"

"Yes, I..." My voice cracked. "I remembered things I had meant to do, wanted to do. Then I never followed through. I felt terrible about it. I had disappointed my parents."

Mrs. Miller's gaze held a tired, knowing look. "Many shadows hide regret. We probably hold more of that darkness imprisoned here than any other kind. It proliferates at will. We do our best to keep it in check, but there's only so much we can do."

She sounded weary and sad, and I wondered if she had also fallen victim to the glass egg's power. I glanced at it but quickly averted my eyes before it could possess me again. "You mean that's one of the things Ruminato—?"

"Collects and brings home. Yes. The egg is its reliquary. Its prison."

I couldn't hold back anymore. "Mrs. Miller," I blurted, "what is this place? There's magic here. I can feel it. I can *see* it. I don't mean to pry, I'm sorry. But…" I stopped. No matter how I tried to say it, it was going to come out sounding offensive and nosy.

She was watching me with her dark, expressive eyes. "But what?" she said. "It's all right, Phee, just say it."

"Who are you? You and Mr. Miller, Holly…" I swallowed. "You're obviously not like anyone else in Holm. You're not like anyone I've ever met. You all have powers that aren't normal— Mr. Miller turning the river for some reason I can't understand, you baking your bread and blessing it with your protective spells, Holly with her music that can repel evil things and keep them locked away from the rest of the world…and…and Ruminato. Oh, my God, Ruminato. He travels between worlds, in the dark places, taking the harmful shadow things and bringing them here for confinement. Why is he so different from the rest of your family? He looks nothing like you!" *He doesn't even look human,* I thought, but I stopped myself from saying it. I held back the other questions I wanted answers to: Was he really Holly's brother? One of their family? A Miller? Was Miller even their name, or just a cover for who they really were? I knew I was getting agitated. It was just so much to think about, so many questions that it was overwhelming. Finally I asked one more, the most basic question I could think of. "Why—*how*—are you able to do these things you do?"

Mrs. Miller gave me a gently pitying look. "This was the last straw for you today, wasn't it, Phee, dear?" She gestured at the glass egg with a work-worn hand that bore the faint, white scars of old burns.

I was suddenly exhausted and cold. I threw a quick look at the egg where it gleamed on the table, and shivered. "I guess it was. This, and…the school bus. I'm sorry. It's just so much to take in. Sometimes, I'm still not sure if I believe it or not. It's just—"

A tremendous crash tore through the quiet house, and it sounded as if the upper floors would collapse, crushing us beneath tons of slate roof tiles and wooden planks. I stared at Mrs. Miller, dumbstruck and paralyzed with fear. Then came an anguished, howling roar, like an animal in unbearable pain.

Mrs. Miller hastily set down her glass and stood up, suddenly all business. "It's starting again. Come, Phee, let's get you out of here. You mustn't stay any longer." She hurried me out of the room and up the hallway, then flung open the front door.

I stopped on the porch. "What's going on? What's making that terrible sound?"

"There's no time to discuss that now," she said firmly, planting herself in the doorway so I couldn't come back in the house.

"What about you? Will you be okay?"

"Yes, yes, I'll be fine. Now, go. Get yourself home."

Before the door slammed in my face, I glimpsed her already turning to rush back down the hall.

For a moment I stared at the door, not moving, stunned at the sharp turn events had taken. Staying any longer was a very bad idea, however, so I turned and started to leave. Before I could descend the porch steps, another horrific crash sounded from the interior of the house, and it struck such fear in me that my heart began to race. I broke out in a sweat, yet I was freezing cold and so lightheaded I couldn't stand without support. My chest felt like someone was squeezing it in a pair of vise grips, so tightly I could take only shallow breaths. I sat down on the top step and hooked one arm around the porch handrail, hanging on for dear life. What was happening to me? I'd experienced awful, frightening things lately. Had they affected my health? Was I having a heart attack?

Sick to my stomach, unable to move, I lowered my head to my knees. When the feeling subsided, I raised it and saw a shadow closing around my feet where they rested on the bottom step. Like a pool of murky water, it turned my white tennis shoes gray. I stared at them, struggling to breathe calmly, trying not to panic. Did I dare go back in the house? Something was wrong with me, and if I didn't get help quickly, I was afraid I would die. Then a gentle voice spoke.

I am not your death. Do you not know me? I am your death shadow. Your greatest fear. And your salvation.

I thought at first I was hallucinating. The voice seemed to fill my head, winding its way among the stillborn hopes and feeble dreams the glass egg had just shown me, but with a helpful intent instead of cruelty. I tried to sit up straighter, still clutching the porch handrail, and looked around. The shadow had clouded everything, as if I wore gray-tinted glasses. Was it really that big? Or did it cover only my eyes? Again it read my mind.

I am vast. I am your fear of everyone you love dying. Your fear of being left alone. I am your world.

My heart pounded faster as sadness overcame me. How could it know that? It replied to me with kind assurance.

I always know. You made me. I am part of you—the part that keeps you whole.

Why was this thing so pleased with itself?

Because you need me. I protect you against the future. Against loss. With me, you will always know how enormous is the realm of possibility. You will always be prepared for whatever comes.

There was a reasonable, mesmerizing quality to the voice, and I wanted to give in to it. What it said made a peculiar kind of sense. Instead I fought it, and gradually my panic lessened. My alarming symptoms eased, allowing me to stand up and let go of the handrail. Now I understood.

I took several deep breaths, filling my lungs. Part of me was aware I'd heard no more commotion coming from the Miller house, and that helped calm me. At last I was able to speak.

"I did make you," I told the voice. "You're right. I made you when my father died. Then I allowed you to grow. But you can't protect me. No one can prepare for a loss like my mother and I suffered. There's no readiness for it, no way to soften such a tragedy. No matter how tightly you cocoon yourself in anxiety."

You cannot walk into the future unprepared. You need me with you.

I heard hesitance creeping into its tone. "No," I said. "My father would hate that I did this to myself. He would want me to unmake you."

I inhabit every corner of your mind. You cannot unmake me!

It was begging now. I felt the small weight of the sardonyx pendant resting against my breastbone. I reached into my jacket and pulled it free, enclosing it in my hand. All these months I'd been carrying my own shadow, my own being of strife, and never known it. Wearing my pendant again had brought it out of hiding.

I remembered what I'd learned when confronting Ruminato, how the love for my father had reached in to fill my heart and mind. I hadn't allowed myself to feel it that deeply since he died. The pain of his loss had been too great. Now I believed I could mourn for him even while loving him just as I always had. No shadow being had the power to help or hinder that.

I looked out over the front garden—at the mailbox and driveway, the trees, the gazebo, the river.

Leave! the voice urged, its agitation growing. *Leave this house before something terrible happens!*

I ignored it. What I saw around me now, with the help of the insight I'd just been granted, was more important. The garden was a little scraggly, the rusty mailbox wouldn't close properly. The house was a collection of piecemeal bits, oddly placed windows and inexplicable dimensions, a little slumped, but every bit of it was beautiful. For the first time since I'd been going there, I allowed myself to appreciate it fully. I wondered how many other things I'd failed to see clearly since Dad died, simply from the fear of losing someone or something else I loved.

I sighed. "I don't need you anymore," I told the death shadow. "You have to leave me alone. I'll take my chances without you."

There was a moment when I felt its uncertainty. It lingered, as if hoping I would change my mind, welcome it back. "Go on, now," I said.

A chill breeze slipped around my neck and rested there briefly. Then it slithered free, and at once I felt relieved of a burden. I watched a fine trail of gray mist float down the porch steps and drift across the driveway. When it neared the mailbox, something unexpected happened. The rusty flap opened just a tad wider, and in an instant, the mist was sucked into the box. The flap closed. This time, all the way.

I didn't see Holly at school the next morning, and didn't expect to. Not after the uproar I'd heard at her house the previous afternoon. Now I was seriously worried for them. It was all I could think about on the morning bus ride. Only something huge and in agony could have made that godawful sound. Of course, when the bus reached the old steel bridge, I braced myself before we crossed it as I always did. Not for oncoming cars this time, but because I thought Ruminato might suddenly reappear. That didn't happen, but I was still tense all morning. I jumped when Mrs. Gilpin spoke to me as I was gathering my things to leave English class.

"Sophia, hold on a moment, please."

Jack was still at his desk, too, and I had the feeling he was hanging back to wait for me so we could walk together. We're both shy, but we'd been exchanging smiles and a few awkward words almost since the start of the school year. Quite a few times during lunch, I'd caught him looking at me from his table across the cafeteria. At first, I got embarrassed and dropped my eyes, but when I finally felt brave enough to smile at him, he'd smiled back. Lately, the frequency of our interactions had increased. We'd been walking from English to history together, and I'd begun to hope that maybe he would ask me to the Winter Holidays dance a few weeks away. The theme that year was "Snow Globe," and I could picture the two of us dancing in the gym beneath a gentle fall of soft, white flakes. I was thinking of it right then, in fact, and when Mrs. Gilpin asked me to wait, I snapped out of my daydream.

Jack raised his eyes to give me a questioning look. I smiled at him apologetically. "I'll see you in a minute," I murmured, then took my books and went to Mrs. Gilpin's desk. She was seated behind it, blinking at me through her owlish glasses, her thin hands folded on a stack of papers before her.

"I won't keep you long," she said, "but I wanted to ask how you're finding life in Holm so far. Are things working out for you here? I've already spoken to your mother about it, but I wanted to speak to you, too. I know how difficult it can be to change to a new school, and I've been concerned about you."

I gaped at her in surprise. "You have? Thank you, Mrs. Gilpin, that's really nice of you. I'm fine, though. Mom and I both are. I mean, you know, we're…adjusting." I knew Mrs. Gilpin was aware of Dad's death. All my teachers were. To protect me from painful moments, Mom had asked the principal to tell them when she registered me for school. I liked Mrs.

Gilpin; she was my favorite teacher, always friendly and personable, but her question was unexpected. I couldn't imagine why she cared enough to ask. Then she surprised me even more.

"I'm glad to hear it. You may not know this, but your mother and I grew up together. We're from the same small town. Distant cousins, actually."

"Really? I had no idea!"

She smiled and waved a dismissive hand. "You wouldn't. It's ancient history. We were close, but when we hit our late teens, we both moved away. We never lost touch completely, but it had been a while. Until you moved here, the last time I'd seen her was just before you were born." She hesitated. "I also wanted to tell you how sorry I was to learn of your father's passing. I met him when I went to see your mother that day. Even that brief visit was enough to tell me that Ian McKean was a good, good man."

I nodded, unable to speak just then.

"I wanted to check in with you and tell you…" She paused and removed her glasses, revealing bright, appraising eyes. She looked younger without her glasses, I noticed. "If there's anything you need, anything I can do for either of you—" She pointed them at me for emphasis. "—you be sure to let me know."

I was unexpectedly moved, and it took me a moment to answer. Her words were so sincere, and the look in her eyes was firm, but kind.

I nodded. "Yes, ma'am. Thank you. I'll tell Mom what you said."

"Good."

She slipped her glasses on again and resumed her usual appearance, at once ten or fifteen years older, and softer, more willing to bend. With them off, she'd looked uncompromising. A person who tolerated no nonsense. That was the real Mrs. Gilpin, I was sure. I decided I liked her even better than the milder version.

"You'd better get going, Sophia. Jack might come looking for you if you don't." One side of her mouth quirked upward, and a dimple appeared.

I ducked my head. "Yes, ma'am. Thank you again." I hurried from the room, my cheeks warm.

Jack and I ate together that day for the first time. After world history, he'd walked me to my locker where I stowed my books and got my lunch. Then I went with him to drop off his books, and we went to the cafeteria. It just happened naturally, as if we'd been doing it for months. As he moved through the lunch line, I watched him from our table. His back was to me, and while I waited, I took in the slope of his shoulders, the dark blond hair cut close to the back of his neck, feathering down, and felt a quick thrill of pleasure. Jack was getting his food, and then he was coming to join me at my table. *Our* table. What had I done right? And what about that quick smile of understanding Mrs. Gilpin had given me as I left her classroom? It was as if she knew we'd end up having lunch together. Had she maybe cast a little spell of blessing to make it happen? Anything was starting to seem possible to me. It wasn't important, though. The only thing that really mattered was to enjoy these moments.

When Jack joined me, we talked for a while about school as we ate. It was so easy. Then I asked him a question.

"This is fun. Why haven't we done this before?"

He gave me a surprised look. "You don't know?"

Now it was my turn to be surprised. "What is it I'm supposed to know?"

He gazed at me steadily, then lowered his eyes, put his fork down, and pushed his tray back from the edge of the table. "Well…" He stopped, balling up his napkin with such force I saw his knuckles turn white.

"What, Jack? What is it?" The change in his mood shocked me. Was it my fault? Had I ruined things before they'd even started?

He raised his eyes to me then. "It was impossible. Most of the time you've been with—"

He broke off, and we both turned to look at the person standing beside our table, holding a lunch tray in her long, fine-boned hands.

"Holly!" I exclaimed. "I thought you weren't in school today!"

"I was able to come for the second half of the day," she said breezily, sitting down next to me. "Hi, Jack," she tossed across the table. "How are you doing?"

I saw his jaw tense as he studied her a moment before answering. She hadn't bothered to look at him, I noticed, just started cutting her cheeseburger and fries into small morsels and lining them up into neat rows, as if making a plate of tasting samples at a supermarket.

"Fine, thanks," he said in a flat voice.

He looked back at me, and my heart sank. I could see him pulling away already. Our nice lunch was over.

"I have to go, Phee." He got to his feet. "I need to look over my physics homework before I turn it in."

I tried to smile up at him, but it was hard. "Okay, Jack. I'll see you later."

With a quick nod, he picked up his tray and was gone.

"Physics, wow," Holly said, her eyebrows raised. She was still playing with her food, not looking at me.

I fought back the urge to snap at her. I was annoyed at the way she'd just barged in on my lunch with Jack, but I was relieved to see her all right after being so worried for her. "Yeah. He's a sophomore like me, but he's a year ahead of me in science. Math, too." Then it dawned on me. "Wait a minute, you should know that already. Don't you take those classes with him?"

She was still looking down at her plate, but her face wore a small, secretive smile. "I guess. I don't really pay that much attention."

I couldn't think of anything to say to that. It seemed unbelievable, yet a very Holly thing to say. So instead, I watched her set her knife down, then aim her fork at the first food morsel on the left, in the top row of the grid she'd arranged on her plate. With a sigh, she stabbed it and stuck it into her mouth. As if eating was the least pleasurable activity on the face of the earth, she proceeded to chew and chew, and finally swallowed. Then, instead of moving her fork to the next bite to the right as I'd expected, she hovered it over the next vertical row, as if making a decision.

Abruptly she lowered it and stabbed a bite three horizontal rows down. When she did the same thing on the next vertical row, choosing a morsel right beside the empty space where bite number two had been, I had to ask.

"What, exactly, are you doing?"

"Composing," she answered, her mouth full.

"Composing what, an art installation? 'Still Life with Crappy Cheeseburger, Minus a Few Bites?'"

She snorted with amusement and covered her mouth.

I sat back, strangely pleased I'd made her laugh.

"No," she said finally. "But I'll have to remember to tell my father that one; he'll appreciate it."

"Not your mother?" I asked, surprised.

"She's not the one with the sense of humor."

Before she could stab another morsel, I said, "Composing what, then?"

"Hang on…" She looked thoughtfully down at the grid, then made her choice from the fourth vertical row: the bite resting on the second horizontal row. As she forked it, I saw what she was doing.

"You're kidding. Music?"

She nodded, chewing. She wiped her lips and took a drink from her chocolate milk carton. "Yeah. It's elementary, just stringing together some notes for a simple little tune, but sometimes it's interesting to see the ideas I get from cafeteria food."

"You can hear the notes in your head?"

She gave me a pitying smile before nodding again. I felt like an idiot. Obviously, she could hear them in her head.

I pointed at the drink carton. "Where does the chocolate milk fit in?"

"It doesn't. But, hey, if I can't have a chocolate malt with my cheeseburger, this is better than nothing."

I watched her nudge a bite in the fifth vertical row upward a bit, until it nearly touched the bite above it. "What are you doing now?"

She threw me an exasperated look. "Sharpening the note, of course."

I watched her for a time in silence. Soon she cut up more food to replace the bites she'd eaten, then began the grid again. I thought if she wasn't going to mention it, I shouldn't either. Except for what happened on the school bus, it wasn't my business. Mrs. Miller had told me they had everything under control, but I'd gone to check on them anyway. Was I just being nosy? After all, it's not as if I could have done anything. I had to ask, though. "So everything's okay at your house? I was a little worried yesterday."

Holly put down her fork, and this time, gave me her full attention. Her expression softened. "It's fine, Phee. Thank you. Mama would like to explain things to you a bit more clearly, so you know what we've been dealing with. She said if you still want to come for your bread-making lesson this Saturday—"

"Of course I still want to!" I broke in, shocked that there would be any question of that.

Holly held up her hands. "Well, she didn't know. She thought you might be done with us forever after everything that's happened. And she wouldn't blame you."

I shook my head firmly. "No, I'm not...at all." *Besides, I'm too curious now,* I thought.

"Good." Holly smiled. "She'll be glad to hear it."

thirteen

That Saturday, I helped Mrs. Miller wash the mixing bowl and wipe flour off the kitchen counters. When we finished, she dried her hands, folded the cup towel and turned from the sink to look at me. "This bread bakes in about forty minutes. So while we've got some time, why don't we sit down, Phee?"

I tensed. Was this going to be the explanation Holly had promised me earlier in the week? So far, Mrs. Miller had talked about the bread we were making that day, asked how my mother was doing, then about school, and that was it. Just small talk. I was beginning to think she didn't plan to tell me anything, and that Holly must've been mistaken. Holly was apparently in her own room, but that meant nothing. She'd often left me to my lessons after her mother sent her out of the kitchen for the first one.

Mrs. Miller went to the kitchen table and planted herself wearily in a chair. She pointed to the chair across from hers. "Make yourself comfortable." There were dark smudges under her eyes.

I pulled out the chair and sat down. I was trying not to look too expectant, but the fingers of my right hand were nervously rubbing the tabletop in front of me. It looked like a single, solid slab of tree, and was polished as smooth as glass. Even the edges were smooth, and gently rounded.

Mrs. Miller leaned back and crossed one leg over the other, clasping her hands loosely in her lap. "I know you've been wanting to learn more about Ruminato, and that's fair. We owe you an explanation after the way he's been following you. Frightening you."

I hesitated before nodding, my eyes fixed on her face. She wasn't looking at me but at a point to my left across the room.

"For years," she said, "his dissatisfaction with the task he performs has been growing. He hid it from us, so we didn't know the full extent of it. He steeled his will and forced himself to do it anyway. The other worlds can be ghastly places, you know, Phee. Devoid of light and love, of warmth and flesh."

Her eyes had shifted briefly to mine when she said this, but now they gazed across the room again.

"The more unhappy he became with his duties, the darker his mood became, until he reached a breaking point. Finally, he—" She paused, lifting one hand to her face and rubbing her lower lip. Sighing, she dropped her hand. "He couldn't take anymore. Something inside compelled him to…change his appearance. He mutilated his own face." She fell silent and dropped her eyes to stare unblinking down at her lap, a deep crease between her brows. It was as if she'd momentarily forgotten I was there.

My stomach lurched. This revelation shocked me, but I tried not to let it show.

After a time, she raised her gaze to mine, and I had the courage to speak. "Is that why he wears the flower mask, Mrs. Miller?"

"Yes." Her eyes were sad, and she gave me a bitter little smile. "Holly and I made it for him. He had to wear something to cover up what he'd done." She shook her head. "I can guess what you're thinking. You're asking yourself why anyone would do such a thing to themselves. Aren't you?"

I nodded.

"The answer is that Ruminato doesn't think the way we do. He believed that by transforming his face into a flower blossom he was making himself beautiful."

I opened my mouth, but before I could speak, Mrs. Miller went on. Now that she'd begun to tell me, she seemed determined to get it all out.

"That's what's under the mask, you see. He's loved flowers since he was a little boy. The magnolia was always his favorite. It's supposed to be one of the oldest flowers in the world. Did you know that?"

I shook my head.

She shrugged. "He tried to make himself look like one."

"So he did it on purpose, then? It wasn't just some...I don't know, evil influence from the shadow beings that caused him to do it?"

"No. His task does have its very ugly aspects, and they can be hard on the spirit. They can cause a sort of psychological decay. But he did it to himself, with full awareness of what he was doing. He grew so tired of the ugliness around him that it infected him. He believed himself to be ugly, too, and he wanted to see only beauty when he looked in the mirror. Now he believes he does. He sees a flower, not the disfigured remains of the face he used to have, or the terror and anguish in its eyes."

"Why does he wear the mask you and Holly made if he already believed he'd created the face of a beautiful flower for himself?"

Mrs. Miller actually smiled then. "Because I had Holly stitch my charm for a peaceful spirit into it. Quite simply, Ruminato wears it because it makes him feel good about himself. Or at least, better than he did before." Her face crumpled in an expression of agony, and she tilted her head back to look up at the kitchen ceiling, her fists clenched in her lap. "If only I had done it sooner!" she moaned. After a moment, she lowered her head and wiped the corners of her eyes with her apron. "However, as I said, we didn't know. We had no idea how badly the strife was affecting him until it was too late."

I stayed quiet, just watching her for a while, thinking about what she'd told me. I felt awkward, seeing her in her obvious grief, and wondered if I should leave. I was intruding. The bread was still in the oven, though. And I was still curious. I had a feeling she was leaving something out.

She was. Quite a lot.

"How did he do it, Mrs. Miller? How does anyone make such drastic changes in a normal face?" Her stricken expression told me I'd found the sorest spot of the story for her.

She put a trembling hand over her mouth for a moment and bowed her head. When she looked up again, she met my eyes with a steady gaze. "He'd made a stencil of the flower he considers the most beautiful."

"The magnolia," I murmured.

She nodded. "And he used…a deadly sharp blade."

I stared at her, then gasped in horror. "Your straight razor!"

She looked at me soberly. "Yes. The one I use now—the one I've shown you—is not the same one. I got rid of the first one when I saw what he had done with it."

My eyes blurred with tears. I couldn't help it. I would never have believed I could feel pity for Ruminato, but I'd been wrong.

Mrs. Miller went on, her expression unwavering. It seemed like being truthful with me now gave her some relief. "It also took a rock-steady hand to follow the stencil. One slip would have ruined the effect he wanted to achieve."

I gulped, nodding.

She sighed. "Finally, it took a self-loathing beyond anything that you or I could comprehend. One so infinite, so profound, that it made what must have been excruciating pain seem negligible."

She shifted her eyes from me to stare across the room, her gaze turned inward. I knew she must be replaying that time in her head, remembering it too clearly. After a while, she resumed her story.

"I had quite a few loaves to bake that day. I'd offered a special on a variety I don't make often, one with candied ginger, toasted almonds, golden raisins, and such. Wonderful bread, although a bit more work. Orders had come in from multiple customers, but with those two big ovens and the industrial mixer, I knew I could get most of them done in just one batch. I'd have only a few to make after that."

I glanced toward the wall in which two gleaming stainless steel ovens were set, their spotless glass doors reflecting the light from the overhead. The huge mixer with its massive bowl and metal cage fitted over the top sat on the floor to one side of the ovens. I'd seen it in operation once. It wasn't the mixer we used for my lessons.

She chewed her lower lip, shaking her head. I watched her in silence, horrified at the images I was seeing in my head. My fingernails dug into my palms.

"Anyway," she continued, "as you know, Phee, I don't cut the patterns into the dough until just before the unbaked loaf goes in the oven. I didn't need the straight razor, didn't look for it. Most of that morning was taken up with making the dough. I was out of the kitchen several times, making trips to the basement for supplies. Then I had the ingredient preparation and quite a bit of kneading to do. The first rising was slow, to develop the flavor. The second rising after the loaves were shaped went a bit faster."

I nodded.

"You can see where this is going, I imagine." Her voice was low and bitter as she flicked her gaze toward me briefly. "Finally all those loaves were ready to bake, and I went to get the straight razor out of the drawer. I had to hunt for it. It wasn't where I normally put it, but I didn't think much about it then. I just pulled it out and opened the blade without a second glance. I doubt I would've noticed anything wrong, anyway. I'd uncovered the loaves, and that thin, dry skin had formed—perfect for making the cuts. My eyes were on the first loaf already, judging the precise place where the design would go, keeping in mind the needs of the customer I was making it for. I had to work fast, and before long, I was done. I took a moment to look them over, then slid the pans into the ovens. Soon a spicy-sweet, delicious smell was filling the kitchen. That bread smells so good, and it always used to put me in a cheerful mood."

Mrs. Miller's sadness was hard to see, and I felt awful for her. Her stare was so distant, filled with so much pain. I couldn't imagine the trauma this had caused for the family.

"Well, the loaves were cooling, set out on their racks, as pretty as you please. By then, I'd made the dough for the last few orders and left it to rise. I was humming to myself, I remember, pleased with a job well done. That's when Ruminato walked into the kitchen. I glanced up, about to greet him and ask if he was hungry. Then I saw…"

She stopped. She looked so distressed I thought she couldn't bear to go on. I didn't blame her. When she resumed her story, I realized she intended to leave nothing to my imagination. She wanted me to hear it all.

"He was naked," she went on heavily, "and covered in blood. It looked sticky. Congealing. For some reason, the next thing I noticed after that was that he'd left a trail of bloody tracks coming into the kitchen. I remember thinking, 'I don't have time to clean that up right now. I need him to do it.'" Mrs. Miller looked at me in disbelief. "Can you imagine? Such an illogical thing to be thinking just then!" She shook her head. "I guess it was the effect of the shock. Then I looked—really looked—at his face, and saw where the blood had come from. And the horror he'd made from his nose and mouth."

She squeezed her eyes shut, her mouth stretched wide. The grief I saw in her face broke my heart. After a time, she opened her eyes and went on with her story.

"He was grinning at me. Or trying to. So eager and pleased with himself. He said, 'Mama, look at me! Don't I look better?' It was hard to understand what he was saying because he'd stitched his upper lip to…well, the whittled-down stump that was left of his nose. Watching him try to speak, the blood smeared around his mouth, the raw wounds he'd made in his dear flesh, it was all I could do to keep from throwing up. I started to scream, and Holly came running into the kitchen, then ran to get her father from his workshop when she saw what had happened."

Mrs. Miller shuddered. "After Holly rushed from the room, Ruminato saw the straight razor where I'd left it lying on the counter. He picked it up and unfolded the blade. Even held it up to the light, admiring it! Then he touched the tip to his chin and looked at me with big, excited eyes. I'll never forget what he said next. He told me, 'This isn't just for your bread.

Look how much more it can do!' That's when I realized what he'd used on his face. So I snatched up a cup towel and, wrapping it around my right hand, I threw myself at him, trying to grab the razor away. A foolish thing to do, but I wasn't thinking clearly. I wanted to get it before he could do more damage to himself. He had a death grip on it, too. The fact that I was trying to take it away from him made him hold on even harder."

I was cringing in the chair, my legs tucked under me, one hand covering my mouth. I had no idea how long I'd been sitting like that.

She held up her right arm. "That's how I injured my wrist. The razor cut me as I was struggling to take it from him. But luck was with me, and I got it away from him at last."

I gasped. "So this happened during the summer before school started?"

"Yes. Just a few weeks before."

This shocked me. I hadn't realized he'd hurt himself so recently. "What did you do then?"

She paused and gave me a grim look. I'd never seen her look so serious.

"I took that straight razor and ran out the back door with it. Holly and her father were running up from the workshop when I got around to the front of the house, and I left them to deal with Ruminato. But I went to the river and pitched the razor out over the waves as far as I could. I'll see it in my mind's eye forever. That cursed thing flashed silver in the sun like a jumping fish as it splashed into the water. Then I came back into the kitchen. I had to do something about the bread."

191

"The bread? What do you mean?"

Mrs. Miller gave a weary shrug. "Well, I couldn't give those loaves to my customers, could I? After what Ruminato had done with the razor, it was no good for making protective charms. It was tainted, and now the bread that it had touched was tainted, too. I didn't know what it might do to anyone who ate it. So I took the loaves out to the burn barrel in the backyard and lit them on fire." Her mouth had a determined set, and she looked almost angry as she said, "I burned every bit of it to ashes. That was the safest thing to do, making sure that nothing would ever have the chance to eat it. I called my customers and told them the order had been delayed. A power outage, I said. They believed me. Things happen out here in the country. The next morning, Nick drove me in to Holm to the barber shop, where I ordered a new straight razor. They're not as easy to come by as they used to be, but the barber is a customer of mine. I made up some story about how one of my kids broke the razor's blade trying to pry a stuck lid off a jar. I didn't breathe a word of the truth. I doubt he would've believed me anyway."

I saw a tight, humorless smile touch Mrs. Miller's lips as she recalled the memory.

"He was horrorstruck," she went on. "As he was filling out the order form to the barber supply company, he kept shaking his head. 'It's a miracle nobody cut a finger off!' he said. I was wearing a long-sleeved blouse, and I'm sure he didn't notice my bandages." She glanced down at the thin scar running from the underside of her wrist up her forearm, still pink against her olive skin. "Nick cleaned my wound and stitched me up. He's good with a needle. Holly did the best she could for her brother. We couldn't let a doctor see either of us. There'd be questions asked and written records kept, you see. Anyway, I put the bread orders on hold. In a few days, the new razor came in, and with Holly's help, I was back in business. It was clear we had to make some changes, though."

"Changes?"

"Of course. To begin with, I had to put the new razor under lock and key. Now it's in a safe place that only I know about, and I get it out only when I need to. When I'm done, I lock it up. I realize now that I wasn't as careful with it as I should've been.

"We've also been keeping a much closer eye on Ruminato's movements around the house and property. We had to. He can't be allowed to wander at will; we don't know what he might do. We thought that was enough. We certainly weren't expecting him to be able to evade our watch, but he did. It's you, Phee. I don't know what it is about you." Mrs. Miller gave me a searching look. "Why won't he leave you alone? I'm so sorry about that, and I don't know what we can do. There's no question he's unhappy. That's become obvious. But his task is to bring the strife and that's exactly what he did—and continues to do—for a very long time, now."

When she stopped, looking pensive, I wondered what her idea of a very long time was. I thought of the millions of ground pecan shells paving their driveway and knew it must be longer than mine.

"I can't put my finger on exactly when it happened…" Her voice trailed off.

I waited for her to finish. When she didn't, I prompted her. "When what happened, Mrs. Miller?"

"When the shift happened," she said. "I know it was before he cut up his face."

"What shift?"

"The shift from simply bringing the strife. It was as if one day a switch had been thrown inside of him. The three of us were aware of it, and talked about it, unsure of what to do. Watching him change has been a terrible sadness for us. It's just as Holly told you. He's as much strife now as any of the shadows he brings us."

She drummed her fingers on the table, then uncrossed her legs, smoothing her apron in a determined fashion. "Well, Phee, I wanted to tell you a bit about what's been going on with us. Not that it fixes anything. I just didn't want you to feel you were alone in this or that we didn't understand your fear. Now that you've told us what you saw, we know he's gone. We don't know when we'll see him again, but at least you can breathe a little easier until we do.

"Speaking of breathing, my nose is telling me this bread is getting close to being done. I'll take a quick peek at it, if you could set out the cooling rack, please, dear."

Before she could stand, I leaned forward. "Mrs. Miller, when I told you what happened on the school bus, you said you had an idea of what that thing was that took Ruminato away."

She looked at me and gave a slight nod. "Possibly."

"Is it as…" I swallowed. "… as big as it seemed?"

She appeared unsure of how to answer me, as if debating

whether the truth or a lie would be kinder. Then she nodded again. "If it's what I think it was."

The finality with which she pressed her lips together prevented me from asking her what she thought it was. Something else bothered me, though. "But what happens if…" I stopped, unable to finish the sentence in a way that wouldn't cause her more hurt. She finished it for me.

"If we never see him again?"

"Yes. What happens to the strife?"

She stood up and gripped the edge of the table, leaning on it. "I'm trying not to think about that possibility, Phee. I need to believe he will be back, that whatever took him will return him." Her mouth was a hard line as she shook her head. "What I worry about is how I feel about it. Sometimes I wish that thing, whatever it was, would keep him forever. That's how much he's changed. At those times, I think I'd be glad to see the back of him for good. The rest of the time…I want him home. Desperately. No matter what he's done, he's my child. What I want isn't important, though. He must return to us. We need him. How would we manage without him? The strife is endless." She straightened up and rapped the table with her knuckles. "Let's check that bread."

I uncurled my legs from under me. "I still don't understand about his hooves."

She stared down at me steadily. "What about them?"

"How did Ruminato change his feet into hooves?"

She surprised me when she chuckled. "Oh, he didn't do that to himself, Phee. He's always had hooves. It made for an uncomfortable birth, as you might imagine. I didn't mind, though. I would suffer willingly for my beautiful boy."

Then she turned and went to the ovens, and pressed a switch in the control panel. I saw the light come on in the top one and watched her lean forward and peer through the window. The heating elements inside gave a faint reddish glow to her face.

"Oh, yes, very nice," she murmured. "Not much longer."

I stared at her for a second, badly jarred, before I forced myself to stand and get the cooling rack.

———

As I walked home, I thought about everything Mrs. Miller had told me. She'd been much more open than I expected. Her story about Ruminato's self-mutilation horrified me. I could see how badly it pained her to talk about it, and I was shocked at how recently it had happened. When she first began describing the incident, I'd imagined his face already healed, the blossom's curves and flowing swells bearing only the ridges of old scar tissue. As she went on, I imagined something quite different, and the thought of the fresh, raw ruins hiding under that mask made me sick to my stomach.

When she spoke about Ruminato's hooves, the look on her face was disturbing. In that moment, she looked proud and fierce, willing to make sacrifices, capable of doing anything to protect that inhuman monster. I was certain that was how she *really* felt about her son. All of her talk about hoping that he might've been snatched away into the darkness forever was just that: talk. It was nonsense. Did she care so deeply about her daughter? Somehow,

I doubted it. For the first time, I realized I hadn't seen Holly once that day. She'd never come into the kitchen, and I'd been too absorbed in Mrs. Miller's story to notice.

So far, I'd kept my mother out of the situation. I hadn't told her anything about Ruminato or his persecution of me. I didn't want her to worry about me, and I certainly didn't want her to tell me to stop seeing the Millers. Holly was still the only real friend I'd made at school, and I didn't want to surrender that relationship, no matter what her brother had done. But now, I decided I needed to tell Mom what was going on and ask for her advice. Maybe she could help.

fourteen

That night over dinner, I told Mom everything—about the dreams I'd had, the magic of Holly's music, Mr. Miller turning the river, Mrs. Miller's protective breads, the power of the glass egg, the struggle with my death shadow, and, of course, about Ruminato intercepting the school bus and the strange noises I'd heard in the Miller house. I left out nothing. Toulouse was lying across my feet, happy to see me after my absence that day. I didn't learn until I got home that I'd spent more time at the Miller's than I thought I had. I couldn't account for it. Whether it was making the bread, or talking with Mrs. Miller, everything seemed to unfold in the normal way. But time had a way of slipping sideways on me whenever any of the Millers were nearby. I brought that up to Mom, too.

She listened attentively, sometimes nodding, every so often asking a question or two, mostly just letting me talk. She raised her eyebrows when I got to the part about Ruminato's hooves but she made no comment. I was surprised at the relief I felt after getting everything out into the open. It was exhausting, and when I finished I was ravenous. I guess I'd been carrying a greater burden than I thought, keeping it inside, hidden from the one person left in my life who would truly listen and believe me.

As I looked at Mom's face, so grateful for her calm acceptance and faith in me, I suddenly recalled a conversation I'd had with Dad the previous school year.

He told me, *If you have a problem you can't solve, tell your mother.*

What about you? I'd asked him. *Why can't I tell you?*

You can always tell me anything, he said, *and I would move heaven and earth to fix it for you. But, babe...* He'd taken my hands then, his eyes full of love, his face serious. *I won't always be here for you to talk to. Your mother, on the other hand? She will.*

Remembering this, I teared up a little, and my heart filled with longing. Across the table, Mom had finished her dinner while I was talking and now sat thoughtfully toying with the last bite of her bread. I brushed at my eyes with my napkin before she could see my mood. Finally, I started eating, and my appetite took over.

When I next looked up, she still held it, a bite of the crust, and even from across the table I could see it was marked with a small part of the pattern Mrs. Miller had slashed into it. Mom was studying it closely.

She held it up. "So these markings were meant for the protection of the person who eats the bread?"

I nodded, my mouth full.

"Well…" She paused, giving me a meaningful look. "They haven't done a very good job of protecting you, have they?"

I stopped chewing, startled. "Sure they have," I said once I'd swallowed. "If we hadn't been eating the bread for the past couple of months, there's no telling what Ruminato could've done to me on the bus. Mrs. Miller let me make the pattern only once, just to get a feel for it. I didn't do it on this loaf." I pointed at the piece in Mom's hand. "She did. She said she wants to be sure I get the best results from the charms."

She glanced at it once more before dropping it on her plate. "Perhaps."

Her tone sounded somewhat dismissive to me. It might've been my imagination. "So what do you think is going on, Mom?" I asked. "Why is Ruminato after me? What does he want?"

She hesitated for a second. "I have an idea about that. First, though, tell me again about the death shadow."

So I went through it again, repeating the death shadow's exact words to me as closely as I could recall them, and what I'd replied. I told her about the deep feeling of love and protection I had from wearing the sardonyx pendant Dad had given me, and how, in the end, it gave me the strength I needed to banish the death shadow. Forever, I hoped. When I finished, she nodded and stood up from the table.

"How about we finish off the evening with some hot chocolate in front of the fire?"

"Oh, yes, please. I'll clear the table."

I ferried the dishes into the kitchen and got them scraped and loaded into the dishwasher while she stirred the cocoa powder and sugar together. By the time I started it, she had the milk stirred in, and I could see steam rising from the saucepan. As she got the mugs ready with marshmallows and spoons, I ran into the family room and put another log on the fire, stirring up the coals with the poker. When Mom came in with our mugs, I had a cheerful blaze going. I looked around the cozy room, at the firelight flickering over the dark walls hung with a few of her bright watercolors, the braided cotton throw rugs on the oak floor. By making myself busy, I'd avoided thinking about what she might tell me. Soon I'd know, and I was getting very uneasy. What if there was no way she could help? What if all I'd done by unburdening myself was to make both of us worried?

We settled on the sofa so we could face the fire. My hands were a little shaky, so I set my hot chocolate on a side table and brought one foot up under me, clutching it like it was a life preserver in the open sea.

I took a deep breath. "Okay. What's your idea?"

She watched me in silence for a moment, her slender fingers curled around her mug. My eyes were drawn to a lingering blotch of crimson paint on one of them, a result of her work in the studio that day, I knew. The color, so like blood, was startling.

"The appearance of your death shadow has made the situation much clearer, I think," Mom began. "From what you've told me, Ruminato's duty is to seek out the strife that populates the cosmos. He then captures it and brings it back in that sack he carries, so that his fellow guardians can imprison it forever, where it will do no more harm. Correct?"

"Right. I don't know anything about guardians, though. Nobody in the Miller family has mentioned that word to me." I was gripping my foot so tightly I could feel my heartbeat in my fingers. I forced them to loosen.

"No. They wouldn't." Mom sipped from her mug and licked marshmallow froth from her upper lip. "But 'Guardians'—" She lifted one hand to indicate air quotes around the word "—is what they are."

I nodded slowly. "Okay. That makes sense."

"From what Mrs. Miller told you today," she went on, "Ruminato has become increasingly unhappy about performing his duty and wishes it were not his burden to bear anymore. Also correct?"

"That's what she said. But what does his unhappiness have to do with me?" I reached for my mug and took a careful sip.

"He's looking for a way to get out of his responsibilities by passing them on to someone else. As soon as you were brought into the Miller fold, he sensed that you, too, understood strife. That not only did you understand it, you inhabited it. You were strife just as much as he is."

I sat forward, nearly spilling my hot chocolate. "How can that be? I'm not strife! You should have seen the misery that glass egg caused! That was strife!"

"I said you *were* strife," she pointed out calmly. "Not that you *are* strife."

"All right, that's a little better," I admitted. "But I still don't see—"

"Your death shadow, darling," my mother said gently. "Your death shadow brought you strife. In the form of fear and anxiety, worry about the future. In the name of protection, it brought you strife. It inhabited every atom of your being. It even told you so."

I sat back against the sofa. "Oh. Now I see." I stared down into my mug, watching the creamy raft of floating marshmallows slowly dissolving. "Ruminato came after me because he thought he could force me to take over his job for him."

"That's exactly what he did."

I took a swallow, thinking. "I don't see how that's possible, though. He can't force me to do something I don't want to. Can he?"

She gave me a long, serious look. "You need to remember something. Nothing is impossible. But you did just what you should have: You sent your death shadow on its way. From what you said, it's now imprisoned with the other strife at the Miller house, which means—"

I laughed a little, but not because I found it funny. "I never thought that mailbox could actually close."

"—which means it will never bother you again. If you hadn't succeeded in ridding yourself of it, you would still be vulnerable. Very vulnerable indeed."

Sudden fear chilled me at the thought of what could've happened, and I sent up a quick prayer of thanks for the strength Dad's love had brought me. I set my mug down and got up to stand by the fire. I turned my back to it, letting the warmth toast me. Toulouse, who was lying by the hearth, uttered a small groan as he stretched and put a comforting paw on top of my foot.

"Mom? Can I ask you something?"

"Of course, sweetheart."

"Why do you believe me? I keep thinking this must sound absolutely crazy to you."

Her gaze on me was steady and calming. "Because I've known something of the darkness myself, Phee." She gave me a faint smile. "Something of Guardians, too."

Questions bubbled up in my head, but before I could ask them, she went on.

"That's not a story for tonight. Tonight we're discussing your problem and what's to be done about it. So let's get back to Ruminato, shall we?"

I nodded, already feeling more hopeful. My parents had always been the most capable people I'd ever known, and Mom's take-charge attitude now went a long way toward improving my mental state.

"After doing this task for such a long time, Ruminato has developed a keen nose for the strife-ridden," she said, her face thoughtful. "That's obvious. And I can understand why being forced to collect the strife would cause him such pain. Not that I'm sympathetic toward him. Especially not when he targets my daughter," she added in a tone so cool it gave me goosebumps. "I'm just saying, I can see why he wants to be done with it."

I came back to the sofa and sank into the cushions. "You should see what passes for his nose on that mask he wears, Mom. I can see him as clearly as if he were here in the room with us." I shuddered. "What's underneath sounds even worse. Mrs. Miller told me what he did to it when he carved up his face. Just thinking about it makes me sick."

Mom studied me a moment, then set down her mug. "Can you describe his appearance to me?"

"Yes. What I can't do is forget it."

"Wait here." She got up and left the room. Toulouse raised his head to watch, then got up from his place by the fire and trotted after her.

In a short while she returned, Toulouse following her. She was carrying a sketchpad, a couple of drawing pencils, and a gum eraser. She sat down on the sofa, opened the sketchpad, and settled in. Toulouse gave himself a hearty shake and flopped down by the hearth again.

Mom saw me looking at her materials. "Drawing always helps me think more clearly. Okay, then." She picked up a pencil and pointed the blunt end at me. "Go."

Over much of what remained of the evening, she drew not one, but four sketches of Ruminato based on my descriptions. I was careful to be as precise as possible. The first was of his masked face. I had the hardest time with this one, especially when trying to describe the cone-shaped area in the center of the mask. After a few minutes and a few erasures, Mom held up a drawing that was frighteningly accurate, even down to the way his dark eyebrows lifted up sharply at the outer corners. She'd made no comment when I told her about the coin-slot pupils of his eyes, just nodded and penciled them in as if they were a feature she saw in human beings every day.

The second sketch was of his head and upper body as he'd looked through the school bus window just before the enormous black thing snatched him backward into oblivion. That scene was so vividly imprinted on my mind that it was easy to describe for her how he looked that morning, with his creamy white magnolia blossom face and his thin, bare forearms pressed against the glass like pale worms. Draped from one was the brown sack, so dark against his skin. The third sketch was a full-length rendering of how I'd seen him in my dream, robed in the carpet runner and with his feet bundled as he thumped down the hall toward me.

"Of course," my mother muttered to herself, frowning in concentration. "So his hooves wouldn't make noise on the wood floor." Her pencil strokes swept across the drawing paper.

The fourth sketch was of only his hooves, the way I'd seen them just before he abducted me in the woods outside the Miller house. Those were a difficult feature for me to recall accurately, as I'd had only a glimpse of them. When Mom asked me to describe them, at first I couldn't even remember if they were cloven like a goat's hoof or single-toed, like a horse's hoof. I'd never stopped to think that there were different kinds of hooves. So she did a rough sketch of each and held them out for me. Seeing them on paper helped me to remember. They were cloven.

"Larger and more solid," I told her. "Think more like a cow, not a goat. But a younger cow."

"A younger bull, you mean," Mom said, raising her eyes briefly to mine.

As she finished each one, she tore the page out of the sketchbook and placed it on the coffee table. Now I leaned forward to inspect them side by side. Her artistic skill, how easy she made it look to do what she did, always amazed me. She had perfectly captured the strife. These drawings were exactly what I'd seen, yet their subject was so impossible in the world I thought I knew that the next words came tumbling out of my mouth without any conscious intent from me.

"Mom, who *are* the Millers?"

She studied the four drawings, then sat back, satisfied with her work, before answering. "Not who they pretend to be, or rather, not who they pretend to be to most people. They've made an exception with you." She reached for her forgotten mug and drank down the last of her hot chocolate.

"In what way?" I asked.

"For one thing, they've given you some broad hints about their capabilities. I'll bet none of Mrs. Miller's bread customers know those aren't just pretty designs she slashes into her loaves."

I thought back. "You know, at my first lesson she told me not to tell anybody what those designs were for. When I asked her if I could tell you, she agreed, but said nobody else needed to know."

"Did you ask her why?"

"She said her customers probably wouldn't understand, and if they knew the reason for the markings, they could misinterpret and even stop buying her bread. I think she meant they'd probably read dark purposes into what she was doing."

"Black magic, witchcraft," my mother said dryly.

"Right. Anyway, she told me she couldn't afford to lose their business."

"What did you say?"

"I told her I understood. Her reasoning made sense to me, and it seemed like a harmless deception. At first I thought the designs were something Mrs. Miller did more to help herself than others, something she could do that would let her feel she was making a difference." I stared at Toulouse, not really seeing him, but mulling the many strange things I'd experienced over the past few months. "It was only later that I began to believe what she'd told me. By then I'd grown to like them so much, and was so glad for Holly's friendship, that I wouldn't have given away the things I'd learned about them."

"Why do you think Mrs. Miller said you could tell me?" Mom asked.

"I'm sure she knows how close you and I are. Holly knows, because Dad's accident was one of the first things I confided to her. I figured getting it out into the open would make our conversations easier." I sighed. "I'd been feeling so lonely at my old school. The people I'd thought were my friends just didn't get it. Holly did. She was sympathetic. She understood how awful it must be for us both and how we've come to count on each other."

"So Holly told Mrs. Miller," my mother said flatly, "and from this information, Mrs. Miller knew that if she insisted you keep your new knowledge from me, she would lose your growing trust."

I jerked my head around to look at her. "Hang on. What are you saying, Mom? That passing his job to me isn't just some wild scheme Ruminato's come up with on his own?"

Mom just waited, watching me.

I couldn't believe the idea taking shape in my head. "Are you telling me that this is some kind of... *plot* the Millers have hatched together? To have me collect the strife instead of him?"

Mom didn't answer right away. Instead, she asked, "Did you tell Holly anything else about us?"

I thought about it, then shook my head. "No. Just that you're an artist. I told her how proud I was of you and how happy it made me to see you stretching your wings and embracing your talent for once, instead of keeping it hidden like some secret hobby of yours. What's that expression you use?"

"Hiding it under a bushel."

"Oh, right." I'd heard her say that a few times over the years. She told me it was something her country kinfolk on her mother's side used to say. It was from them that she'd learned how to cook, and to can and preserve. I'd never met any of them; they'd mostly died out long ago. Now it occurred to me that Mrs. Gilpin might be one of the last left of those country kinfolk.

Mom was still watching me. "Anything else?"

"No. I don't think so. Only that you have a one-woman show coming up in January at the fine arts gallery." I shrugged. "What else is there to tell? Neither you nor Dad had any close relatives left alive. It was always just the three of us. I would never tell Holly about our family life together before…we moved. It's only for us to know. It's special…private."

Mom gave me a small, sad smile.

"We talk about normal, day-to-day stuff—books, school, her music. What life is like in the world outside of Holm." I stopped, thinking. "Actually, we don't really talk much about school. Or boys, either. Come to think of it, Holly hasn't mentioned ever having a boyfriend. It's like she doesn't notice cute guys at all."

"Okay, sweetheart." Mom reached across the sofa cushion to pat my knee. "I just need you to be really careful in the future—even more careful than you've already been. Don't reveal anything else about us. Keep your eyes open. I don't want to alarm you, but I think they've got something in mind. Still in the planning stage, I think. Don't let your guard down when you're at the Miller house."

Her warning disturbed me, but mostly I felt an overwhelming sadness. This was breaking my heart. "Why can't I just not see them anymore? It would hurt less."

"You can't stop abruptly, not after you've spent so much time there. If you did, they'd suspect that something was up on our end. They probably would guess that you'd told me everything and that I was suspicious." She gave my knee a squeeze and released it, sinking back into the cushion. "A better plan is for you to cut back on your Saturday visits. And when you see Holly at school, don't avoid her. That would seem odd to her, so just be normal."

I looked down at my lap. My fingers were twining together and I hadn't realized it. "What happens when I do go
to their house? I can't stay on guard the whole time." I sniffed.
"Sometimes it's as if I lose consciousness. I can't help it and
there's no warning it's going to happen. I told you that."

My mother nodded. "I understand. You'll just have to do
the best you can. We'll come up with something you could be
doing on Saturdays instead of going over there, some sort of
activity. Maybe studying for the PSATs. Don't worry. You're
not alone in this. We're going to fix it."

I stared at my fingers, feeling helpless. They seemed to have
minds of their own. They looked like a snarl of nightcrawlers,
the earthworms Dad and I used to fish with. "Mom, why did
this have to happen? *Why?* I like the Millers so much!" I looked
up at her. "I thought I'd lucked out, finding a really nice family,
a good friend to spend time with! The fact that they live so close
to us, too. It seemed as if it was meant to happen!"

My mother gave me a serious, level look that startled me.
Her eyes were so sad and filled with ancient knowing, green as
the tides washing the seashore under moonlight. "It was, my
darling. Just not in the way you believed."

fifteen

The winter holidays were coming not long after our conversation that night, and I couldn't wait. Not only would I get a break from seeing Holly at school and pretending everything was normal, but also I wouldn't need to come up with excuses not to go to her house. I found this out over lunch one day.

I'd grabbed a table and saw her crossing the cafeteria toward me as I unwrapped my smoked turkey sandwich. Her pale face wore a slight frown as she plopped her lunch tray down and pulled out a chair.

"What's wrong?" I asked.

She shook her head. "It's not a big deal. It's just disappointing." She opened her carton of lemonade and took a sip. "We won't be able to see each other as much as I'd hoped over the break, that's all."

"Oh, how come?"

"Around the holidays, Mama gets extra orders for breads and cakes. I always help her with them because there's too much for one person to do. For some reason, this year she's *really* swamped. She's already taken twice as many orders as usual, and there's no telling how many more she'll get. She may even have to start turning people down."

"Wow!"

Holly's frown deepened as she looked down at her plate and began to pick at her food. "Anyway, I'm sorry. I hoped we'd be able to spend more time together, but it's not going to work out."

"Oh, it's okay, I understand." I tried to sound disappointed while hiding the huge sense of relief flooding through me.

Holly suddenly looked up at me, her eyes wide, as if she'd been struck by an idea. "Hey, it's not too late for you and your mother to order something special if you'd like to. When you pick it up, we'd get to see each other for a few minutes, at least." She laughed. "Just make it something easy, like dinner rolls!"

So I acted excited about her suggestion and told her I'd talk to Mom. Then I gave her the excuse I'd prepared, pleased that it sounded natural when it came out of my mouth. We were busy in my house, too, I told her. Mom's art show was coming soon after the winter break was over. I enthused about it—the easiest part of that conversation for me—but stopped short of suggesting that Holly and her parents come see it. I would've invited them before everything got strange, but at that point, the last thing I wanted was to have the Millers there.

Somehow I managed to keep a smile on my face, and that lunch passed just like any other normal one.

———————

Mom was constantly wired during that time, a ball of buzzing, nervous energy. She drove back and forth from our house to Holm; transported the smaller finished pieces to the gallery; met with the owner, Mrs. Bruner; made sure the lighting would be perfect; proofed the handouts; measured the spacing on the gallery walls and countless other things. She was also finishing up the last couple of pieces—watercolors, she told me—and doing holiday grocery shopping for us.

Over dinner one night she said, "This will be our first Christmas without your father, and I want us to honor his memory. I'd also like to form new traditions for the two of us. A way to celebrate going forward."

I watched her face in the flickering light of the red and green pillar candles she'd arranged on the table. I could see our reflections in the windows, glowing against the night-black world outside. It was a rare moment when she'd stopped her constant running from task to task. Toulouse lay on the floor, already taking up much more space than he used to. His dark head rested on his outstretched front legs, and his brown eyes moved from one of us to the other, relaxed, but alert.

"We need to try to move on," Mom said. She was holding back tears, but her face had a determined look. "Dad would want that…for both of us. In less than three weeks, it will be a year since the accident."

"I know." I nodded reluctantly. A lump in my throat made it hard to swallow; I was struggling not to cry. I pulled the sardonyx pendant out of my sweater and gripped it tightly for a moment. "I can feel him. He's here with us."

That night was a brief respite of peace. By the next day, Mom had resumed her nonstop activity. Toulouse and I watched her as she rushed about. It seemed like a nightmare of last-minute details to me, and it made my head hurt to think of all the balls she was keeping in the air. I did wonder if she might be overcompensating, staying busier than she needed to be to keep from thinking about the approaching anniversary. At the same time, I was so glad to see her thriving. She had truly come into her own. In the end, since there wasn't much we could do to help, she shooed the two of us outside to enjoy the winter weather.

Toulouse's first snowfall was fun for all three of us. It began overnight, and the next morning the ground was covered in several inches, with a few flakes still drifting down. Toulouse stood by the windows in Mom's studio, fascinated by the new view. When we opened the back door, he went out, stepping cautiously, sniffing at the ground. Soon, he put his black nose to the white surface and trotted around the yard, plowing furrows. Next he went rolling and romping in the drifts, emerging with a big doggy grin, his thick, reddish-black coat glistening with white flakes, his lolling tongue very dark against his snow-covered muzzle. Then he shook himself, and the air gleamed with a sudden fall of crystals. He'd become a living, breathing snow globe.

Watching Toulouse play took my mind off Ruminato and the Millers, which was what I needed then. It did make me think of the snow globe-themed dance I'd had such hopes for, though. I didn't get to go. Jack never asked me to go with him, and I couldn't go with Holly because I was avoiding her. Jack had retreated again after Holly horned in on our lunch that day. I wished he'd had time to finish what he'd begun to tell me. I was sure it had something to do with Holly—something negative. I hoped that eventually, once I was free of the mess I was in, Jack and I could pick up where we left off. If I ever *could* be free of it.

Mostly, I tried not to think about what the future might hold after vacation was over. I just wanted to watch Toulouse enjoying himself, and live in those good moments as the days of the winter break whirled by. Only much later did I wonder if Mrs. Miller had found it odd that we didn't order any of her bread for our holiday dinner.

————

New Year's Eve was early and quiet for Mom, Toulouse, and me. Well before midnight, we stood outside for a few minutes to watch a shower of fireworks in the cold, black sky over Holm's modest nighttime glow. The new semester at school began a few days later.

I still wouldn't be seeing much of Holly, which eased my mind. She was busy practicing with the Holm High orchestra—as concertmistress, of course—for their spring performance coming near the end of March. The few times I did see her, she was always carrying her violin, always in a rush, and otherwise seemed like her normal self: beautiful, much more sophisticated than her age and small-town background would make you think, and her personality somehow always larger and cooler than life. If it had been the start of the school year, those early days when I didn't yet know anything about her, I would've been weak with envy.

She didn't mention Ruminato, and neither did I. I wondered if he'd returned from wherever the blackness had taken him that morning at the old truss bridge. I also wondered if he'd ever been a student at Holm High. I couldn't ask Holly; the less I saw of her, the better. After the talk with Mom, I was afraid of interacting with any of the Millers. It was possible they'd see straight through me to the bottom of my distrust for them.

So I decided to ask Deb, the older girl who'd spoken about the first movie vampires during book club early in the school year. She's a senior, a year ahead of Holly, and by then, I'd gathered that her family had lived in Holm for a long time. I caught her in the library before the next book club meeting started. We went into the meeting room together, several minutes early. While we waited for everybody else to arrive, I brought up her discussion about *Nosferatu* from months before.

"Hey, Deb, I told my mom what you said about *Nosferatu*, and she was so intrigued that we decided we'd both like to see it.

The only problem is, we don't know how. We've been checking the TV listings, but…" I broke off as Deb started nodding.

"I know," she agreed, "it's hard to find. It's not shown on TV much."

"How did you see it, then?"

"The first time I saw it was a couple of years ago. One of the TV stations features old horror movies in October, and I just stumbled across it. Since then, I've seen it quite a few times."

"But if it's not shown much, how have you—"

Deb gave a shamefaced little laugh and flushed bright pink. "Don't tell anybody, okay?"

"Of course I won't!" I said, wondering what the big secret was.

"When my grandfather found out how much I enjoyed the movie, he gave me a release print."

"Release print? I don't—"

"The film reels."

I stared at her, speechless for a moment. *"What?* How on earth—"

No one else had arrived yet, but Deb hushed me with a finger to her lips, still blushing. *"Shh, shh.* I don't know how he got them, and I'm not asking. He was a Hollywood cameraman years ago, and he had a lot of friends in the business. He's the reason my dad got interested in electronics." She turned her head to glance around the room, and her fine, reddish-blonde hair caught the light.

I remembered then that I'd heard Deb's father owned a small electronics store in Holm. "And you can play the reels at home?" I asked.

"Sure! We've even got a movie room. Dad converted our garage years ago."

"Wow!" I said, surprised and impressed.

Deb shrugged. "He's a tech fanatic, what can I say? And it's fun. Halloween is my favorite holiday, and it wouldn't be complete anymore without *Nosferatu*." She smiled at me then, the expression in her eyes open and honest. "Hey, I've got an idea! Do you want to see it with me next Halloween? We can do it on a weekend when I'm home from college. Your mom's welcome to come, too. My parents enjoy the movie almost as much as I do!" Deb gave a delighted little shiver. "I think you'll like it. They knew how to do creepy in those days."

I grinned at her. "Thanks, we'd love that!" Watching her face, her enthusiasm for a weird old movie not many people our age wanted to see, I realized I hadn't done myself any favors when I latched onto Holly from the beginning. Why hadn't I tried to broaden my group of friends? I suspected Holly was the reason my relationship with Jack had ended almost from the moment it began. Thinking of him gave me a sharp pang. He'd backed off so far that he was just giving me a little nod, sometimes a "Hi," in our shared classes. I hadn't seen him with any other girls, and that gave me hope. Maybe it wasn't too late. But this was my chance to make a friend of Deb. Halloween was my favorite holiday, too, and I had the feeling there might be other things she and I had in common. So instead of trying to ease into it slowly, I decided to just ask her.

I got serious. "Listen, I've got a question. Do you know Holly's older brother, Ruminato?"

For a long moment Deb was silent, her expression blank. The change in her was startling, and I began to think I'd committed some huge *faux pas* that she'd found deeply offensive. Or maybe that she'd lost track of the question. Then a light of comprehension came on in her gray eyes, and her freckled cheeks went pale. "Why? Do you know him?"

I took a deep breath. "I do. I've had some unpleasant experiences that involve him. I thought if he went to Holm High, too, then you might know something about him."

She gave me an uncertain look. "'Unpleasant experiences?' Can't you just ask Holly about him? You two seem to be pretty good friends."

"We are. She and her parents know what he's done and they've apologized and been supportive. I thought I could trust them to keep him away from me, but they're his family, after all, not mine, and now I think they might be trying to protect him. I think it's possible they're even trying to set me up to take the—" I almost said "the strife," but stopped myself. "To take the blame for the things he's done, make it seem like it's my fault."

Deb watched me carefully while I was telling her this, then gave an apologetic half-shrug when I finished. "Now that you mention it, I did know him a little. Not from school, though. For a while, Holly and I were friends, too. I was a freshman, Holly was a little older. I can't remember now why we stopped seeing each other. My mom used to drop me off at her house sometimes. I don't think she ever came to mine. I do remember how nice her parents always were to me, though."

As Deb spoke, I could see her losing focus again. "But what about Ruminato?" I looked over my shoulder. A couple of other book club members had entered the meeting room. I lowered my voice. "Did he ever do anything to upset you? Scare you, even?"

Deb shook her head. "I'm sorry, Phee, I can see this is bothering you, but I don't think I'll be much help here. My entire freshman year was extremely difficult for my parents and me. My mom was having health problems, and our family was stretched to the breaking point. That's really all I remember about that time."

"Oh, I had no idea, I'm sorry. I shouldn't have brought it up."

"No, it's okay. Everything's fine now." She smiled. "Better than ever, in fact."

"I'm so glad," I told her, meaning it, feeling bad for stirring up painful memories for her. I glanced at the clock on the wall. There were still a couple of minutes to go before the meeting started, so on a hunch, I decided to try one last question. "Could I just ask, though... Do you by any chance remember what Ruminato looked like?"

Deb's brow furrowed as she tried to recall. She started to shake her head, but then her lips parted and her eyes grew wide with shock. She darted a look around the slowly filling meeting room and dropped her voice to a whisper. "Oh, my God, no—I mean yes, I do now, but what just hit me is how he *smelled!* It turned my stomach! Like a dirty farmyard on a sweltering day. So weird." She made a face, but then inhaled sharply and put a hand over her mouth. "Wait—I even had a dream about him! I can't believe I forgot that!"

"Wow, you did?"

"It was terrifying." She shivered, looking ill. "Even in the dream, I could smell him. Disgusting. And the worst part? He had *hooves!*"

We had to stop our conversation then. Mrs. Gilpin had just entered the room, and the book club members were taking their seats. As Deb and I moved to take our usual chairs, I threw her a sympathetic look and mouthed the words, *I've seen them, too.*

Mrs. Gilpin shut the door behind her. "Okay, everybody's here." She clasped her hands together and broke into a mischievous grin. "Let's get started on our next selection. Who made time to read Matheson's *I Am Legend* over the holidays?"

I didn't get to talk to Deb again for a few days, so I was glad I'd taken the opportunity when it arose. It was good to have my experience confirmed by her own, and equally good to know that somehow, she'd managed to get free of the Millers before anything far more awful happened to her. Something she'd said kept nagging at me, though. How was it possible that when Deb was a freshman, Holly was older? That wasn't the case now. Deb was in her senior year. Holly was a year behind her.

———

Mom's birthday had come shortly after the spring term started. It was a gloomy Saturday, a couple of days before I'd had the chance to speak to Deb. The sky was low and gray, and freezing rain was falling. Nevertheless, we went into Holm for a small celebration over ice cream. We didn't have the heart for doughnuts anymore, and the anniversary of Dad's death was only three days later, a sad remembrance we had to get through the best way we could.

Thankfully, the opening night of her art show was three days after that, coming so quickly that it gave us something else to focus on. Mom was gratified with the efforts Mrs. Bruner had made to publicize the event. She'd advertised it in the Holm newspaper and also in papers from surrounding towns. The ads featured black-and-white photos of a few of the pieces to give people an idea of what they could expect to see.

I'd gone with Mom on one of her art gallery trips over the holidays, and that's when I met the owner—a nice, older woman. I liked her immediately, because she appreciates Mom's work as much as I do.

"People will love your work," Mrs. Bruner told her that day. "Even the ones who say they don't understand art." The gallery owner had clasped Mom's hands between her own, the blue veins prominent but her rings and rose-pink nail polish gleaming with subdued elegance under the gallery lights. "Do you know why, Livia?" she said. "Because people don't need to understand your art. All they have to do is stand before it and look, really *look* at it, and it will possess them."

Even though I agreed with this statement, I was kind of stunned by the fact that someone else saw my mother's art the way I did—as something special to be sought out and admired by total strangers. I was hugely proud of Mom and happy that

Mrs. Bruner truly *got* her work, but Mom didn't seem to be nearly as thrilled by this as I was. She'd given Mrs. Bruner a faint smile and thanked her kindly for the "lovely compliment."

As the event drew closer, I was becoming a nervous wreck. Mom, up until that point a sizzling, fizzing Roman candle of frenetic energy, grew calmer, radiating peace with everything she'd accomplished. She reminded me of the Madonnas I'd seen in Renaissance paintings, with her downcast eyes, her modest air, her benevolent smile. It was unnatural, and I told her so.

"Shouldn't you be excited?" I demanded. "This is your moment! People are coming to meet you—to see your work!"

I was glad when her response was a snorted laugh. That was more like Mom as I knew her.

"We'll see," she said. "We can't know how it will go until it's over, Phee. Frankly, I'll be happy if we just have a couple of sales. Holm isn't exactly the big city, you know. Most people here have better things to spend their money on."

I rolled my eyes at that. What could be better than seeing an amazing piece of art every day? "Sure, I know," I said. Privately, I hoped for much more than the lukewarm response she seemed to expect.

———

The show was on a Friday evening, nine days after the start of the spring semester, and Holly and I had lunch together in the cafeteria that day. She was her usual self, treating me with warmth and kindness. With what appeared to be complete sincerity, she told me she hoped my mother had a successful show.

"If her art is half as good as her cooking," Holly laughed, "she'll probably sell all of her pieces in one night."

I laughed too, pleased she was so generous with her good wishes. On the rare occasions Holly had been to my house, she'd never seen Mom's studio, only the few watercolors in the living room, all scenes from nature, which she'd admired in a polite way. I had no idea what she'd think when she saw the large acrylics, their colors so brilliant, the subjects so fantastical, the monstrous horned creatures glistening with scales, winged figures half-bird and half-human, bronze fish with their toothy mouths gaping wide enough to swallow the world. Each painting seemed to have a story behind it, a tale from a far-distant time and place. I could stand facing any one of them, absorbed, and hear the whispering of ancient voices in my head, speaking a language that might never have existed. As much as I loved these paintings, I understood that Holly—or anyone else—might have a different reaction.

She was still the girl I couldn't help thinking of as my friend, no matter what Mom and I suspected her family wanted from me. For just an instant, seeing her across the table from me, where I'd seen her so many times, I forgot about that. Everything seemed normal again.

"It's going to be great!" I said. "You and your parents should come!" Then I wanted to bite my tongue. Inwardly I was horrified, which I thought probably showed on my face, so I ducked my head and got busy on my sandwich. When I glanced up, still chewing, I was confident I'd hidden my expression. I gave Holly a cheerful smile but noted her cool, speculative look.

It vanished almost as soon as I'd seen it, replaced with wide-eyed enthusiasm.

"Thanks, Phee," she said, "we'd love to!"

She picked up her fork then, and her face clouded as she looked down at her tray. A thin slab of grainy meat bathed in a slightly gelatinous brown sauce rested on her plate. Tentatively, she nudged a piece of what the cafeteria menu had described that day as "Salisbury Steak." With a sigh, she turned her fork sideways and sawed off a small bite, then examined it carefully before putting it in her mouth.

I watched her, fascinated, as she chewed and chewed. Finally I had to know. "So based on your first impression, what's the state of humanity today?"

She chewed a few more times before washing down the meat with a swallow of pink lemonade and making a face. "Unimaginative, yet with…surprising resilience."

I had to laugh, and for the rest of our lunch, it was almost like the old times before Ruminato came between us and ruined it all.

sixteen

Mom's art show started at five o'clock that evening and was to run until nine when the gallery closed. We'd brought Toulouse in the pickup truck with us, and he stayed there while I ran back and forth between the gallery and the small corner parking lot to check on him. Even though he was much bigger by then, he was still a puppy, and we didn't want to leave him at the house alone for that long. We'd brought his toys, his food and treats and water, his dishes and his leash. The weather was in the forties, not supposed to freeze until after midnight, and the floor in the back seat of the truck was covered in blankets. Every time I went to check on him, he greeted me with happy kisses, and after I walked him, he jumped back into the truck and burrowed down into his warm nest.

Having him there gave me something to occupy my mind for the first forty-five minutes of the show when only three visitors walked through the glass front doors: an older couple and a middle-aged woman who came in by herself. I was getting more than a little nervous that the show would be a dismal failure, until Mrs. Bruner took a look at my face and pulled me aside.

"Don't you worry, Sophia," she said in a confidential undertone. "In my experience, the first hour tends to be slow. People are getting off work, or they're picking up their kids from after-school band or sports practice or whatever." Mrs. Bruner waved her perfectly manicured hand. It sparkled with some understated pieces of what I knew must be expensive diamond jewelry. "It's the second hour when things really start to pick up." She patted my arm. "Just wait and see."

I thanked her and went to check on Toulouse again. When I came back about ten minutes later, four more people had come into the gallery and were still standing near the front, reading the handouts, chatting among themselves. Then I watched a lone man walk in after them. He cast his eyes about, and when he spotted Mrs. Bruner, went to hug her. Before long, they had their heads together and were moving from one painting to the next, conversing in low voices. Mom and I discreetly exchanged wide-eyed looks and soon were watching, with pleasant smiles pasted on our faces, as a steady stream of people entered and milled around. Most sipped from complimentary glasses of wine and nibbled morsels of cheeses and tiny sausages on toothpicks.

Many recognized my mother from her picture on the handouts and came to introduce themselves. A remarkable number of them were from out of town.

It was a nice surprise to see Mrs. Gilpin come through the front doors in this wave of people. She stood stripping off her gloves, scanning the gallery, but soon was heading our way. Before I knew it, she and Mom had wrapped each other in a huge hug.

"Stacy, I'm so glad you could come!" Mom exclaimed.

Mrs. Gilpin held her at arm's length and gave her a look I recognized from the classroom.

"Don't be silly, Livvy, did you really think I was going to miss this?" Mrs. Gilpin turned to me. "Your mother was always a shining star, Sophia, even when we were children. We all knew her talent would take her far." She cast a beaming glance around the gallery, which was becoming increasingly crowded. "Now look at her. How I love being proved right!"

Mom gave an embarrassed laugh. She'd blushed a bright pink. "What malarkey, Anastasia! Now who's being silly?"

I was enjoying myself, seeing this unexpected window open on Mom's past, and gaining some insight into my teacher, too.

Mrs. Gilpin gave Mom's arm a squeeze. "Knock 'em dead, Livvy! I'll leave you to it, but I'll stop by before I leave. There are people here who want to meet you, and I mustn't be in the way." She took off her glasses and gave me a mischievous look, tapping her front teeth with the tip of one temple. "I'm told there's some stunning artwork to see in here somewhere."

Mom and I were both laughing as Mrs. Gilpin slipped back into the crowd. I could feel my nervousness melting away.

"Wow. So this is an art show," I said in a low voice to Mom after checking that no one was nearby. "This is like something you'd see in the movies." I took another look around. "But without the fancy clothes."

As I watched the crowd, I saw that most of the visitors had, like Mrs. Gilpin, stopped to peel off their gloves and stuff them in their pockets when they first entered. Many, however, had left their jackets on as they moved through the rooms. In close quarters, jackets are easier to wear than carry. With a flash of understanding, I realized why Mrs. Bruner had turned the thermostat down. Otherwise, these potential customers would've grown too warm in a short time and probably left before spending what she considered to be enough money. I was impressed. The nice old lady was also a shrewd businesswoman.

"This is amazing," I said. "Who knew that Holm could be this sophisticated?"

Mom nodded. "I'm in shock," she whispered. "Mrs. Bruner told me she has a lot of contacts, but still…I never thought this many people would come."

Then I sensed her stiffen beside me. I followed her gaze and saw Mr. and Mrs. Miller enter the gallery, accompanied by Holly. When they saw us, Holly gave a little wave and they began to slowly wade through the crowd toward us. My face felt frozen in a grimace, but when I turned to look at my mother, she wore the most natural smile in the world and was even moving forward to meet them, her hands held out in welcome.

"Holly, are these your parents? Well, hello, you three, Phee told me she invited you. I'm so glad you could come!"

She sounded every bit the gracious hostess as they exchanged first names. I detected no false notes in her voice, and I tried to follow her lead. I greeted them and said how happy I was to see them. I hoped my face didn't look as stiff as it felt.

I don't remember what else was said. There were pleasantries and polite nothings exchanged, and Mom encouraged them to help themselves to the drinks and hors d'oeuvres.

"Do please take a look at the art while you're here," she urged them. "Some of this installation represents what I've been working on for the past year, and I truly want to share it with people." Her smile broadened. "Especially the people in Holm who've been so welcoming to us, like your family. Phee and I are very grateful for your kindness."

I watched the Millers as they returned her smile and assured her they were eager to see her work. Mrs. Miller's eyes traveled from wall to wall. I thought she looked a little surprised as she turned back to us.

"My goodness," she said, "you've done several of these pieces just in the past year? You've been very busy then, haven't you?"

Mom murmured something modest and gave a self-deprecating shrug, and before long, the Millers politely took their leave and allowed themselves to be absorbed back into the crowd. From time to time, I saw them moving through the rooms, gazing intently at the pieces on display. I never saw them eating or drinking, which made me wonder. At the time, I thought perhaps it was because Holly got enough information on the "state of humanity" from eating the awful cafeteria food. Only later did I wonder if maybe they simply didn't care enough to learn much about the type of people who'd come to support Mom's work.

Several times over the course of the evening, Mrs. Bruner materialized beside us to update Mom on how the show was going. She spoke in a low voice, her face glazed in a practiced smile that conveyed nothing to anyone watching. At eight-forty-five, a delighted Mrs. Gilpin flitted by to tell us goodnight, and Mom walked her to the front doors. In the meantime, Mrs. Bruner began winding up the evening, thanking a handful of departing attendees and twice dimming the lights in the main showroom to signal the gallery's imminent closing.

Once Mom had returned, Mrs. Bruner came to stand with us again. She had an air of suppressed excitement. When she told us that fourteen of the thirty-five pieces had been sold, I was over the moon. She also informed us she'd received phone calls from several collectors across the country—people who were always on the lookout for the next big name.

"At least two of them are showing serious interest," she said. "I'm certain of it. You can be proud, Livia. This has been an excellent first showing. I wouldn't have expected anything less. You have a marvelous career in front of you."

I caught sight of the Millers approaching. Mrs. Bruner knew them, just as everyone else in Holm seemed to.

"I'm glad I finally have the chance to welcome you to the show," she said, beaming. "I couldn't get to you before, with all the people packed in here. Did you enjoy your neighbor's gorgeous art?"

Mr. and Mrs. Miller nodded and smiled stiffly. Holly's smile appeared more genuine to me.

"I can't get over how much talent there is in your section of the county," Mrs. Bruner went on. "Such a range of artistic gifts! There must be something in the water around there."

"There is. It's the River Buckle," Holly said, catching my eye in a wickedly knowing glance. "It's got a magical influence."

I saw Mrs. Miller's eyes widen before she started to laugh, and soon everyone joined in. I don't know why the rest of them did, but I laughed because it struck me how close to the edge Holly was skating, seeming to be right on the verge of spilling secrets.

"That must be it." Mrs. Bruner chuckled and then turned to my mother. "Well, Livia, I'm going to start closing things up here. I believe we're about done for this evening. You'll hear more from me tomorrow, of course."

"Phee and I can stay. Let us help you," Mom offered.

"I'd love to help," I said.

Mrs. Bruner waved a hand. "No, no," she began, but then Holly broke in.

"Why don't Phee and I stay?" she suggested. "It's Friday night, so we don't have school tomorrow."

"That's a lovely offer, Holly," my mother said. "I could get Toulouse home and settled and then come back to pick you both up when you're done."

Mr. and Mrs. Miller, wearing faint smiles, remained silent during this discussion, only looking at each of us in turn. Mr. Miller's hair looked very black in the lowered gallery light.

"I love that idea, girls," Mrs. Bruner said. "Thank you so much. And I'll be happy to drive you home. You don't need to come back for them, Livia. It's on the way to my granddaughter's house in Berwick. She and her husband invited me to spend the weekend with them after the gallery closes tonight."

"The gallery's not open tomorrow?" I asked, trying to hide my disappointment. *Not open on a Saturday?* I wondered. What if somebody decided against buying one of Mom's pieces tonight but changed their mind tomorrow?

Mrs. Bruner smiled. "Oh, we're open, all right." She seemed to sense the anxiety behind my question. "But a big opening with a lot of people coming through is like a very exhausting party. I'm not as young as I used to be, so your mother's marvelous work will be in the capable hands of my assistant tomorrow."

I nodded, relieved.

Mom dashed off to take Toulouse home then, and the Millers left, too, after a bit of awkward lingering near the entrance. They didn't seem to know whether to stay or go. I thought their hesitation was because they weren't too thrilled with the idea of Mrs. Bruner driving Holly home, though I couldn't imagine why. Holly finally escorted them through the doors, probably to their car, and returned alone a short time later.

It took the three of us less than an hour to get the gallery tidied up. Holly and I gathered up the leftover food, the discarded plates and other trash, and put the food away in the gallery's tiny kitchenette while Mrs. Bruner swept noisily through the airy display spaces with a vacuum cleaner. Then, after wiping down the small tables where the food and iced wine bottles had been set out and disposing of the garbage bag in the parking lot dumpster, we were ready to go.

Mrs. Bruner took a last look around. "There, that looks lovely; everything is back in place and ready to open at noon tomorrow. Thank you, girls, you were a big help."

The three of us headed out the front doors, and Mrs. Bruner locked up.

She has a huge old boat of a Cadillac, and that night it sat, black and sleek, under the street lamps of downtown Holm. I guess most people would say it's quite elegant, but to me it seemed like a lumbering dinosaur, although it really was comfortable. Holly and I got into the back seat and sank down into the luxurious turquoise upholstery. I assumed it was leather, because I was sure that Mrs. Bruner would have nothing less.

In no time, we were on the outskirts of Holm and heading out into the countryside. Mrs. Bruner had the radio turned on low to an FM classical music station. It was quite soothing, and I began to relax, letting the excitement of the evening go, and the nerves from seeing the Millers. I had to admit it was nice to be with Holly again. I knew it couldn't last, so I wanted to enjoy those few minutes while I could.

We cruised, softly floating along as Mrs. Bruner drove with both hands clamped on the steering wheel, following much the same roads the bus took on the way home from school. We'd reached the fields of winter wheat that lined both sides of the road, and had a couple of miles to go before the truss bridge. Mrs. Bruner had leaned forward and now hunched over the wheel as she peered out the front windshield.

"These country roads are dark as the devil himself at night," she muttered. "I can hardly see a thing." More loudly, she said, "Your turnoff is coming up first, Sophia. I'll run you down to your house, and then I'll get you home, Holly. It won't take long after we get back to the main road again."

Holly glanced into the front seat, where Mrs. Bruner was still staring fixedly out at the road. "It's okay, Mrs. Bruner, you don't have to go to that much trouble. If you could just drop us off at the turnoff to Phee's house, that would be great. Her house is less than a hundred yards down that road and I can cut through her back-yard to my house. That way, we'll both be safe, and you'll get back to the main highway a lot sooner. It'll be much easier for you."

Mrs. Bruner leaped at this suggestion with obvious relief. "Thank you, Holly, that's a wonderful idea, if you're both sure it's all right and your parents wouldn't mind. These old eyes just can't see as well at night as they used to."

"Oh, no, ma'am, it'll be fine," Holly assured her, and I said something in agreement.

Before long, I could see the dark outline of the bridge ahead. My fingers tightened on the upholstery, but as we drew closer I saw there was no need to be nervous. Even with the trees lining the banks of the stream and the road's blind curve at both ends, the light of approaching headlights would be easy to spot through the blackness. I relaxed, easing back into the seat. Mrs. Bruner slowed, then cautiously drove onto the bridge and crept across the stream to the other side. The night remained black, of course, with not a headlight in sight. I released the breath I'd been holding, feeling a little foolish.

Less than two miles later, we reached the turnoff to my house. There was a wide shoulder there, and Mrs. Bruner pulled well off the main road.

"You're sure this is all right, girls? Do you want me to at least take you down to Sophia's house, so you don't have to walk all that way in the cold?"

"Thank you, Mrs. Bruner," I said, "but it's really only a short walk, and I'm looking forward to the cool night air. It's a beautiful, clear sky, and I'd like to see the stars." That was perfectly true, and the interior of Mrs. Bruner's car was so warm and stuffy that my head had started to hurt.

"Maybe we'll see a shooting star, Phee," Holly said. "I think the Quadrantids meteor shower is still going on."

After a little hesitation on Mrs. Bruner's part, only because she was doing her duty as the responsible adult in the car, we thanked her for the ride and piled out. The huge black Cadillac pulled back onto the road with a gravelly spin of its tires and motored sedately away.

I inhaled a deep breath of the brisk air and felt my head start to clear. "What a gorgeous night. Great suggestion, Holly. I'd had enough of that hot car." I started walking toward my house, but after only a few steps realized Holly hadn't moved. I turned to look at her. "Why aren't you coming?"

"Because…I have a favor to ask."

What a weird time to be asking for a favor, I thought. "Now? Can't it wait?"

She shook her head. "No. I'm sorry. It's already been too long."

"What is it, then?"

"I need you to go back to the bridge with me, Phee. Please."

I stared at her. Her dark hair was glittering with starlight. She looked magical just then, and it wouldn't have surprised me if she'd sprouted delicate, translucent wings and flown up into the sky. "Why?" I said. My teeth started to chatter, but not from the cold. When she didn't answer right away, I asked again. "Holly, why would we go back to the bridge?" I hadn't moved yet and didn't want to. I knew what she was going to say.

"I have to find my brother. And I don't think I can do it alone."

"What am I supposed to do? You think I can do something you can't?"

"Yes, of course! Don't you see it?"

Her voice broke, and I watched her bury her face in her hands. She was obviously struggling with her emotions. I'd never seen her distraught, and it upset me.

After a while, she dropped her hands. "He's got some strange connection to you. My parents don't get it; I don't get it. But for some reason, he's compelled to come to you. He can't seem to help himself." Her voice was low and tired. "I hoped that having you with me would draw him. We've already tried, and it didn't work. You've got the best chance of any of us to get him back home where he belongs. I've been trying to think of a way to ask you, and then this…this opportunity arose, as if by magic. I had to take it."

"You've tried to bring Ruminato back?"

She turned her face away and stood, shoulders slumped,

looking forlorn. "Yes. Twice." She wiped a tear from her face. "It was no use. I wouldn't have asked you if there was any other way. But I'm desperate, Phee. He may be odd, but…he's all I've got. I miss him." She sniffed, then wiped her nose with the back of one hand. "If you don't help me, I'm going to try once more. I have to. I can't live with myself if I don't." She hesitated. "And there's the strife, too. Something has to be done. It's getting out of control."

She turned and began trudging down the road to the bridge.

At first, I could only stand watching her, too many thoughts running through my head. What if I went with her? I didn't think the Millers would be concerned about their daughter, but Mom would definitely worry about me. When would she start wondering where I was? Wasn't she bound to come looking for us if I didn't come home soon? She had no idea how long it would take to clean up the gallery, though. I knew neither Mom nor the Millers had heard from Mrs. Bruner; she hadn't called anyone before we left. Now she was unreachable, in her car on the way to Berwick.

Holly was already well down the road, a dark shape vanishing into the night. Reluctantly, I reached a decision. She was still my friend, even after everything that had happened. She'd always protected me, and I couldn't leave her alone to face whatever dwelt in the nothingness surrounding that bridge. Her last words about the strife concerned me, too. Would there come a point when the strife would overpower us? I didn't know and didn't want to find out. I ran after her, hoping whatever she planned to do wouldn't take very long.

seventeen

Holly said nothing, only stopped to wrap me in a big hug when I ran up to her. Then the two of us continued on at a good pace.

The night was making me feel exposed, vulnerable. Two teenage girls out on their own on a dark, lonely road at ten-thirty at night would catch any driver's eye. The thought of what might happen after that unnerved me. "We need to keep a lookout for cars," I told her. "We don't want to be seen."

"Good idea," Holly said.

Luckily, only two cars passed us on the way to the bridge, and the yellowish glow of headlights approaching in the distance gave us plenty of time to get off the road and hide. It was

Susan Rooke

all farmland, no wide-open pastures, and most of the properties were unfenced. The wheatfields came within a few feet of the road on either side and were bordered by tall weeds that grew the rest of the way to the pavement. So twice we dashed into the wheat, crouched low behind the screen of weeds, and when the vehicle had passed, we came out and resumed walking. We moved quickly, and before I knew it, we were at the bridge. Too soon.

It loomed before us, a complicated-looking framework of steel posts, struts, and triangles. With the night sky above, it reminded me of those constellation maps with straight lines drawn from star to star, showing the designs they supposedly make in the sky. Those maps have always disappointed me. Ursa Major looks nothing like a Great Bear to me—although it does look something like a Big Dipper—and I can only think the ancients had much better imaginations than I do. But that night, each sharp angle on the upper part of the bridge seemed to hold a faraway star flickering in the tight crook of its elbow. In the moment, I could believe that boundaries were crossed here, that magic happened.

"Now what?" I don't know why I was whispering. There was no one to overhear—not physically present, anyway. But even a whisper sounded too loud to me.

Just then, a coyote howled from somewhere on the Holm side of the bridge, and I jumped. Then a whole horde of them joined in, or at least that's what it sounded like, and the night was filled with crazed yipping and cackling. However many there were, they were too close.

"Can we please hurry this along?" I hissed.

Holly was in control of her emotions now and had an air of purpose, of certainty, about her. Her assurance was intimidating. "Don't let them scare you," she said in a low voice. "They're just worshipping the moon."

I tilted my face up to the sky. "What moon? I just see stars."

"That's because it's behind the trees. The last sliver of the waning crescent. What we call the old moon."

"We"? I wondered. *"We" who?* And I'd never heard the term "old moon" before. Holly was talking again, so I tried to ignore the horrible racket the coyotes were making and pay attention.

"We won't be on the bridge," she was saying, "so don't worry about that. I know you don't like it, but that's not where we need to be anyway."

I was glad to hear it. I didn't like driving over it, and I certainly didn't want to be standing on it where a car could hit me. I was shivering, so I hugged myself, tucking my freezing hands under my arms. I'd left my gloves in Steve's back seat the last time I finished walking Toulouse. Holly wasn't wearing gloves, either, but she seemed not to notice the cold.

"We'll stand beside the bridge," she said, "on the bank, close to where it drops off down to the creek. Right there by that post so we can have our hands on it." She gestured to the spot she meant.

"We have to touch the bridge? Why?" This was surprising, and made me uncomfortable. I watched her profile, the way she stood, her posture erect and poised. She looked confident and quietly relaxed as she faced the bridge, her focus sharp. She looked like she did in the moments before the first touch of the bow on the violin string. The coyotes had fallen silent. I envisioned them loping toward us across the fields through the darkness and pushed the image out of my mind.

"Because I've been giving it some thought, and I believe that to have any hope of reaching Ruminato, we must be near the liminal space where he disappeared. Having our hands on the metal will channel our energy toward him and bring us as close as it's possible to be."

Unpleasant thoughts were crowding my head. Why did I have the feeling she'd had this planned long before I invited her and her parents to my mother's art show? "What's a liminal space?" I asked, not sure I wanted to know.

"A place of transition," Holly said. "Like a crossroads. A bridge. A doorway." She turned to me again. "A hallway."

The tone of her voice chilled me to the bone. I thought of the entry hall in her house where I'd first seen Ruminato in a dream. The doorways, and the rooms with impossible dimensions, the upstairs rooms that endlessly opened into and out of one another, where the unwary had been lost. Even the pecan grove I passed through on my way to the Miller house, and the river. The river! Oh, my God, the river. The river that turned. I began to see the picture more clearly.

"That's what you and your family live in, isn't it, Holly? It's all a big liminal space."

I saw her lips curve in a smile, but it was too dark to see what her eyes might show me.

"Now you're getting it, Phee," she said gently.

I was feeling more unsettled by the moment. I wanted the whole charade to be over with, and I was regretting my decision to come with her. "Well, let's get to it," I said, more sharply than I'd meant to. "I'm freezing, and I want to go home."

She nodded. "Then follow me."

We stepped off the right side of the roadway onto the grassy verge and made our way down a gentle slope. Now we stood beside the first steel post that thrust its way upward toward the struts. A few feet in front of us, the land dropped off sharply down to the creek. I could hear it gurgling below. Scattered everywhere were the trunks of fallen trees. I looked up and saw the creaky bodies of those still standing, leaning perilously over us. I prayed they stayed upright until we were done here tonight.

Holly reached out her left hand and grasped the post. "Put your right hand with your thumb against mine, here," she instructed. "You'll have to move down the bank a foot or two."

Of course I would. Holly was facing the creek, and I would be standing farther down the slope, my back to the water. A scream for help was building inside me. I fought it back and did as she told me. When I was in position, I turned to her. Her hand was shoulder height, so I put my right hand beside it, our two thumbs touching, and gripped the post. I gasped. The steel was like ice, and a bolt of cold shot up my arm. But having gone this far, I'd be damned if I was going to quit now. I wasn't about to let her see my fear.

I felt her take my left hand with her right one. We were facing each other, making a rough circle, with the bridge as the anchor.

"Everything will be fine," Holly said. "Just don't let go."

If these words were meant to soothe, they failed. They struck me as so ominous that I closed my eyes and said a brief, silent prayer.

When I opened them, only moments had passed, but I was enclosed in a black emptiness so suffocating it was hard to breathe. My senses felt deadened, and I couldn't tell if I still had hold of the post, or was even touching Holly's hand. I felt neither warmth nor icy cold, neither the rigidity of metal nor the flexible strength of fingers. I thought I was alone in this hell, and I nearly let go, feeling nothing either inside myself or outside—no breath, no heartbeat, no tongue behind my lips. *No lips.* Right then, I lost myself—floating, numbed and deaf inside the void, forgetting everyone I had ever loved.

After a time—I don't know how long, it could've been an instant or a year—a thought flared, a lit match in an unused corner of my mind. I wondered, was this what it was like to be Ruminato? Was this the horrifying place he was forced to inhabit every day in his pursuit of the shadows? The idea was so bleak, so hopeless, that I started to weep, then could feel myself weeping, my sobs and the wet tears on my cheeks, and it was such a relief to know I was alive and not an empty speck, dormant in the larger whole of nothing.

I became aware of Holly's voice inside my head, just a murmur at first, nearing and receding, again and again, as if it were traveling along my bloodstream in time with the beating of my heart. I couldn't make out what she was saying, but there was a rhythm to it, like a chant, or a prayer. Then her voice became clearer, and I understood words. "Yes, good," she said. "He needs to know decency and kindness. Keep feeling."

Feeling was all I was capable of. It was too black to see, to hear, too black to speak, to taste. I pitied that monster as I had never pitied anyone who might have deserved it far more. Then I saw what seemed impossible, a pair of hands so white they looked bleached, reaching up toward me out of the infinite darkness, as if surfacing from some unimaginable depth in the sea. The arms came into view, those limp, pale stems reaching for me, as if they twined toward the sunlight. Then Ruminato's face appeared.

It was like that morning on the school bus, but this time he wasn't trying to terrify me. He was the one in terror, his black, sweeping eyebrows angled sharply up at the outer corners as if they were screaming the words the dreadful little cone in the center of his mask could not.

He kept rising higher, approaching, and I could see his nakedness—the dark haunches, coarsely furred, the blocky split hooves. I wasn't ready for how *other* he looked, the top half, except for the blossom mask, much like that of any normal young man, the bottom like a creature from myth. Had he really been trying to beautify himself with his use of the straight razor? Did he believe he was so hideous that self-mutilation could make him lovely?

As he drew closer, I acted without thinking. I felt so sorry for him that I held out my arms to him, and he surged desperately into my embrace. In that moment, I forgave him everything, and I understood his need to escape this awful fate. I had to do it. I had to help bring him out of the void.

As I felt his arms close around me, a loud rushing, roaring sound like a waterfall dropping off the edge of a flat world filled my ears, and I felt myself plunging backward, down and down. I shut my eyes, terrified, knowing what I had done—I had broken the circle. I had done exactly what Holly had told me not to. I had let go.

The roaring ceased suddenly, the way it had begun. I couldn't bear to open my eyes at first, too fearful, too stunned by the abrupt change in the atmosphere. Something was lying on top of me, and the earthy barnyard funk told me it was Ruminato. He was sprawled on me at full length, his breathing heavy, difficult, one thickly furred leg thrown across me. I couldn't hear anything else. Where was Holly? Had I accidentally left her in that blackness when I broke the circle?

My worry for her made me open my eyes. I was relieved to see her above me, her shape a silhouette on the night. She was bent over the two of us, and I saw her put a hand on Ruminato's shoulder.

"Come, brother," she said. "You're free now."

He reached an arm up to her, and she helped him stand. She hugged him, and the two of them blended into one large, ungainly shape in the darkness, a thing with two heads. It looked unnatural and I cringed from it, wishing I could disappear into the earth.

They separated then, and both of them looked down on me. Neither one made any move to help me get to my feet.

"I'm sorry, Phee," Holly said. "You always knew I had to do it, right?"

My mouth opened as I stared up at her. She sounded genuinely regretful. "You had to do what? What are you talking about?"

She lifted a hand. "I had to save my brother. He couldn't do it anymore; it was too much for him. Someday, it'll be too much for you, too. I really hope you'll have someone who can save you from it. I'm sorry it won't be me. You may not believe me, but I didn't foresee it coming to this."

I struggled to sit upright, too dizzy to stand. I felt tired and achy, and my head hurt. "What are you saying?"

"The strife is your job now," Ruminato said. "It's not mine any longer."

At least I think that's what he said. His speech impediment made him hard to understand, and I couldn't bear to dwell on the reason for it. Even if I'd understood him perfectly, none of this made sense. They couldn't mean what it sounded like, could they?

Then I noticed something about Ruminato was different. He didn't have his sack. I looked down at myself, and was bewildered to see a dark, coarsely woven length of fabric lying across my lap. When I picked it up, the black mouth of a sack gaped open, exposing an interior with a distant glimmer in its depths, large enough to swallow worlds. I knew then where I'd gone when he kidnapped me in the woods. I didn't care what Mrs. Miller said. I doubt I ever made it into their house. He'd held me in his sack.

A car was coming toward us down the road, slowing as it neared the bridge, neared us. It was an old, wood-paneled station wagon, and I knew who it was. It pulled partway off the road and stopped. Mrs. Miller got out of the front passenger side. She rushed to her son.

"Oh, my darling boy, we've been so worried about you!" Then she burst into tears and threw herself into his scrawny arms. Holly joined the two of them. Ruminato began to cry, too, as he hugged his mother. His sobs sounded like a calf bawling.

Mr. Miller got out of the car more slowly, then went to them and clapped a hand on his son's shoulder. "It's good to have you back, boy," he said. He turned and looked at me where I still sat on the ground in a daze. "Here." He came over and put down a hand. "Let me help you, Phee."

"Thank you, Mr. Miller." I was glad for the hand but wondered why he was the only one being nice to me. I took it and he hauled me to my feet. The sack dropped to the ground and he picked it up.

He watched me brush myself off, then in a low voice, he said, "I'm truly sorry about this. I'll need to turn the river again in a few days. Things in this part of the world are on a downhill slide. I want you to know I'll put in a good thought for you when I do it. It might help you get off to a better start." He handed the sack to me, pressing it into my numb fingers.

All right, things were becoming clearer now. I didn't know what to say to him. Was I supposed to thank him for his good thoughts? How were good thoughts going to help me? Now that I'd had a chance to recover a little from my experience with the blackness, I was beginning to get angry. I kept silent, though.

He was still talking. "I don't want you going into this duty blind; that wouldn't be fair. I want you to be prepared for the things you'll face. So I'll try to see that you're eased into it to make sure you know what you're doing before you take over completely."

I stared at him so long he began to look uncomfortable, which gave me a warm satisfaction. Finally I said, "That's very kind of you. Thank you." I sounded like a robot to myself, my voice toneless, but I didn't care. I wasn't going to put myself out just to make him feel better about his part in this betrayal.

The tearful reunion of the other three broke up, and they started toward the station wagon. Mr. Miller patted my arm. "You and I will meet tomorrow so we can get you started. The strife is getting worse. If we wait too long, it will be immensely difficult to regain control. We can't have that."

By now I was so furious that I didn't even feel the cold anymore. "Oh, gosh no," I snapped. "Just give me a call. Holly knows how to reach me."

As she was getting into the car, Mrs. Miller tossed a few words my way. "Good night, Phee, dear. Take care on your walk home."

It was obviously an afterthought, and I didn't bother to answer her. Then something occurred to me. "Wait!" I called out.

The other three were already in the car, but Mr. Miller was lowering himself in on the driver's side. He paused with one foot in, looking my way.

"How am I supposed to explain this to my mother? She's going to wonder where I disappear to when I'm gone for hours at a time!"

"You can collect most of the strife overnight," Mr. Miller explained, clearly relieved. That must've been an easy question for him. "She'll never suspect anything is going on."

I saw Mrs. Miller lean across the seat and say something to him. "And Ria will put a charm of unknowing on the bread she bakes for you and your mother," he added.

That gave me a bit of hope. The charm would make me unknowing, too. I might still get out of this mess after all. Then Mr. Miller squashed this idea.

"Of course, the charm would have no effect on you," he said. "Your duty supersedes such spells."

With that, as I stared at them, still in stunned disbelief despite every indication that they meant what they'd said, Mr. Miller turned their old station wagon around and they drove off into the night. Leaving me standing by the truss bridge to walk home alone. As their red taillights grew smaller in the distance, I realized I was getting cold again. I started walking.

I was halfway home when I saw headlights coming toward me. I had a moment's paranoia and was tempted to hide in the wheat. How could I know what dangerous thing might be driving that vehicle? I was already staring a terrible fate in the face, though. What good would it do me to hide myself from this one? Then I saw that it was a pickup truck, pale against the dark road. Thankfully, it was Mom.

She swung Steve around so I could get into the passenger seat, and before I could even put my seatbelt on, she said, "What happened?" Her eyes dropped to the sack I held in one hand, and her lips tightened to a hard, cold line. "Talk to me, honey."

At first, I hesitated. I needed to carry this burden alone. To tell her anything about what the Millers had done to me would only worry her. She thought I'd be less susceptible to

Ruminato's torment after I banished my death shadow. What would it do to her to learn that wasn't the case at all? That I had walked into a trap? She had told me I'd have to be careful, but we would fix the situation. She hadn't known what the Millers were capable of, though.

Just when I'd resolved not to reveal anything, I looked up and met her eyes, and saw a stony, grim determination there. So I told her everything while she drove us home, her hands clutching the steering wheel like it was Ruminato's throat.

eighteen

Mom said nothing more in the truck as I told her my story. When we got home, Toulouse came running to greet me, so ecstatic that his whole body was wagging. He stopped short when he reached me. The fur on his spine stood stiffly upright as he sniffed at my jeans, front and back, sniffing at the sack, too, circling me, growling low in his throat. Mom and I looked at each other. She pointed to the sack and held out her hand.

I gave it to her, feeling a sense of unreality as I watched her take it from me. She pinched it between her thumb and forefinger, an unreadable expression on her face. Holding it upside down by one corner, she went to her studio. I heard her shut the door, and when she returned, she didn't have the sack. Once I was free of it, Toulouse was much happier. He yipped at me, jumping up and begging to be held. I dropped to the floor and put my arms around him, and he covered me with kisses. It was as if he'd thought I had turned into someone else, and he was never going to see the real me again. It made me cry, because I had a horrible feeling the real me was gone forever.

Mom knelt, too, and squeezed us both in big hugs before rising and going into the kitchen, not saying a word. I was still holding our sweet boy, my face buried in his neck, when she called me to the table. She'd made me a big bowl of oatmeal with hot milk and melting butter swirled through it. She'd topped it with an extra spoonful of brown sugar. I wiped my face with a sleeve and sat down. After everything that had happened, I thought I'd have no appetite, but I was wrong.

She sat in silence at the table with me and watched me eat, and only once I'd scraped the bowl and set it on the floor for Toulouse to lick did she finally speak again.

"I want you to go to bed, Phee, and I want you to sleep. No matter what you think is going to happen, don't let worry keep you awake."

I nodded, staring down at the table. I wanted to believe her, but I just couldn't. I'd seen too much. "You know, Holly told me they'd already tried to get Ruminato back but couldn't do it. I don't believe it. I'll bet they didn't even try."

"You're probably right. But even if they had, I doubt it would've worked."

I looked up. "Why not?"

"Because you're Ruminato's compulsion. For reasons we'll likely never understand, you're the one he's fixated on. Not his family."

The thought of this disgusted me, and I made a face.

Mom reached across the table and grabbed my hand. "Look at me."

I did. Her green eyes were so steady, so serious, and I felt my own eyes wanting to close. I was exhausted.

"Everything is going to be fine," she said. "I promise." She gave my hand a squeeze. "Now go to bed. You've had a long day."

I nodded. "I love you, Mom."

"I love you, too, honey."

Toulouse followed me into the bedroom and jumped into bed to wait for me. When I climbed in beside him, he snuggled up to me, and I fell asleep at once.

———

I woke to the sound of our telephone ringing, and after the few disoriented seconds it took me to realize it was morning, I jerked upright in bed. I was positive the call was for me, and that I knew who was on the other end of the line. I waited, my heart thumping, for Mom to come and get me. I could hear her speaking quietly, but I couldn't make out anything she was saying. After a time, I think she must've hung up. When a couple of minutes passed and she still hadn't appeared at my door, I gathered the courage to get up and go look for her. Maybe the call had nothing to do with my problems. Probably it was Mrs. Bruner, I decided. She'd said she'd be in touch today.

The Music and the Strife

I found Mom in her studio standing before an easel with Toulouse on the floor next to her. I didn't see Ruminato's sack anywhere. On the easel was her largest pad of drawing paper, a good two feet tall. She was working on a drawing that looked unfamiliar to me, but she was partially blocking my view, and I couldn't be sure. When Toulouse jumped up to come greet me, she turned around, pencil in hand. I was stunned to see a big smile on her face.

"Good morning, sweetheart. Why don't you grab yourself some breakfast?" Her eyes shifted to the T-shirt I was wearing— Dad's black one with the Dickens quote on it. She gave it a slight, approving nod. "Take your time. I have a little finishing up to do here before we go to the Millers."

"*We're* going to the Millers?' You're coming with me?"

She was back at work on her drawing. "That's right," she replied briskly.

I watched her for a few moments, her swift, sure pencil strokes, the details and shading growing beneath her hand as if by magic. I still couldn't tell what I was looking at, but I thought I saw…horns.

"Is that who was on the phone?" I ventured.

"Mr. Miller," she answered. "Yes."

This wasn't making sense. "Didn't he ask to speak to me?"

"Of course he did. It was some nonsense about a gift, a special bread Mrs. Miller had meant to give me at the gallery last night. You know, to celebrate the show. He asked if you could meet Holly at their fence to pick it up." Mom snorted and shook her head. "As if he really thought I'd allow that.

I told him we'd come by their house later this morning. Honestly, those people," she muttered. "Sometimes I just want to…" She trailed off, absorbed in her drawing.

Now I was certain I saw horns. The rest of the drawing, I couldn't make out. She seemed to be in a fine mood, though, so I tried to calm my anxiety. "Okay," I said, "when are we leaving?"

"About an hour, I'd say." My mother took a step back from her easel and tilted her head critically. "No rush. They can wait on us. I've got a little something for them, too."

Puzzling over this, I went into the kitchen to get something to eat. For no reason I could think of, my heart felt a bit lighter.

———————

A little over an hour later, Mom and I left our backyard and headed through the barren winter woods toward the Miller house. It was a frigid morning. We were both wearing warm jackets, and Mom had a canvas tote bag slung over one arm. I'd offered to carry it for her, but she turned me down, assuring me it weighed scarcely anything. In that hand, she also carried the drawing she'd been working on that morning, rolled up and secured with a rubber band. She'd thrown a striped wool scarf around her neck. It was knitted in cheery colors of sky blue, crimson, and tangerine. That and the faint smile she wore made her look as if she didn't have a care in the world.

She'd never been to the Millers' before. When we needed bread, I'd bring loaves back from my lessons. Then around Thanksgiving, I felt confident enough to start making our own at home. I was glad to do it; making something beautiful and nourishing with my own hands was deeply satisfying. Nothing else I'd ever tried could quite compare to it. As we tramped through piles of dead leaves, I wondered if I would ever want to do it again. Mom seemed so confident, and I wanted badly to believe in the promise she'd made just twelve hours before. She'd looked so certain when she told me everything would be fine. I couldn't think of a way that this would have a good ending, though. I stared at the ground, my hands stuffed in my pockets, and kept trudging.

When we came to the stile in the fence, my mother put her foot on the first step without hesitating. I held out a hand.

"Can I take your things for you until you're on the other side?"

She threw me a questioning look.

"In case you'd feel off balance," I explained.

She laughed and shook her head. "I'm fine, Phee, thank you." Then she stepped lightly up and over, as if she did it every day. Once on the other side of the fence, she stopped and gazed up through the branches at the sky, her face intent, evidently listening for something.

"What is it?" I asked.

"There are no animals in these woods. Haven't you noticed?"

"I did, but I kept thinking I must be mistaken."

"No, you were right. As soon as I stepped off the stile, I could tell." She shook her head. "I imagine the things the Millers keep imprisoned here have driven them away."

"Too bad they didn't drive me away," I mumbled.

258

Mom gave me a stern but loving look. "It's going to be fine, honey. Trust your mother." She resumed walking, and I followed her.

I would rather have walked all day and into the night, but that wasn't an option. Before long, we'd reached the pecan grove, and beyond that, there was the roofline of the Miller house. Mom stopped walking and studied the trees before us Then she lifted her eyes to the slate roof visible through the winter-bare limbs. Her jaw tightened, then relaxed.

"First, the river," she murmured, tucking the roll of drawing paper under one arm.

I had the impression she was talking to herself, so I said nothing, only watched her. Unexpectedly, she reached for my hand, startling me. When she turned it palm-up and spat in it, I was shocked.

"What was *that* for?"

She still gripped my hand, and now pressed her palm to mine, holding us tightly clamped together for maybe ten seconds. Her head was bowed and her eyes were closed. I had the idea she might be praying. She finally released my hand and lifted her head, meeting my eyes.

"Sorry, sweetheart."

I waited for an explanation, but she didn't give one. Instead, she pulled the scarf from around her neck. She used one end of it to carefully wipe both our palms. Then she moved forward into the pecan grove. Baffled, I followed her.

When we emerged from the trees, the shining River Buckle was before us, and we both halted. No matter how many times

I saw it, I always caught my breath. The setting was so lovely, and I thought how wonderful it would be to wake up to every morning. For the first time, I felt something else, too: bitter resentment. Why did the Millers deserve this beauty after their cruel betrayal? Thanks to the way they toyed with and deceived me, I was cursed to a life of darkness and misery. Collecting the strife, a never-ending task, would be no life at all.

I was so preoccupied with these thoughts that I jumped when Mom abruptly turned to me. She was holding out the tote bag and the roll of drawing paper.

"Hold these for me, please, honey."

When I took them, she began walking toward the river, winding up the scarf in both hands.

At the riverbank, she didn't hesitate. Before I could think what she might do, she pitched the scarf out over the rippling water. It unwound in flight—a long, fluttering streamer with those cheerful stripes. It was so vibrant and full of movement that it almost looked alive—some long-tailed tropical bird dropping out of the sky to skim the waves for a drink. It was her favorite scarf; I couldn't imagine why she had done such a thing.

When it landed on the water, I expected to see it float quickly downstream and be lost from view. Instead it stayed in place, as if caught on something below the surface. Then without warning, it was yanked under, out of sight.

I stared at the water. I may have uttered a small cry of shock. A swirl lingered briefly at the spot where the scarf had disappeared, then it, too, was gone.

My mother turned and faced me with a bright smile. "I'll take those again, thanks." She extended her hands and I gave her things back.

"What was that about?"

"That was an offering. A small token of our esteem given to the river."

"What about the spitting?"

She laughed. "Oh, that. I marked you as my offspring. The scarf was to be a gift from both of us."

"But *why?*"

Mom looked at me, suddenly serious. "This is the River Buckle, an arterial pathway of great power. We needed to introduce ourselves and pay our respects. Why do you think I've been wanting to see it since we moved here?" She smiled again, and it made my heart lighter. "Ready?"

I hesitated, my eyes moving from her to the river again, half-expecting a water monster to rise from the surface in a geyser of foam. I wanted to ask what I was supposed to be ready for. The past few minutes had made little sense to me. Still, her take-charge confidence, no matter how inexplicable it seemed, gave me a spark of courage.

"Um...I guess?"

"Good. Then let's get this over with."

She started walking swiftly toward the house and I hurried to catch up with her.

We didn't have to wait long. The door opened within a few seconds of Mom's knock, and there stood Mrs. Miller. Even through the screen door's wire mesh I could see a range of expressions—from astonishment to displeasure to wariness—cross her face in the brief time it took her to master herself.

"Hello, Phee." She inclined her head in Mom's direction. "Livia. I wasn't expecting to see you this morning." Her tone was unwelcoming. Her lips were turned up, but it wasn't a smile.

"Good morning, Ria," Mom said pleasantly. "Since Phee was coming to see Holly this morning, I thought I'd come with her. I've got a couple of things for you." Mom held up the tote bag and the roll of drawing paper.

Mrs. Miller said nothing, only stared through the screen at us, her face chilly, her eyes hooded. It was a far cry from the way I'd been used to seeing her. What had happened to the woman who gave such comforting hugs? Had she even existed?

Mr. Miller and Holly appeared in the hallway behind her.

Mom waved her free hand at them. "Hello, Nick. Hi, Holly." She turned her attention back to Mrs. Miller. "May we come in? We won't take much of your time."

Mr. Miller stepped past his wife to the screen door and pushed it open. "Good morning. Yes, of course, come in, both of you. I spoke to Livia on the phone earlier, Ria. I told her we'd be glad to see her if she wished to accompany Phee."

I saw Mrs. Miller shoot a look at the back of his head. It could've melted iron.

"Thank you. Come on, honey." Mom gave them all a cordial smile as she breezed past them and into the house.

Apprehensively, I followed her, unable to guess what I was in store for.

Mrs. Miller had stood to one side, but the expression on her face had hardened further. As I passed, she glanced at me as though I were nothing more than an annoying gnat to be slapped away. Her focus was on my mother. Mr. Miller watched Mom, too, but his eyes kept darting nervously to his wife. Holly had remained silent. I saw her gaze shifting between her mother and mine. She didn't look angry or concerned, or cowed, which was Mr. Miller's expression at the moment. She looked carefully neutral.

In the murky light of the entry hall, Mom stopped and looked around, still smiling and polite. "Where is Ruminato? I'd hoped I might meet him."

Mrs. Miller's eyes widened. "My son is resting," she snapped. "It's been a difficult few days."

"Ah," Mom nodded. "Let's get to it, then. I know you'll be sure to fill him in later on anything he may have missed."

"If I may ask, what are we 'getting to?'" Mrs. Miller inquired in an icy voice. "You seem to have come here, to my house, with some purpose in mind. You'll have to enlighten me."

She had dropped any pretense of courtesy. It seemed that hearing Ruminato's name from my mother's lips incensed her. She must have known at once that I had told Mom about him and what his family had done to me.

Mom's friendly smile never left her face. "We need to clarify a few things."

Mrs. Miller took an enraged breath, her throat swelling up like a bullfrog's. Mr. Miller chose this moment to try to pacify his furious wife.

"It's all right, Ria, I'm sure Livia just wants to—"

Mrs. Miller turned on him, an ugly expression on her face, and Mr. Miller took a step back. "Just wants to what?" she spat. "And what were you thinking, telling this interfering busybody that she could come here?"

I gasped. Hot anger boiled inside of me, but before I could speak, Mrs. Miller again addressed my mother.

"The summons was for Phee alone," she said in a hard voice. "Why are you here?"

Mom actually laughed, a response I couldn't believe.

"Why on earth would you believe you could summon Phee? *My* child?"

This bewildered me. Why would the Millers care whose child I was?

Mrs. Miller was glaring steadily at my mother, and again, Mr. Miller tried to placate her.

"Ria, just go along with it," he begged. "Don't make this worse than it needs to be. Soon this whole encounter will have faded." He waved a hand vaguely at his forehead. "She'll forget."

I glanced at Holly then. She was staring at the floor, shaking her head.

Mrs. Miller scowled. "Very well. 'Clarify' all you like. But don't think for one second it will change anything."

"You're quite right about that," Mom said agreeably. "A room with a table would be best." She held up the rolled drawing and waved it at the Millers. "I've got something to show you all." She pointed one end of it at Mrs. Miller. "Especially you."

Mrs. Miller's face turned brick red, and she looked so angry I thought for a moment she was going to burst. I was astounded to realize I was actually beginning to enjoy myself.

"The dining room, then," Mrs. Miller gritted. She went down the hall to a set of pocket doors near the kitchen and flung them open so hard they rebounded, nearly crashing shut again. Impatiently she swept them aside, then marched into the room and turned on the light without looking to see if anyone was coming after her. We did, of course, my mother being the first one to follow.

"Oh, this will do very well," Mom said, sounding pleased. She glanced around the room, and when her eyes lifted to the low ceiling, I saw a brief flash of surprised interest on her face. When I followed her gaze, I could swear I saw a ceiling that soared thirty feet or more. It even had a skylight of stained glass. I blinked, and the illusion was gone.

Mom went to the dining table, an antique, by the looks of it, with seating for eight. She pulled the tote bag free of her arm and hooked it over the back of a dining chair. A pair of silver candlesticks stood in the middle of the table. My mother casually grabbed one, put it on a corner of the sketch paper, and began to unroll it. She released it when the candlestick began to vibrate. Soon, its mate joined in.

We stared at the table as the candlestick slowly jittered off the drawing, which curled into a tight roll again. The vibrating didn't stop, though.

I saw Mom raise an eyebrow. She turned to Holly. "These are reliquaries for shadows?"

Holly nodded.

Mom gestured at her with one hand. "You know what to do."

Holly hesitated only a moment before pulling her panpipes from her back pocket. She put the instrument to her lips and played a low, sweet tune that reminded me of a lullaby. In less than a minute, both candlesticks had ceased their agitated motion.

Mom tried again, and this time successfully unrolled the drawing, placing a candlestick at each end to hold it open as the rest of us gathered around. I heard a sharp exclamation from Mr. Miller, and saw him put a hand to his mouth. Mrs. Miller was staring at the drawing with eyes so wide they looked like a pair of hard-boiled eggs. Holly only pursed her lips and gave a slight nod, as if what she saw confirmed what she'd been expecting. I'd been too busy watching everyone's reaction, but now I finally looked, too, and my mouth fell open. I don't know what I thought I'd see, but this wasn't it.

On the table, drawn so skillfully as to give the thing a look of living, breathing life, was a stunning beast: a magnificent, powerful bull, his deadly sharp horns spreading out and upward from his huge skull, a gaze of forceful, knowing ferocity in his eyes, their horizontal pupils plainly visible. My own eyes traveled down the drawing. This creature had only the bull's head and tail. The rest of it was human, with a man's muscular body. And there at the bottom right, Mom's signature: L. McKean.

"The *Minotaur?*" I whispered.

No one was paying attention to me. They were staring at my mother.

"How long have you known this?" Mrs. Miller finally said.

My mother gave her a pitying look. "Since soon after we arrived, Ria. But until recently, I believed you were all doing as you are supposed to do. I saw no reason to upset your lives."

I watched, fascinated, as Mrs. Miller's mouth opened and closed a few times. She looked like a guppy. "*You*? Upset *our* lives? Who are you that you think you're capable of that?"

"Oh, Mama." Holly was shaking her head.

We all looked at her in surprise. All of us but my mother.

"She's an Old One's daughter. The daughter of one of the three who—" Holly broke off, looking at her father, before going on. "—who sentenced us. Who sentenced *you*, Mama." Holly shrugged. "She can do anything she likes."

"How did you learn this, Holly?" her mother cried. "And why haven't you told me before?"

"I ate at their house one night, that's how. As soon as I tasted her food, it was obvious."

Mrs. Miller's jaw tightened. "You didn't think it was important enough to tell me that very night?"

Holly seemed defeated. "Would it have made any difference? When you're that determined, you usually get what you want." She turned her striking caramel eyes on me. "For what it's worth, Phee, I just wanted my brother back. I never meant for you to take his place. That wasn't my idea."

My mother looked at their three faces for a few moments as if sizing them up, then moved the candlesticks aside and rolled the drawing back up.

"I think we're done here," she said, still with that pleasant smile on her face. "Keep Ruminato away from my daughter, and we should be fine."

Mrs. Miller, her olive-skinned cheeks flushed a deep pink, opened her mouth to protest, but my mother cut her off, smacking the roll of drawing paper on the table with a loud *crack*, her smile fading.

"Stop it, now. Enough of this nonsense. This is a vile and cowardly thing you've tried to do, Ria. Imagine taking advantage of a fifteen-year-old girl grieving the loss of her father. You know what you did and why you're here, and you have to bear it for the rest of your long life. Don't try to force anyone else to live with the consequences of your actions. I notice you didn't tell Phee quite everything that was in store for her as collector of the strife. You didn't, for instance, tell her what *really* made Ruminato ruin his own face."

Mom took a step toward Mrs. Miller, who backed away, staring at her, her lower lip trembling.

"You didn't tell her," Mom went on, her voice like a sharp steel blade, "that these shadow beings you keep here finally succeeded in spreading the dark they carry to him. That it's their purpose, the reason they're so dangerous, especially to humanity. That they'll make you so tired of your life that you harm whatever makes it harder for you to bear. It could be your pets. Your spouse. Your children. That some of them spread a numbness so deadening that you'll do whatever you have to, just to feel something...*anything*." Mom stopped, her face hard as she held Mrs. Miller with her eyes. "Even awful things to yourself, like Ruminato did."

Horrified, I put a hand over my mouth.

"How long do you think my daughter would have lasted," Mom asked, taking another relentless step toward Mrs. Miller, "collecting the strife day in, day out, if your misbegotten son—so very far from human!—couldn't keep from self-harm?"

Mrs. Miller's face was wet with tears now, and her mouth gaped open in an awful expression of gut-wrenching pain, but no sound escaped her. She seemed unable to do anything except bear my mother's fury.

"Then what would you have done?" Mom said. "You would've tossed her aside and set your sights on some other poor soul." Mom stepped back now, shaking her head, her face flinty and unforgiving. "No. I won't allow that to happen, Ria. Ruminato and the rest of your family will continue to fulfill their duties, whether it's collecting the strife or turning the river or bringing the music. They have no choice. You will be baking an endless supply of the bread. And your son, your husband, and your daughter have no one to thank for their fates…but *you*." Mom looked at the three Millers then, and her eyes seemed to hold pity. "Neither does that poor beast you keep in this labyrinth of a house. That creature you claim to love."

I was so stunned, trying to process what Mom had said, that I was barely aware of what was happening around me. I saw Mr. Miller drop his head into his hands and his shoulders begin to shake. Holly was staring sadly at the table where the drawing had been.

"Here," Mom said. "A keepsake for you."

I watched Mrs. Miller gazing helplessly at my mother,

and saw her clearly for the first time. I didn't understand how I could've been so deceived. She wasn't who I'd thought she was. Not one bit.

She reached out to take the drawing as it was extended toward her. It was an automatic gesture, as if her hand had a will of its own.

Mom nodded to me, a signal it was time to go. The two of us had reached the pocket doors when Holly said, "Wait, you forgot your bag!" She unhooked it from the chairback and started toward us.

Mom stopped and turned to her. "No, I'm returning Ruminato's sack. Someone mislaid it last night, and somehow it ended up at our house." She gave Holly a dazzling smile. "Just keep the tote. I've got others."

Mom and I walked out of the dining room and up the entry hall. When we came to the front door, a sudden scream tore the air, a scream of such agony that it twisted my gut to hear it.

Mom's eyes narrowed, and she put her hand lightly on my arm. "Come on, honey, let's get out of here. I've done what I came to do."

Mrs. Miller screamed again, and then we heard her crying. "*I DO LOVE HIM!*" she sobbed. "*I'LL ALWAYS LOVE HIM!*" What followed was a deafening sound, a piercing bellow from some monstrous beast, so loud it left my ears ringing. Then came a tremendous crash that seemed to shake the entire house to its foundation. By then, we were out of the front door and on the porch steps, wasting no time in leaving the Miller house behind.

I thought the anguish in Mrs. Miller's screams would last in my head forever, but by the time Mom and I reached the stile again—not walking fast, but not strolling, either—it was already fading. Once we crossed the fence and slowed down to an easier pace, I asked her the question uppermost in my mind.

"Mom, you've told me the Millers are Guardians, but what does that mean?" I heard rustling in the branches overhead and looked up to see a dove huddled there, its feathers fluffed out in defense against the cold. It was good to be back in nature's proper realm again.

Mom glanced up at it and smiled. "Primarily, Guardians are charged with collecting and confining the shadows. Shadow beings of all types have been a threat almost since the beginning of time."

"Where do the shadows come from?"

"They're born of the original darkness, a being that arose from Chaos. That's with a capital 'C,'" she added. "Chaos is the formless matter that existed before the universe."

I nodded. "I remember reading that in a mythology book. You said 'primarily'. What else do Guardians do?"

"They monitor humankind, and they'll try to alter the course of harmful patterns that threaten the world. Sometimes successfully. Sometimes not."

I thought of the Buckle's fire-tipped waves. "Is that what turning the river does?"

"It is. And these are big jobs, as you can imagine. The Millers aren't the only ones. There are others like them. Some are self-sacrificing, but most are sentenced to Guardianship for their past failings, like Mrs. Miller. Her family just has the poor luck of being connected to her."

"What is she being punished for?"

Mom made a sound of disgust. "Strictly for her own pleasure, Ria Miller did something that altered the course of fate. The Old Ones frown on that."

I stopped walking as a dizzying wave of disbelief washed over me. "Hang on. How old are the Millers, really?"

Mom stopped beside me. "Do you know the story of the Minotaur, Phee?"

"I thought I did. Now I'm not so sure."

"Tell me what you think you know, then."

"Ariadne fell in love with Theseus and helped him find his way into the labyrinth when he went to kill the Minotaur. After that, she helped him find his way back out again. They went away together, but after a while he dumped her, didn't he?"

"That's one version," Mom said. "There are several. But critical aspects of those stories are wrong. Beginning with the obvious one. The Minotaur didn't really die."

"So what did happen?"

"Ariadne wept and begged Theseus not to kill the Minotaur, throwing herself on his mercy. The beast is her half-brother, and she leaned heavily on that, claiming a deep love for him. Which was true, but not because they were half-brother and half-sister. Theseus, however, thought rather highly of himself—"

"Wait a second," I said. Something had rung a bell in my head. "Ariadne? Mrs. *Ria Miller*?"

Mom nodded. "Bingo. Anyway, Theseus was determined

to be seen as the hero of the affair. Sparing the Minotaur's life wasn't part of his plan, and he refused to consider her request."

Mom started walking again, and I fell into place beside her. My mind was racing, trying to wrap my head around the idea that she and I were talking about these things as if they'd actually happened. That the Mrs. Miller I thought I knew, the baker, small businesswoman, seemingly kindly mother of my best friend, was a real person from a myth over two thousand years old. Then again, I'd seen with my own eyes a young man who was only part human.

"The way Ariadne finally convinced Theseus," Mom was saying, "was to promise to help him find his way into and out of the labyrinth. Only, however, if she was allowed to accompany him. Then when they reached the center, she would soothe the Minotaur's bloodlust by making love to him—they'd been having relations for quite some time by this point, and the beast was mad for her—while one of King Minos's subjects, a man who made swords and other weaponry for the king's forces, would provide a bull for Theseus to kill. Theseus would cut off this poor creature's head and later display it in triumph when he emerged from the labyrinth. He would still look like the hero, and no one but Ariadne would be the wiser."

"What would stop her from double-crossing Theseus once she got him to spare the Minotaur and kill some random bull instead?" I asked.

"Her father, Minos, would've been furious with her. The Minotaur was the way Minos took vengeance on Athens every nine years. The Athens thing is a whole other story," Mom added, holding up a hand when she saw my mouth open for a question. "No, Ariadne was perfectly content to keep the secret. She had what she wanted most out of the bargain: her beloved man-bull. Theseus had what he wanted, too."

"Another heroic claim to fame," I said.

"Exactly."

I looked at the ground, thinking, as we walked. "There's another person who knew Theseus didn't really slay the Minotaur, isn't there?"

Mom glanced sideways at me. Her face wore a slight smile. "Mm. Who would that have been?"

"It was the man who provided the bull."

"Good girl. He's the one who put the big kink in Ariadne's future plans. She didn't think of him as a threat in her plot to free the monster. To her, he was just a useful tool, there only to do her bidding. But he was in love with her, and even though he knew he had no chance with the daughter of King Minos, he couldn't stand to see her with the Minotaur. So he went to the temple and petitioned the Old Ones to hear his prayers."

"Did they?" I asked.

"They did. He had the positive notice of the gods. He was a hard worker, a blacksmith, and well respected for his art. So the Old Ones granted the smith the favor he asked for. Ariadne's company. Forever."

I gasped as the vision of a strongly built man in a leather apron standing before a flaming forge flashed through my head. "Mr. Miller! Mr. Miller was the blacksmith!"

Mom nodded, staring thoughtfully down at her feet as we scuffed through the fallen leaves.

"What kind of favor is that?" I said. "All this time he's had to put up with Mrs. Miller having the Minotaur as her lover!" I shook my head. "That's so unfair!"

Mom gave a contemptuous snort. "Don't feel too sorry for him. He walked into his own fate with his eyes wide open."

"What do you mean?"

"He knew what sort of woman she was, with her taste for the unnatural. She was already pregnant with the Minotaur's child when he petitioned the gods. It takes a certain kind of man with his own inner darkness to love a woman like that."

I frowned. Obviously, I'd misjudged Mr. Miller, too.

"And anyway, the Old Ones have often granted favors in ways that strike them as humorous," Mom said in a dry tone. "I think this was probably one of those. You have to wonder if he's come to regret his petition, don't you?"

"What about the Minotaur?" I asked. "Nobody asked him what he wanted, I bet "

"No. Poor beast. He's been kept locked up in one labyrinth or another all his life, almost entirely by Ariadne, wherever she and her long-suffering husband happen to be living at the time. The Miller house is just the latest version."

We were both quiet for a few moments. I now knew the source of those loud noises I'd heard in the Miller house. No matter how monstrous the Minotaur was, Mrs. Miller had treated him horribly. How could I have been so wrong about her? I hadn't known her at all. I remembered Ruminato's rank odor as he lay on top of me after I pulled him from the void. My skin crawled with revulsion, and I rubbed my arms. How did she do it with his father? How could she *stand* it?

Thinking aloud, I said, "So Ruminato is Mrs. Miller's son by her half-brother, the Minotaur. That explains the hooves and the haunches. And the pupils of his eyes."

Mom only nodded. She was looking tired now, as if the demands of the day had finally started to wear on her.

"What about Holly?" I asked.

"She's Mr. Miller's daughter, not the Minotaur's."

"That makes sense. They needed someone to bring the music. They couldn't risk a child with hooves for hands." I stared open-mouthed at the ground. The pieces were falling into place, but it all seemed too fantastical to believe. We'd reached our back fence, and Mom opened the gate. I followed her into the yard. It's never looked so welcoming to me as it did at that moment.

———

By the time we finished dinner and cleaned up that night, both of us were exhausted. I wasn't quite ready to let the day go yet, though. I'd learned too much, things that changed what I thought I'd known all my life. My mind was on fire, and I knew I wouldn't be able sleep for a while. So I asked Mom if we could sit in the living room for a time to unwind. She agreed, and while she poured herself a small snifter of brandy and put a last log on the fire, I made myself a mug of Ovaltine. Soon, we were seated at either end of the sofa where Toulouse was already curled up on the middle cushion waiting for us, bright-eyed and expectant. It made us laugh to see him there and how confident he was that we'd be joining him. His understanding of our habits and of the English language grew more impressive daily.

For a time, we stared into the flames unspeaking, each of us lost in our own thoughts. Finally, I brought up something that had been bothering me since we'd returned from the Millers' house that morning.

"It scares me so much when I think about what could've happened if you hadn't…taken care of things. What if Mrs. Miller tries again with somebody else? Is there anybody who makes sure the Guardians do what they're supposed to? I mean, look what she almost got away with!"

Mom took a sip of brandy and held it in her mouth for a moment before swallowing. "Yes. There are Overseers."

I considered this and gave a humph. "I think the system needs more of those."

"You're probably right," Mom said with a little smile. "They're stretched quite thin. I do think they'll be keeping a closer eye on the Miller family activities from now on, though."

"Somebody needs to," I grumbled.

Mom laughed outright at this, then got serious. "Thank heavens for Stacy Gilpin, though. She's the reason I found you when I did last night. She called to congratulate me again after Toulouse and I got home. When she heard you'd stayed behind with Holly to help Mrs. Bruner clean up, she told me she'd seen the Millers behaving in a suspicious way—almost furtively— near the end of the evening. So I called the gallery, and when nobody answered, I decided to try to intercept you on your way home. I just wish I'd come after you more quickly."

I'd felt so alone. I'd thought my poor choices, my naïve trust in people who didn't deserve it, were problems that only I was fated to bear. It was a huge relief to know I'd never been as alone as I thought. I sank back into the cushions with a contented sigh and closed my eyes. "Better late than never, though."

Mom made a little murmur of agreement. Toulouse yawned, stretching his front and rear legs out until he could touch us both. He was turning into a sofa hog. We sipped from our drinks in companionable silence for a time, then something occurred to me. There was still a mystery that Mrs. Miller had never addressed. I sat forward.

"Mom, what do you think snatched Ruminato at the bridge?"

"Hmm. You told me you had the impression of something very large…"

"Huge! And unimaginably old. Powerful. As if darkness has its own god."

Mom nodded slowly. "That's a very apt description. I believe you used the words 'the absence of all light,' didn't you?"

"I did."

"There's only one thing I know of that matches that description. You know the answer, too, Phee."

I shook my head, drawing a blank.

"Remember on the way home today when I told you about Chaos? And the being that arose from Chaos?"

"The original darkness!" I exclaimed. "Where the shadows come from!" I collapsed back against the sofa, feeling as if the wind had been knocked out of me. "Wow."

"It's a lot to think about," my mother agreed. "So much knowledge has been left in the past. Yet it's claimed to be the way of progress."

"Does the darkness have a name?"

"Erebus. One of the first beings in existence."

Her tone was so matter-of-fact, so sure, that at first I could only stare at her. I guess even after what I'd seen on the bus that day, I still hoped to comfortably dismiss it and put it out of my head. Finally, I said, "Why would it waste its time on some trivial life form like Ruminato?"

"To teach him a lesson? To scold him? To get his attention focused back where it belonged? Probably all of the above. We'll never know." Mom shrugged. "I think that's what you saw in your first dream of Ruminato, though. Then, after he continued to come after you, I imagine Erebus believed Ruminato needed a more forceful lesson in his duties." She sipped from the brandy snifter. "But it's best not to spend too much time thinking about it. Because, well…it's darkness."

A chill pierced me, and I took a gulp of Ovaltine. She was right, so I tried to think of more pleasant subjects. After a few quiet minutes, I decided to bring up one last thing.

"You know, Mom, you haven't explained about…you."

She'd been thoughtfully gazing into the fire, but now she turned to look at me. "No," she agreed with a smile. "I don't suppose I have."

"Well, at least tell me this. *Were* you ever an Army wife?"

Her eyes widened for the briefest instant at that, then she reached across Toulouse and patted my leg. "I don't know about you, but I feel like I could sleep for a week."

The subject of who she was or wasn't was closed for that day, and for weeks to come.

nineteen

A few months have passed since that evening, and it's almost the end of the school year. Now that I'm free of them, I've come to understand that something about the Millers causes amnesia. The people in Holm know Holly and her parents on sight, appreciate them as members of the community, but they don't know who the Millers really are or notice from year to year that they never change. The Millers are persuasive, somehow. It's as if they persuade people to not notice them in any meaningful way. They persuade us to forget.

I've seen this forgetfulness in my teachers, my fellow students. When Deb told me about her former friendship with

Holly, she never noticed that she got older while Holly stayed the same age through the years. In fact, it's likely she wouldn't have remembered any of her time with Holly if Ruminato hadn't caused her such revulsion and fear. Deb and I are friends now, and I've learned that her parents were separated and close to divorcing when Holly took a sympathetic interest in her. During that time, Deb's mother was diagnosed with breast cancer, and things got very dark for their family for a while. That was Deb's brush with the strife, and if her mother's treatment had been unsuccessful and her parents hadn't reconciled, she probably would've been forced into collecting the shadows for the Millers until (and unless) an Overseer stepped in to prevent it. Who knows how long that would've taken? It might've been too late for her by then. She and I don't talk about it much, though. Forgetfulness can be a blessing.

Jack knows on some level that the Millers aren't normal, but it's instinct, not anything he can explain out loud. He's distrustful, and it was that distrust that caused him to get up from the lunch table that day. I often think about what he said to me then. *It was impossible. Most of the time you've been with*— I knew he was going to say I'd been with Holly. To him, it seemed as if I had lunch with her nearly every day. But that wasn't the case. Or was it? Were there days when I'd had lunch with Holly and then forgotten as soon as I stood up from the table? I suppose it's possible. Whatever happened, his perception, my forgetfulness, it caused him to pull back from me until I was free of Holly for good. I'm thankful he gave me another chance. He's a really good person, and we just seem to click together.

I haven't just grown closer to Jack and Deb. I've made several new friends, mostly girls I've met in book club. Making friends feels easier now. Maybe it was my death shadow that kept people away before, some signal from me that said, *Don't come near.* A few other people might be like Jack: instinctively feeling something was "off" about Holly and avoiding me, too, because of her. I was so dazzled by her talent and her quirky way of looking at things that I couldn't see it. Well, I could, but I didn't often admit it to myself. Her quick, unquestioning acceptance of me should've been a clue. It was as if she singled me out. And she did.

I can feel myself starting to forget, though, just like Mom told me I would. As I was putting together this record from my journal entries over the past year, I found some I don't remember writing, things I can't remember happening. Even though they touch something inside me, ring a chime of warning. *Be aware,* it tells me, *so this doesn't happen again.* It may be too late for that, though. I'll become like nearly everybody else in Holm. I'll greet the Millers when I see them, smile back at Mrs. Miller's kind face, think of Mr. Miller as a good guy who I'll remember only as her husband and Holly's dad. I won't notice that Holly is always a junior at Holm High. Or that every year she's the concertmistress for the Holm High orchestra's spring performance.

Ruminato, though… That could be a different situation. Smell and memory are closely connected, after all. It's possible that on some level I'll always remember him, remember his reek, always know he's a monster—the son of the monster who sired him. I hope I do. And I pray I never see him again.

The Music and the Strife

Certainly Mrs. Gilpin and Mom won't forget any of the Millers. She and Mom are just different from the rest of us, and I don't know if that makes them luckier than we are, or less so. When I think about Mrs. Gilpin's remark that her past with Mom was "ancient history," it makes me smile. The times I see the two of them together, I think they must be picking up where they left off, renewing the closeness they had when they were girls, before life intervened. It's clear to me now that Mom's choice of Holm wasn't random, and that's a good thing.

Mom's been very busy in the aftermath of her gallery show. Mrs. Bruner had been right about the power of her art. People are drawn to it, and soon, thanks to Mrs. Bruner and her contacts, Mom's reputation began to grow. Just yesterday, she was interviewed by a fine arts magazine. A journalist, a very nice woman, came to the house and taped the interview, then took pictures of Mom's studio. She told us her magazine would mail Mom's copies of the issue over the summer.

"The title I'm going with is 'Livia McKean and the Art of Fabulism,'" the journalist said, waving her hands in the air with enthusiasm as she spoke. "Even collectors who've never been drawn to fabulist art will see the passion and the magic of your work."

I loved seeing the intensity in this woman's eyes. She'd been captivated by Mom's work, too.

With everything that's been going on, the Millers have been pushed to the back of my mind, and Mom hasn't mentioned them, directly or otherwise. Then at breakfast yesterday morning, she surprised me when she brought up something completely out of the blue.

"You know I'll always be here for you, don't you, Phee?" she asked. "You can always count on me. You don't ever need to wait before asking for my help. I'll love you and your father forever."

I was reading *Interview with the Vampire* as I ate, and I glanced up at her, startled. Her eyes were unnaturally bright, as if she was about to cry, and her face was sad, but so proud as she looked at me. A lump formed in my throat. "I know, Mom. I love you, too." Something in my voice made Toulouse come to me and put his cold nose against my bare arm. It was comforting to feel his nearness, and I looked down to see the handsome, tall boy he was becoming. He was watching me with concern.

After a moment, Mom nodded, then went back to her scrambled eggs and her gardening magazine.

I believe her wholeheartedly. Dad told me she'd always be there, too. He must've known who she is.

Then last night at dinner, we were talking about college. It's still two years off, but the guidance counselor has already started meeting with the sophomores about it. Mom asked me what I thought I'd like to study.

I took a bite of my garlic toast and thought about it as I chewed. It was a slice from a sourdough loaf I'd recently made after poring through a ton of cookbooks and magazines at the public library for information on starters and fermentation, then flipping through Mom's collection for recipes. I got lucky and made a loaf I was proud of on my first try. The flavor was well-balanced with only a mild tang, perfect with the lemony chicken piccata and asparagus Mom had made. I closed my eyes to savor it and didn't open them until Mom cleared her throat. She was watching me with raised eyebrows and a smile.

"Oh, sorry!" I said. "I've got an idea. I think I'd like to…" I trailed off, suddenly shy, and felt my cheeks grow warm.

Mom leaned forward, waiting for my answer. "What would you like, honey? Tell me."

"I'd like to make the bread that Mrs. Miller only pretended to make." The words were out of my mouth before I knew what I was saying. When I heard them, I couldn't quite grasp what I'd meant. Mom did, though.

"You want real feeling, real love and kindness, to go into what you make for people," she said. "Instead of just doing what you've been ordered to do by someone who holds power over you." Mom sat back and reached for her wineglass, shaking her head. "While resenting every moment of it."

"That's right. I think I could really enjoy that." Toulouse was lying on the floor beside my chair, his nose working, and then he rose to sit upright. He stared at my fingers, which held the last bite of bread. When he leaned forward and huffed at me, I laughed and offered it to him. He swallowed it in one gulp and then licked my hand with his dark tongue.

Mom's smile had faded as she watched the two of us. Her eyes had drifted to a point over my shoulder, her mind evidently lost in thought, a million miles away.

"What about you, Mom? Are you doing what you wanted to with your life?"

Her eyes came back to me, and she didn't speak at first. "I am," she said. "Only I wanted to do it with your father here, too, to share it with us."

I rubbed Toulouse's ears and stroked his head. "Are you ever going to tell me who you really are? I'm pretty sure you must've told Dad." I didn't look at her while I waited for her answer.

"Yes. Someday I'll tell you about it, sweetheart."

"When is 'someday?'"

"When you're older."

"How old?" I raised my eyes to her face and saw the sorrow there.

She extended her hand across the table to me. I took it, and held it tightly.

"When you reach the age of mother to your mother."

It sounded like a riddle to me. Maybe it wasn't. I stared into her eyes, trying to work it out, and it slipped away from me.

I've done what I can to record here what happened. For now, I'm closing the book on it.

The End

Also by Susan

The Space Between: The Prophecy of Faeries
The Realm Below: The Rise of Tanipestis
Across the Worlds: Finding Hope
The Space Between Series: The Box Set

Of Stars & Smoke: Poems for the dark wane of the year

About the Author

Susan Rooke is an award-winning poet, multiple Pushcart Prize nominee and the author of the Space Between series. Her poems and short stories have appeared widely in national and international journals and anthologies. She resides on a square of green, peaceful country in Central Texas with her husband, a smattering of cows and two irascible donkeys.